THE **XANDER KING** SERIES

WHISKEY
&ROSES

ALSO BY BRADLEY WRIGHT

Xander King Series

WHISKEY & ROSES
VANQUISH
KING'S RANSOM

WHISKEY
&
ROSES

Bradley Wright/King's Ransom Books
www.bradleywrightauthor.com

Whiskey & Roses/ Bradley Wright. – 2nd ed.
ISBN 978-0-9973926-0-9

For my parents, Tom Wright and Deborah Wright

It's never an easy thing to follow your dreams. Once you make that difficult decision, it's even harder to make those dreams come true. However, it is a hell of a lot easier when you have two amazing parents cheering for you all along the way. Picking you up when you fall down and reminding you that nothing great in life is ever easy.

My dad showed me that I could be anything I ever wanted to be, no matter what it was or where I was from. My mom showed me that life is about more than just what you want to be. That it's just as much about *how* you are as it is *who* you are.

With the two of them in my corner, there is no such thing as failure. For me, *that* has always been the real dream come true.

Mom and Dad, thank you for everything. I love you with all that I am.

"None of us will ever accomplish anything excellent or commanding except when he listens to this whisper, which is heard by him alone."

-Ralph Waldo Emerson

WHISKEY
&
ROSES

The Xander King Series
XK1

BRADLEY WRIGHT

The Legend of Xander King

"Some people don't deserve to live. One man is *exceptional* at making sure they don't," Director William Manning announced as he addressed the roomful of the CIA's finest. "The decision that lies before us is whether we make this man an ally or an enemy. And I'm afraid we can't afford the latter."

Just before Director Manning blasted into the room and uttered those chilling words, Sarah Gilbright sat alone trying desperately to keep from nervous-sweating through her blouse. She knew it wasn't all that unusual for the director of the CIA to call a top secret meeting of the seven highest-ranking officials in the agency. However, it was highly unusual for the eighth person involved in that meeting to be a comparatively low-ranked special agent like herself. Sarah knew there could only be one reason she had been invited to a meeting so far above her clearance level: they had decided to do something about Xander King.

Sarah fidgeted in her seat and shuffled through her prepared portfolios. She felt as if she were back in college. The plain white walls of the square room, the cheap collapsible faux-wood tables, and the metal folding chairs were almost enough to give her that familiar college hungover feeling.

That was when the heavy wooden door flung open, clanging against the painted cinder block wall with a loud crash, and Director Manning buzzed into the room. Though he didn't look anything like the TV character, his clumsy, hurried entry reminded Sarah of Kramer from *Seinfeld*. No, Director Manning couldn't have looked less like Cosmo Kramer. Manning's short, stout frame and his cloud-white hair made certain of that.

Director Manning finished his morbid opening remarks about Xander.

"Either way, enemy or ally, we've got to do something. Let's get through this as quickly as possible." His tone was more of a growl as he dropped his black leather briefcase onto the table. The button on his light-gray suit jacket seemed to be holding on by a mere thread.

Sarah imagined the button on his pants probably shared a similar stretch.

"All of you know each other, with the exception of Special Agent Sarah Gilbright here." Manning pointed to Sarah.

The palms of Sarah's hands filled with sweat at the sound of her name among all those important people. This was a big damn deal. She played it off as best she could, tucking her long blonde hair back behind her ear.

"Sarah, if you could please hand everyone a file and come up front with me."

She did as Manning asked and began passing around

2

Xander's file. She worried that her slim-fitting black skirt and tight royal-blue silk blouse might be inappropriate. She had decided to button one more button on her blouse in the bathroom just moments ago. It was hard for her to contain her mother's gift of large breasts, but she wanted the men in this meeting to take her seriously. The women too. She wanted them all to listen because of her merit, not because of her curves and slender waist, as had all too often been the case since she joined the agency.

Director Manning continued. "Six months ago I gave Sarah an assignment to keep an eye on a man named Alexander King. I'm sure that all of you have heard the name at one time or another due to the legend of his time in our military, but his service to our country has taken on a much different role these days. Sarah is going to fill us in, and then we are going to figure out just what in the hell we are going to do about him. Sarah?"

Sarah handed off her last file and took the podium in front of the deputy and executive directors, the head of admin, the head of espionage, and the head of public affairs for the Central *freaking* Intelligence Agency of the United States of *freaking* America.

Wow.

Her voice was shaky. "Good afternoon, everyone. It's an honor to—"

"Sarah . . . all due respect, spare us," Director Manning broke in. "We have other things to worry about so please keep this short."

"Yes, sir, Mr. Manning. Alexander King." She did as she was told and got right to it, swallowing the growing nerves and digging in. "All of you are familiar with the name?"

The roomful of stuffy higher-ups all nodded in unison.

3

Sarah continued. "The Alexander—Xander—King of today is known to the world as the billionaire son of Martin King, of King Oil. After his parents were brutally murdered in front of him, Xander decided not to follow in his father's footsteps. Instead, he sold King Oil and, as you well know by his *legend*, as Director Manning put it, he joined the navy. If you will, please open to the first page of the portfolio."

"And he's handsome," Mary Hartsfield, Director of Espionage, remarked when she opened the folder and saw a picture of Xander holding a bottle of bourbon.

"Mary, please. Could you wait till you get the portfolio home before you start drooling over it?" Director Manning scolded.

The group laughed at Mary's outburst, and Sarah, for the first time since entering the room, let the tension fall from her shoulders. She looked again, for probably the thousandth time, at the blue eyes staring at her in that picture and wholeheartedly agreed with Mary.

"I'm with you, Mary, he is quite handsome."

Director Manning rolled his eyes and motioned for Sarah to move on.

"That bottle in his hand is from his own bourbon company—King's Ransom—that he launched recently, and as some of you may or may not have heard, he has a horse by the same name running in the Kentucky Derby this coming Saturday. Those are the things he's known for to the outside world. However, the reason we are here today is because of what the public doesn't know, what Xander King doesn't know we know, and the reason Director Manning has had me monitoring Xander for the last six months. Xander King is an *assassin*."

The air in the room changed, shifting with the dark word Sarah uttered, surprising them all.

"Now, before you get the wrong idea about Xander, let me brief you on exactly what I mean."

Sarah turned the page, and the picture this time was of a beautiful dark-haired woman whose stern demeanor suggested she had seen her share of cruelty in the world.

"If you'll turn the page, you'll find Samantha Harrison, or Sam, as Xander calls her. Sam had quite the reputation at MI6 in the UK for being what used to be an unparalleled agent. We aren't exactly sure how she and Xander initially connected, but together they have formed quite a team. Sam is in charge of finding and coordinating the targets, and Xander goes about eliminating them. She is the coach, and he is the talent, if you will."

"Targets, Ms. Gilbright?" Mary asked.

"Yes, targets. The scum of the earth. The most evil and vile human beings on the planet."

Deputy Director Richards, a silver-haired, tall, and lanky man, spoke up. "And he just kills them? No justice system? Vigilante style, he's the judge and jury? I see now why we are here. This is a problem."

Sarah felt the mood in the room shift again, and she wanted to make sure she gave the rest of the facts in such a manner to show that what Xander was doing, though not legal, was just about the most noble and honorable thing a man with his particular set of skills could do. She had been watching him for months. All of the charity events he had hosted, all of the people he had saved by taking out these miserable targets. She didn't want this audience to get the wrong impression of him.

"Well, I understand your skepticism, Mr. Richards, but I

assure you this isn't some amateur running around killing random people he thinks *might* be doing bad things. Sam painstakingly researches each and every target, and if you will turn the page, I'll introduce you to some of these evil people."

They all turned the page. There was a picture of a forty-something man with an emptiness to his stare.

"The first man you see was killed by Xander three months ago. Jerrold Connors. Jerrold was—"

"Hey, I remember this guy," Deputy Director Richards interjected. "We were building a case against him when he was suddenly killed. Horrible, the things he was doing. Didn't we find the bodies of more than seven male teenagers out in his shed?"

"Yes, that's the guy."

"Awful. I remember, they were all drugged and tortured over a span of months, if I'm not mistaken."

"You are not mistaken. I'm glad you remember, Mr. Richards."

Director Manning cleared his throat. "Move along, Sarah."

"Right. The second target on the list, Mitch Boyle, was eliminated last month—"

"Oh God." Mary winced. "I remember him. He was the guy—the nurse—who was going around stealing newborn babies from the hospital nursery, then taking them home, killing them, and stuffing them like dolls."

"Good God," the Head of Public Affairs blurted.

Sarah could already feel that they were coming to understand Xander like she did. She had been skeptical at first too. She had thought there was no way this could be right, a man exacting vigilante justice; then she spent time getting to know him from afar. "I know. It's terrible. Mitch Boyle was a monster."

Director Manning cut in again. "Look, I think we get the point. The other six *monsters* on this page all deserve what Xander gave them, but that isn't what we need to focus on. Get to that please, Sarah."

Director Manning paused, then held up his hand. "You know what, actually . . . let me just take it from here." He stood up and shuffled Sarah to the side.

"But Director Manning—"

"Thank you, Sarah," he said, dismissing her. Sarah took a seat by the podium. She wanted to give them a better sense of things. She wasn't sure they understood Xander yet. She didn't want them to stop the good things he was doing to right the wrongs the judicial system couldn't manage to take care of. There was nothing more she could do now, though; it was Manning's show. She had assumed he was thinking the same way she was, but he had called this meeting for a reason.

Manning took the podium. "Now, the way I see it, we have three options here. One, we could shut Xander down and bring him up on charges . . ."

Sarah's stomach dropped.

"Two, we could let Mr. King continue to go about this, what I think we all would agree is noble work and just continue to monitor him—"

"What, and just let him play like he's Batman?" Richards interjected.

"Deputy Richards, I understand that concern, and that's why I think my third option is the only way to go. We will just have to be careful how we go about it."

"Which is?" Richards said.

"Which is, we get him to go to work for us."

7

Sarah tried to hold her tongue, but she couldn't. "Xander will never work for the government, Director Manning. You're wasting your time on that notion."

"Now hold on, Sarah. I just told you we would have to be careful how we went about it."

"I don't understand, why wouldn't we just *make* him work for us?" Mary asked. "We do have evidence that he has killed these people."

Again Sarah couldn't help herself. "He just simply won't do it—"

Director Manning gave Sarah an "I'm warning you" glare and continued to explain. "What Ms. Gilbright is so passionately stating is that Xander doesn't agree with how the United States government goes about some of its business. He made this very clear when he abruptly left our Special Ops team. He loves his country, but not its governing body."

"Xander was Special Ops?" Mary said.

"Xander King was everything you could be in our military. After his parents died, his sole mission was revenge and he wanted to be trained by the best. He joined the navy, quickly becoming a Navy SEAL; then in record time he was running Special Ops missions. I'm not sure what you have or have not heard, but he just might be the best damn soldier this military has *ever* known."

"So what happened?" Mary asked.

"Well, like a lot of our soldiers, he didn't agree with the missions he was sent on and frankly, as you all know, some of the innocent casualties that go along with keeping this country safe. So he'd had enough. To be honest with you, I'm not so sure this wasn't his plan all along."

"What do you mean?" Richards asked.

"I mean, I think he used our military."

"Used us?"

"Don't get me wrong, he laid his life on the line every single day for his country, but yes, I think ultimately he used us. I think the only thing Xander ever wanted was to find the people responsible for the murder of his parents."

"And he used the military to train him to do so," Mary Hartsfield said as she let that sink in.

"That's right. But we *need* a man like this. A man with his skills. Sometimes a surgical strike works far better than bringing in the entire army. Saves a lot of lives too. As you know, things are getting downright scary on the terrorist front and we could use a silent weapon like King."

Mary stood up. "So what then? What are we supposed to do?"

"The only thing we can do. Use our resources to find what he wants before he finds it. Then we give it to him . . . at a price."

"We find out who killed his parents and force him to do jobs for us for the information." Richards recognized the direction Manning was suggesting.

"It's the only way it will work." Manning hiked up his pants. "He will go to prison before he stops hunting their killer, and we can't have that happen. We can't lose him. He wouldn't go to prison anyway; he has too many resources. If he really wanted to, he could just disappear. That is why we have to take our time and get this right, and that is why Sarah is going to head up a team that will monitor Xander and Sam while finding the information that King desires."

Sarah couldn't contain the joy she found in that news, and a smile grew across her face.

"When we find that information—who killed Xander's family—we will approach him. But . . ."

Manning paused and looked over to Sarah.

"We have to be careful. If something goes wrong, if Xander were to kill the wrong person and it gets out that we knew what he was doing and we let it happen, we kiss all of our jobs good-bye."

Richards stood and gathered his things. "If you don't mind me asking, sir, why take the risk? You ask me, we should shut him down and find a soldier who *wants* to work for us. There has to be a hundred guys in our great military who can do the jobs we need done, the jobs he can do—"

"I assure you there is not."

Director Manning's expression was dead serious.

"There isn't one. Not in our military, or any other military. That's the only reason I would even call this meeting. If it was someone besides King doing this, we *would* just shut it down. But this soldier is special. We just have to make him an offer he can't refuse, and we need to do it fast. As far as I'm concerned, this is of the highest priority. The United States needs Xander King."

The King Is in the Building

The black Cadillac Escalade glided down the 5 freeway, heading south. The tangerine evening sky hovered over downtown as it admired its own reflection in the glistening waters of San Diego Bay. A 737 commercial airliner pulled its wheels up into itself and floated out over the Pacific Ocean, carrying passengers headed to all sorts of different final destinations. Some flying back home from vacation, others just starting theirs, and others unfortunately leaving for work or maybe, even worse, a loved one's funeral. Xander King took in the scenery from the passenger seat. His eyes wandered over the airport, trying to pick out the hangar where his own private aircraft awaited his arrival. He wished he were on his way there now, but he wasn't. He had business to tend to.

Xander's phone vibrated in his lap.

"Hey, Sam," he answered.

"Xander." She spoke in a strong, proper British accent. "The two of you are behind schedule. You should only be ten minutes from Juarez's compound at the moment."

"Sam?" Through the phone Sam could hear Xander's wry smile grow as he started speaking. "Are you watching us on GPS again?"

"Of course I'm following you on GPS. Someone has to keep you on schedule. It isn't like you are late to a film. I know this is all second nature to you, Xander, but your life depends on the preciseness of my plan. Every second you are behind is a second that I hadn't planned for, and—"

"Then it's a good thing I know how to improvise, Sam. You act like it's my first time. Relax, darlin'. How many times have we done this?" Xander attempted to reassure her. He threw in the word *darlin'* for good measure, because he knew how much she hated it.

"I hate it when you call me darlin'." Sam over-countrified the word *darlin'*. "I know exactly how many times we have done this. I know, because every single time, we have to have this little chat beforehand."

"And every time, everything goes just as you'd planned. Now, if you don't have anything important to offer about the target, I'm gonna get back—"

"I have confirmed there are at least three young girls being held captive in the cellar," Sam interrupted. "All of them under the age of fifteen."

Her words hung over them with the weight of an elephant. Xander's playful mood instantly switched off, and a sickening rumble permeated his stomach. Live hostages changed the game entirely. His level of precision would have to parallel perfection.

"Jesus, Sam."

"This changes everything, Xander. All yellow targets are now green. I know you never like eliminating anyone but our main target, but there are innocent lives at stake here. You know that everyone working security for Juarez is fully aware of the horrible things he plans to do to these poor young ladies. They all have a hand in the rape and the brutal—"

"All right, all right. I get it. You don't have to tell me why we are doing this."

"I know I don't. As soon as you give me word the compound is clear and you are well on your way, I will send in the authorities to pick up the hostages. Xander, I—"

"I know, Sam . . . They all have to die."

"I'm sorry, Xander. It's the only way."

It never ceased to amaze Kyle how poised Xander could be in these situations. He had been driving for him going on four years now, and still he always felt more nervous than his friend seemed in these moments. His mind couldn't compute how calm Xander could remain, like he had ice water in his veins. He supposed it was because of Xander's training, but still it amazed him. With downtown now behind them and the last of the auburn sky fading to black, Xander read through the target file. Another file full of all things drug trafficking, prostitution, and murder. Yet again, a profile of another of the world's nastiest human beings, and by looking at him, you would think Xander was reading a magazine. Not a fidget or a squirm of nervousness, even though he was about to walk right into the lion's den.

Alone.

Kyle could tell by Xander's conversation with Sam that things at the target's compound had become more complicated. However, you'd never know it by looking at Xander.

"You need some more air or anything?" Kyle asked.

"I'm good. Just doing my homework," Xander replied. "Did Sam brief you before we left?"

"Not really, just the drop-off and pickup points. Sorry. I got back too late from the DMV. They were giving me shit about not having a California driver's license. And . . . I may have been a little hungover."

"No worries. Last night was fun." Xander smiled.

"It really was—"

"Let me catch you up before we get there," Xander interrupted, all business now. Fun and games were over. He shuffled back to the beginning of the profile. He looked down at a photo of a young Mexican man, midtwenties, a gold-toothed snarl on his face, bald head, and a tattoo of a snake winding up and around his neck. Xander thought the snake tattoo seemed rather appropriate. He read aloud to Kyle.

"Okay, the target is Miguel Juarez—son of Jose Juarez— the founder of the Trinity Cartel. About three years ago when his father died, Miguel took over operations and has grown it by more than double. As you know, I don't give a shit about drug trafficking. If it were just about that, I definitely wouldn't waste our time."

Kyle nodded as he navigated the palm-lined roads. They had now crossed over into Chula Vista, California's southernmost city, just above Tijuana at the Mexican border. He knew Xander wasn't worried about petty crimes that only involved drugs.

"But about two years ago our boy Miguel here started dipping his toes in the human trafficking waters. Young teenage girls, to be more specific."

"Wow, who does that?" Kyle said.

"I know. Since then he has bought or kidnapped and sold more than two hundred young girls, to the fate of God knows what. Lately, and the main reason he popped up on Sam's radar of potential targets, Miguel has figured out that young San Diego white girls fetch a lot more money on the black market than his usual lineup of teenage Mexicans."

"Does he have anything to do with the reports I've been seeing lately on the news about young girls going missing?" Kyle asked.

"He has everything to do with them." Xander casually took a sip from his Red Bull. "Listen, I've heard awful stories of what's happened to some of these girls, and it is sickening. Rape, slavery, torture. I heard one girl he sold ended up being a sex slave to an entire cartel in southern Mexico. Fifteen men raped and beat her whenever they wanted, for months, before she finally found a way to kill herself. And it's all courtesy of Miguel here, our dead man walking." Xander briefly flashed Kyle the photo of Miguel.

"Sam did mention I was dropping you off just outside this guy's compound. Any special instructions?"

"No, you can drop me off just around the corner. It's pretty isolated, and as always, I'll see you at the pickup point when it's over."

"No problem. I'll be there," Kyle assured him. "Only about ten minutes away now."

Xander nodded and got back to reading over the blueprints of Miguel Juarez's compound. The glow of the GPS in the middle of the Escalade's dash was all the brighter now that the sun had set and darkness had filled in around them. Kyle always left the last few minutes of these rides for silence. Xander never said he needed it, but he knew his friend about as well as he

15

knew himself. Besides, Kyle always felt that if it were he who was about to walk into a notorious gangster's personal compound in order to kill him, he would at least like to take a few minutes to gather himself. Not that Xander ever needed it, but it was the least Kyle could do.

The semirobotic female voice of the GPS broke the silence. "Turn left onto Palm Bluff Lane, and in two-tenths of a mile your destination is ahead on the right."

"This is close enough," Xander said as he pointed to the side of the road. His voice was calm, as if he were getting dropped at the bus station. It was pitch-black now, and the only light on the isolated road beamed from the front of their Cadillac. Kyle brought the SUV to a stop and popped open the liftgate. Xander opened the passenger door, and the overhead light of the vehicle shined down on his chiseled face as he turned back to Kyle.

"I'll meet you back here in exactly twelve minutes. Any longer and I'll meet you at plan B in half an hour. We really don't have time for plan B, though. We have a launch party to get to," Xander said with a smile and a wink. His deep and tranquil blue eyes showed no signs of fear or nerves.

Kyle smiled back and reached out his hand for their customary handshake—three sideways open-hand slaps and a fist bump. It hadn't been modified in over ten years, not since the first touchdown he threw to Kyle senior year against their cross-town rivals, the Ashland Tomcats. Sam thought it entirely immature of them, but Sam didn't know how to have fun. Kyle knew he would see Xander in exactly twelve minutes. Four years in and there had never been a need for plan B. Xander had never missed his mark.

Xander's smile turned to game face as he shut the passenger

16

door. The cool Southern California breeze said hello as it carried the faint salty scent of the ocean. He made his way to the back of the Escalade and inside were a few tools of the trade. He took his sniper rifle from its case and threw the strap over his shoulder. Sam had also left him two silencer-fitted Glock 19 pistols for his shoulder holster, and he slid both of them in their slots beneath his perfectly tailored black blazer and shut the liftgate. He'd had the blazer custom made to allow for plenty of movement while maintaining a snug athletic fit. He chose Glock 19s as his preferred piece because he liked the way it felt in his hand. And at that point, he had sent thousands of rounds down the gun range with it, so it felt like a reliable old friend. He gave two pats on the back of the Escalade, and Kyle pulled a U-turn, leaving Xander alone to his mission.

Xander walked down a small grass-covered embankment toward the tree line to avoid being noticed by any potential passersby. As he made his way toward Miguel's driveway, another cool breeze swept through his hair and seemed to awaken the rows of pine and palm trees that stood watch over him. With only a sliver of moon visible, there wasn't much to light his path. Branches and pinecones snapped and popped beneath his feet as he moved methodically toward the now visible light of the gate and guardhouse at the foot of the compound. About a hundred meters, he figured.

Cloaked in the shadows of the freshly fallen night, he took a knee and pulled the rifle from his shoulder. The ground was soft under his weight. He checked his Apple watch—8:00 p.m. An iron gate—the only way into Miguel Juarez's completely walled-in, drug and slave money–funded mansion—opened and a black SUV drove through. Xander crouched lower and watched with a keen eye. It stopped for a moment, then proceeded out onto the main road, just as Sam had said it would. According to her calculations, there was a 50 percent chance that Juarez was in that SUV and a 30 percent chance he wouldn't return for at least forty-three minutes. Sam was never wrong. However, in this case the intel wasn't absolute, and as she had stated in her briefing, this left Xander with a probable success rate of only 14 percent. She always teetered on the side of caution.

Xander did not.

The exhaust rumbled as the driver stepped on the gas, and the red glow of the SUV's taillights disappeared in the distance. Xander loaded two specially made tranquilizer bullets into his silencer-modified, bolt-action M24 sniper rifle. It had a range of over eight hundred meters, but only about a hundred of those would be necessary to take out the guard stationed at the gate. Xander had read that the gate guard was employed by an outside security firm, so there would be no reason for him to die. He readied the sniper rifle. Every time he used this rifle, it reminded him of his time as a Navy SEAL. Moreover, it reminded him of his course manager, Sergeant Marx, who used to never let a moment go by without giving Xander a hard time about being the son of a billionaire oil tycoon.

Marx would always joke: "I don't understand why in the hell a good-lookin', rich-ass son of a bitch like you would want to practically kill himself to become a Navy SEAL. If I were you and I had all of my daddy's billions, I'd be at the titty bars throwin' money around till somethin' came home with me!"

Ever charming was Marx.

Xander laughed to himself as he peered through the rifle's

scope. He adjusted for the slight but steady SoCal breeze, and he wrapped his black leather glove–covered finger around the trigger. The crosshairs danced back and forth over the guard's chest. With a deep breath and a steady hand he gently squeezed the trigger and hit his mark directly in the right shoulder. He continued his gaze through the scope, studying the guard as he grasped his shoulder in pain. A small spatter of blood saturated the entry point of the bullet on the guard's white short-sleeved button-down shirt. In a matter of seconds he slowly folded over as the tranquilizer settled into his bloodstream. Xander panned the rifle a few feet to the right until he spotted the camera on the gate in his sights. One more squeeze and the bullet exploded directly through the lens, disabling the camera. Xander lowered his rifle and tossed it just outside the tree line, where his intended exit route would take him. He made his way through the rest of the trees to the opening of the driveway and continued past the guardhouse to the gate's keypad. He entered the four-digit code he had memorized from Sam's intel, and the gate opened, giving way to the compound and its grounds. He moved through, and the gate closed behind him. Ahead of him lay a long narrow driveway that wound its way up a hill before dead-ending into a massive Mediterranean-style mansion. Instead of taking the driveway and further exposing himself, he made his way up the manicured hill beside it, through various tropical plants, pines, and palm trees. He took notice of the soft but firm ground, just in case a quick exit from the premises would be necessary.

As he approached the outside of the mansion, there were no sounds or signs of movement coming from inside. It was, in fact, much quieter than he had expected. His intel had shown, especially on the weekends, that many parties took place here.

There were no signs this was the case tonight. The driveway was free of souped-up Chevy Impalas and other tacky retro cars fitted with thirty-inch rims.

Sam's 14 percent probable success rate might just be right on the money, he thought.

He quickly erased this thought from his mind, as there was no room for any doubt that Miguel and his crew would be anything but ready and waiting for him. He spotted the first security camera and pulled one of his pistols. With minimal effort he shot out the camera. Xander, one time, after a few too many bourbons had joked with Sam that he was going to start bringing a paintball gun along just for the security cameras. Sam didn't find the idea amusing at all. She was the best in the world at building these missions, but she was a little uptight. A lot uptight actually, the yin to Xander's yang. Sam was supposed to have already hacked in and cut the cameras, but since it was on his way in, he figured it couldn't hurt to be safe.

Xander reholstered his pistol and made a move for the side door when a window lit up on the second floor toward the rear of the mansion. He couldn't help but feel that at that moment the 14 percent probability Sam had given him to succeed had just gone to 100. A shade was drawn, but he could see a shadow moving in the background. He surveyed the outside of the compound for an easier way to reach his target. If he could avoid having to scour the entire mansion, it would be far more efficient. To his left, in the yellow floodlight, he could see a substantial concrete balcony protruding from the second floor of the back of the mansion, connected to the very room that showed the signs of movement above him. With three quick-bursting bounds he used his momentum to propel himself up the side of the stucco wall. Without stopping, he pushed off of the wall, and after a catlike leap over the back gate, he had a hold on the bottom of the balcony on the other side. Pulling himself up with one arm, he kept his right hand gripped around his pistol, which was tucked inside his suspender holsters.

Much to the dismay of Sam he had decided long ago to go form over function with his attire.

There was no one out on the balcony, and once he had pulled himself the rest of the way up, he tucked up against the side of the mansion on the outside of the stucco and stone pillar railing. His all-black suit stood out loudly against the light tan stucco he now leaned his back against.

There was a massive sliding door on the other side of the railing. The light was on in the room, but in addition to the window there was a curtain closed for privacy. As he listened for any movement, he noticed the sprawling grounds at the back of the mansion. Multiple floodlights cast their rays over a magnificent pool, complete with a faux-rock mountain holding a slide and what appeared to be the opening to a grotto tucked underneath it. Xander was amazed by how much money was made trafficking drugs and, in this case, prostituting innocent children. That thought brought his blood to a boil and focused him on the task at hand. A sliver of wall on the balcony separated the rail from the beginning of the sliding door, just enough room for him to stay hidden. Xander hopped the rail and paused at that gap before noticing a small opening in the curtain as it had been pulled a little too far to the middle of the glass doors. Just as he began to take a look inside, he heard a woman let out a moan, and he quickly pulled his head back away from the door. For the moment at least, it didn't sound as if she was moaning from being forced into her current situation. Xander figured he could take his time.

21

First things first, he wanted to determine for certain whether or not this was Juarez. Judging by size and proximity, this room had the makings of what should be the master bedroom. He flipped back through his memory to the blueprints he had studied on the car ride over and confirmed in his mind that it indeed was.

Check.

The moans continued as Xander peeked inside the room through the small opening in the curtains. Whatever he was doing to her it certainly wasn't hurting.

Hurt so good maybe.

The bedroom was large with cathedral ceilings and chock-full of gaudy, gold-framed paintings featuring what looked to be Mexican countryside. In the center of the room and on the side of a large bed, a naked man stood thrusting against a woman who was bent over, white-knuckle-clutching the sheets. The thrusts were to a constant beat and with each moan came an opportunity to mask the sound of sliding open the fortuitously unlocked door.

Keep up the good work, my man. This is too easy.

Juarez's Date with Destiny

Xander stepped inside the bedroom and reached inside his blazer, pulling one of his pistols. With the couple's backs turned to him it would be easy to shoot them both without alarming anyone else who might be lurking around the mansion. However, contrary to his discussion with Sam in the car, Xander didn't kill innocent people. Sam always found this notion absurd. Her thought process was, how many innocent people hang out in a drug lord's mansion? She had been on many similar cases during her time with MI6. Though Xander understood her thinking, this wasn't MI6. This wasn't the CIA or the FBI, either. This was his show, and there was only one target on this mission. He would risk his own life to make sure it stayed this way. The only exception to this rule was if someone was trying to kill him or someone else's life was in danger. Even then he did his damnedest to avoid unnecessary casualties. This was one of Xander's few original laws when he decided this would be his life's work.

The naked man's pumping came to an abrupt stop when he was clearly finished pleasuring himself. Xander moved closer as the man exhaustedly slumped over the woman, his body heaving as he tried to catch his breath. The soft yellow glow of the overhead light glistened over his sweat-drenched back and revealed a large tattoo covering the top of it from shoulder to shoulder. Xander noticed it looked like skulls intertwined with assault rifles as he drove the butt of his pistol into the back of the Mexican man's bald head. Now that he was so close, he knew for certain that it wasn't Juarez. This man was short, maybe five eight, and intel on Juarez was that he was closer to six feet. The girl turned in surprise at the sound the man's skull made as it was being smashed, but in the same motion Xander kept her from seeing him by burying her head in the mattress with his elbow, stifling her from alerting the rest of the house. With the one arm pinning her down, he holstered his gun and shook the adjacent pillows out of their tan silk cases. The first one covered her head, and as gently as he could he tied the second pillowcase around her mouth as her naked body squirmed beneath him. She continued moaning, but the cloth in her mouth muffled the sounds. She also tried screaming, but even if she was heard it certainly wasn't as loud or as alarming as the voluntary moans she had been making just moments ago. He lowered the unconscious man to the floor, then used the sheets to tie the woman to one of the large cherrywood posts at the top corner of the bed. First her wrists, then her feet; she lay there looking like a human hammock. Xander checked his watch.

Seven minutes.

He repurposed the king-size comforter, removing it from

the bed and tying it around the base of the stone railing out on the balcony, in the event there might be a need for a quick second-story exit. As he finished tightening the knot, through a gap in the stone balcony railing he noticed a light on in the room below him. It was easy to see because the window to that room was the size of a wall.

Noted.

On his way back through the bedroom he made use of a nearby belt to subdue the still unconscious naked man while constantly being accompanied by the soundtrack of the girl's muffled squeals. Now he could finally turn his attention to the rest of the house and, more importantly, to finding the potential hostages and killing Miguel Juarez. At the front wall of the bedroom was an oversize dark oak wood door that matched the crown moulding lining the tops of the walls of the bedroom. He noticed the light switch on the wall and turned it off to help gauge the strength of the light that was to greet him in the hallway. There wasn't much of a crack at the bottom of the closed door, so this yielded little information about what lay ahead on the other side. He tested the door with his ear. He could faintly hear the muffled sound of music emanating from a seemingly distant part of the house. This was good. Not only did it give him a direction, but it also provided cover for any noise he might mistakenly make. Unholstering a pistol he reached for the horizontal brass door handle. Slow and steady he gently opened the door.

Six minutes.

The alarm went off in his head. One of the many things you learn being a Navy SEAL is that internal clock. Not only did it keep the task on pace, but it also steadied his focus.

He found the hallway empty. The only light shined from

the room below, and the music was much clearer now. It seemed to be coming from a common area like a living room or kitchen. The hallway was a balcony, lined with a wraparound wrought iron railing. At the wall it swirled around and down into a grand half-spiral staircase that ended in a beautiful foyer. He could see through the windows below that surrounded the giant oak front door that there were guards outside keeping watch.

Miguel is here.

A shot of adrenaline flooded his veins, practically floating him along the wall and down the stairs. At the bottom, Xander could hear the laughter of a man and a woman coming from the same room as the music. The man's laugh seemed genuine, but he could tell the woman was nervous. He danced along the inside wall of the open foyer in the direction of those sounds. The floor below him was white marble with a large brown mosaic pattern in the middle of the room. A massive crystal chandelier dangled gracefully above it, and its light cascaded down on him, making it difficult for Xander to stay in the shadows. Along the way he noticed a door underneath the stairs he had just descended. His stomach turned. He knew it was the basement door. What he didn't know was just how horrible what he might find down there would be. He took a deep breath, walked over to the door, and tested the knob. Much to his surprise, it opened.

Five minutes.

Darkness met him at the top of the stairs, not a trace of light below, the only sounds coming from the music and voices on the main floor. He tuned his mind to his hands and feet, and after he shut the door behind him, he began to feel his way down. The stairs were solid, so he was able to move without sound. The smell of mold was thick and the walls felt like splintered two-by-fours. He came to a wall in front of him, and with a turn to his right he continued to find stairs. Finally, he noticed a slight yellow glow from a point at the other end of the basement. He stopped for a moment, bent down, and peered under the ceiling from his spot on the stairs. There was definitely a light, but it was coming from a room around a corner through a break in the wall. The basement looked to be completely empty. The walls were a dark-colored brick and the floor seemed to be poured concrete. He tried to look to the other side, but instead of an open space, that side was all walled in.

Xander pulled out his phone and messaged Sam.

Sam, I need to know how many men are upstairs. Were you able to tap the cameras?

Sam responded, *I told you, there is a special code that couldn't be cracked, otherwise you would have had the feed from the beginning. If you are having a problem, abort. We will find another way to save the girls.*

Find out how many men there are.

I have an idea, but I'll need a moment.

Xander knew Sam would think of something. He put his phone away and descended the last of the stairs. The light was strong enough now for him to be able to see, but there just wasn't anything to see. However, he heard something shuffling around in the direction of the light. He reached for his pistol and moved slowly toward the back wall of the basement. There was a break in the wall just large enough for him to walk through. Beyond it, the light became brighter the closer he moved toward it. He heard more shuffling.

Xander approached the open doorway. The light shined from the right, but the left side was completely dark. There were only about eight feet until there was another wall. Just as he was about to turn the corner, a horrible smell sparked his senses. It was unmistakable to Xander. He had smelled the rotting dead many times in the Middle East. There was nothing on earth like it. He readied his gun and prepared his mind for the worst.

Four minutes.

Xander spun around the break in the wall and pointed his gun in front of him. A sickness came over him. His eyes found a cell, eight by eight feet; the back wall was almost completely covered by a pile of dead girls.

A pile of dead girls.

The smell overwhelmed him. Emotion attempted to overcome him, but Xander didn't have time for emotion. He took a large breath through his mouth to avoid the smell and swallowed the burning saliva that flooded his jowls. Behind the iron bars, tied to a chair in front of the wall of bodies, was a blonde-haired girl who looked to be fourteen or so, her face full of fright and her body devoid of food. In front of her were three more emaciated girls, hands tied, lying facedown, turning their heads to look up at him. They all squealed in fear, eyes wide at the sight of Xander's gun. He put it away and approached the bars, his heart broken.

"It's okay. I'm gonna get you out of here. Is there anyone else down here?" he asked. His voice tried to catch, but he wouldn't allow it. He wouldn't allow these poor girls to see even a hint of anything but strength and resolve in him.

The blonde girl tied to the chair looked up into his eyes, holding them, until suddenly her eyes darted up over his shoulder and she feverishly began to squeal. Xander instinctively ducked down in a twisting motion as he swept his leg out and around his body. Just as he heard a loud clang above him, where his head had been before he ducked, Xander's foot connected with a leg and swept someone off his feet. The man grunted as he lost balance and crashed onto his back on the concrete floor. The girls screamed through their gagged mouths from behind Xander as he pounced on top of the large Mexican man. Straddling him, he pulled back his right arm and dropped a skull-cracking elbow down on the man's head, knocking him unconscious. Xander stood and dragged the body into the other room. The girls had seen enough atrocities, so he spared them the sight of the silenced bullet he put in the temple of the man's head. He searched the man's pockets and found a set of keys. He stepped over the pooling blood, walked back to the girls, unlocked the cell, and helped them to their feet. They were almost too weak to stand. They wobbled like newborn foals. He untied the girl from the chair, and before he could remove her gag, she threw her arms around him and squeezed him as tight as she could. Once again, emotion crawled up his spine, but he couldn't let it take hold of him. Not for a second. Not if he wanted to get these girls out of this hellhole alive.

Xander returned the hug and patted her softly on the back. He took the time to meet each one of their trembling pairs of eyes, making sure they understood him—believed him. "It's okay, girls. You don't have to be scared anymore."

He managed to pry the girl's arms from his neck and put his finger to his mouth as he untied her gag. She nodded, understanding that it wasn't over yet. She began to sob uncontrollably and so did the others.

Once more, Xander focused deep into their watery eyes.

"Listen, I'm gonna need you girls to be brave. Can you do that for me? I have to go back upstairs and make sure all the

29

bad men are gone, okay? Can you be strong for me?" This was especially hard for Xander. When he looked at them, he saw his young niece, Kaley, in their eyes.

Through her heavy tears the little blonde girl spoke in a frightened whisper. "No, please! Don't leave us down here!"

This was tough.

"I know you're scared. It's okay. No one is going to hurt you. I promise." Xander walked them out away from the decaying bodies and into the room with the dead man. "Wait here." He dragged the dead man into the cell where the girls had been held, then rejoined them in the now empty room. "Listen to me now. I'm gonna need you to be brave. Can you girls do that for me?"

Through their sniffles of fear and elation, they nodded their heads. They could see the kindness in Xander's eyes. They could hear the steadiness in his voice. They knew he could help them. Hope returned to their faces.

"I know you can be. You've been so strong this entire time. I have to go now, but I promise you . . . Look at me. I promise you, the police will be here for you within a half an hour. Can you all stay hidden down here for me?" he asked them as he wiped away one girl's tears.

The little blonde spoke up. "You promise you won't leave us down here with them?"

Xander got down on his knee, eye level. "I promise, sweetheart. Pinky promise." He held out his pinky. She stared at it for a moment, then hooked it with hers, and the other girls wove theirs in as well. "I just need you girls, no matter what you hear upstairs, to stay down here and stay quiet. Can you do that for me?"

They nodded. Xander broke the pinky huddle, took off his

right glove, and removed his watch. He made a few clicks with his finger and set the timer for thirty minutes and handed it to the girl.

"By the time this gets to zero, you all will be on your way back home to your families. Okay?"

"O-Okay." The blonde girl took the watch and once again threw her arms around Xander's neck and squeezed with all her might. Xander gathered the other three girls and gave them all a reassuring hug.

"Thirty minutes," he told them. They wiped their tears and nodded their heads. Xander turned toward the stairs, and with a deep breath he refocused on what had once been just another target but now was revenge.

Three minutes.

As he carefully ascended the dark stairs, he formulated a plan. He knew at full speed it would take him exactly 40.5 seconds to get from the mansion to where Kyle would be waiting to pick him up. Two-tenths of a mile, 352 strides, 1.15 seconds per ten strides—40.5 seconds. This is the kind of subconscious math a professional does while thinking of his next move.

For an ex–Special Ops soldier, it is second nature.

He slowly opened the basement door, doing his best not to make any sort of sound as he peered around the frame into the foyer. The music was still playing, some sort of shit Mexican crooner, and the girl continued to laugh nervously in a nearby room. After finding the girls in the basement, he knew now why the girl in the next room seemed nervous. He followed the sounds and walked along the far wall of the foyer until he came to an opening that led to the occupied room. Xander inched his head around the door frame until his eyes found a young girl in a tight royal-blue cocktail dress. She couldn't have been a day over fifteen; her curves had yet to blossom. Her profile was leaning against a dark oak bar. She was talking to a man as he sat on a bar stool in front of her. Xander leaned his head out just a little farther.

She was talking to Miguel Juarez.

Juarez was wearing a douchey dark-colored suit with thick white pinstripes over a white button-down shirt. An extra-douchey purple fedora complete with a white feather—an actual feather cap—and an "I'm a pretentious prick" flowered pocket square, overfluffed, jutted from his lapel. There could be a thousand reasons Xander didn't like this guy, but all the reason he needed was watching his left hand rub all over the captive girl as he sipped from a bottle of beer.

She continued to be polite and gently remove his hand from her ass, but Juarez kept on. Xander quieted the rage growing inside of him.

Two minutes.

Juarez sat exactly twenty feet from Xander and ten feet from the same wall-size window that a moment ago he had noticed was situated directly under the master bedroom balcony. That window now revealed the reflection of a security guard standing just on the other side of the same wall Xander currently peered around. Xander pulled his head back and checked his phone. He had a text message from Sam.

A friend at the CIA tapped into a satellite that has an infrared signal. He said the satellite showed what looked to be five people inside the house and what looked to be two outside. Remember, if YOU are inside you must subtract one.

Xander received the message when he was in the basement, so he knew he wasn't one of the five. With the two he tied up in the bedroom upstairs and three in the room adjacent to him, that left only two other men on site and they were guarding the front door.

In order to protect the girls in the basement, except for the couple he had already subdued in the bedroom, they all would have to die.

Xander turned from the wall back into the foyer and bolted back up the stairs to the second floor. He unholstered a silenced pistol as he walked down the hallway, turned toward the foyer, and fired two shots, severing the decorative chain attached to the massive chandelier. The extravagant fixture dropped from the ceiling and shattered in an amazing crash on the floor. The two guards at the front door rushed in from outside, and Xander promptly put bullets in both of the men's chest and neck areas, then moved along the railing above them. When he opened the bedroom door, he broke into a full sprint. He streaked past the two people he had previously tied to the bed and continued running outside through the open sliding door onto the balcony—grabbing the comforter he had tied to the railing earlier with his left hand and without hesitation leaping off the balcony. His momentum carried him out toward the backyard; then it began to swing him back toward the large wall-size window below. With the comforter in one hand and a pistol in the other, he swung toward the great room window and squeezed off four shots that rocketed through the glass—two shots hit the security guard as he went to check on the commotion from the chandelier, and two more shots met their target: one in the back and one through the back of the distracted Miguel Juarez's head. Just above that hideous snake tattoo.

Target eliminated.

By the time the police showed up after receiving Sam's anonymous tip, Xander and Kyle would already be well on their way to the launch party.

Xander Meets His Match

Kyle Hamilton was the very definition of a player. It was just too easy for him. Six feet two inches tall, dark hair, and a chiseled jaw that matched his chiseled physique. While his physical attributes were important to his playboy triumphs, it was his stark-raving fun personality that won everyone over. Especially Xander. Without Kyle pulling Xander out of his shell, he easily could have become an introvert. Kyle was the exact opposite of the other constant in Xander's life, Sam. The two of them were oil and water. As far left as Kyle's wild side could bring Xander, Sam's far-right, staunch, and by-the-book side could pull him right back to the middle. They really balanced him. As Kyle walked toward Xander, drinks in hand, he sure was happy to have the wild one with him right now. He needed to blow off some steam, to clear from his mind what he had just been through.

Kyle approached, a hop to his step and a smile on his face.

BRADLEY WRIGHT

"Cheers, to an amazing weekend and to saving lives," he said as he clanked his whiskey glass forcefully against Xander's.

"Cheers," Xander replied.

Kyle smiled and took a sip of his whiskey. The room was filled with people dying to talk to Alexander King, founder and proprietor of the reason they were all there at the swanky rooftop San Diego bar—the California launch of King's Ransom barrel-aged Kentucky straight bourbon whiskey.

"I really appreciate you letting me be a part of this," Kyle told Xander.

"Let you? I couldn't do this without you. Thanks for picking up my slack lately. My head has been on the horses."

"I mean, the Kentucky Derby. Wow. What a dream come true. You have to be out of your mind excited for tomorrow."

"I am excited. Win or lose, it's going to be a hell of a fun day," Xander said.

"Launching your own whiskey brand in California tonight, then a horse in the Kentucky Derby tomorrow. X, your dad would have been so proud—"

"Ladies and gentlemen, if I could please have your attention for a moment," a man from the makeshift DJ stage in the corner of the room announced through the speakers. "My name is Jeremy Harrison with Southern Wine and Spirits. We have the distinct pleasure of introducing you tonight to the best bourbon whiskey on the planet, earning *Wine Spectator Magazine*'s first one-hundred-point whiskey grade, and for the first time in California—King's Ransom bourbon!" The man motioned for two beautiful young women in tight white cocktail dresses. They stood, each holding the end of a rope, on opposite sides of a large white silk banner spanning at least ten feet wide and eight feet tall bearing the name of the bourbon brand in large black letters with a regal crown and crest surrounding it. On Jeremy's cue, they each gave the rope a tug, and as the banner dropped to the floor it revealed a magnificent wall of King's Ransom bourbon bottles. They were arranged on multilevel shelves all wrapping around a large ice sculpture of a king's crown in the middle of the wall.

"It never gets old!" Kyle slapped Xander on the shoulder, unable to withhold his excitement.

Xander just sat back with a smile as he took in the moment. It wasn't lost on him how fortunate he was. He watched as the gathered group of Southern California VIPs cheered and held up their glasses in honor of Xander and Kyle's young company, and he couldn't help but laugh at Kyle as he watched him do a happy dance. The venue Kyle had chosen for the event was breathtaking. Sitting thirty stories above downtown San Diego, this half-open-air, half-covered ballroom gave way to views all the way to San Diego Bay. Petco Park—home of the Padres—sat just below them, and strategically placed fire pits all around the moonlight-drenched room helped alleviate the nip in the cool night air. Xander looked around the venue as he leaned against the outside bar. Everyone was having a great time, and as their focus was still on the bottle display, he looked to his left, toward the rail that overlooked the buildings of downtown. There he saw something more beautiful than any of the sights San Diego offered just beyond that rail.

"I'll be right back," Xander said to Kyle as he started his walk toward her.

"But they are getting ready to call you up," Kyle tried to tell Xander, but his words never hit their target. Xander was on a mission.

As Xander walked over to her, the first thing he noticed was the way she smiled. It was a smile bright enough to melt the ice sculpture by the bottle display. Her light-brown hair fell down well below her shoulders in the back, and in the front, it loosely curled down around her sun-kissed face.

Her oddly familiar sun-kissed face.

She wasn't very tall, wasn't overdone, either. This was a formal event, but she wore a basic white cotton sundress that did nothing but enable her slender and undeniably sexy body to shine. She laughed with a girlfriend as he approached, and her smile continued to light up the entire room.

Xander pulled up short of where she stood and turned back toward the event to gather himself for a moment. Where had he seen her before? He didn't really know anyone in San Diego yet. The crowd was still focused on Jeremy with his microphone at the DJ stand. Words were coming out of his mouth, but nothing was reaching Xander's ears. He was busy trying to place how he knew this woman.

He downed the rest of his whiskey and pulled another glass from the tray of a passing waitress. As the gentle burn of the alcohol slid down his throat, he straightened his blazer and turned back to her. As soon as he did, they locked eyes and immediately her familiarity was no longer a mystery.

Natalie Rockwell.

This is going to be fun.

"Excuse me, Miss." Xander gave Natalie a smile. "I noticed the two of you were having a lot more fun than everyone else at this party. I'm a little jealous, what's your secret?"

Natalie returned his smile. "A great sense of humor and some delicious whiskey."

"Two of my favorite things."

"Is that right, Mr. . . . ?"

"King. My friends call me Xander."

Natalie raised a playful eyebrow. "So, we're friends now, are we?"

Xander smiled and played back at her. "Whoa, slow down. I don't even know your name yet."

"Okay," Natalie said. She turned and wrinkled her nose at her friend, then looked back at Xander. "In that case, this is Annie, and my name is Natalie."

Xander shook Annie's hand. "Nice to meet you, Annie." Then he reached his hand for Natalie's. "Nice to meet you, Natalie." Their eye contact lasted longer than it should have, both sensing each other's attraction.

Annie interrupted, "So, are we all friends now? Because I saw you over there with that tall gentlemen, and I know I wouldn't mind being his friend."

Natalie playfully slapped Annie on the arm.

Xander glanced at Kyle, then turned back to Annie. "Well, aren't you forward? You and Kyle will get along just fine."

"So, you seem like a gentleman, Mr. King." Natalie turned up the wattage on her smile. "How is it that you came to be at one of these lame liquor parties? Your friend drag you here like mine did?"

Her smile was all the more dazzling the closer he stood. It was strange how just because he had seen her on the silver screen a dozen times that he felt as if he already knew her. Before he could explain that it just so happened that this was his *lame* liquor party, the MC interrupted their conversation and made an announcement.

"And now, ladies and gentlemen, I'd like to introduce the founder of King's Ransom bourbon, Mr. Alexander King!"

Jeremy announced from the booth. As the mini spotlight moved onto Xander and the crowd all turned his way, he looked Natalie in the eye as he pointed in the air.

"That is how I came to be here."

Xander winked and backed away toward the stage. Natalie covered her mouth, blushing, and with an embarrassed smile she mouthed the words "I'm sorry" to him. Before he could turn his back to her, he saw her hit her forehead with the palm of her hand as if to say "whoops" to her friend. He smiled to himself as he was caught off guard by how humble she seemed for a woman in her position. He took to the stage, shook Jeremy's hand, and took over the microphone.

"Thank you very much, Jeremy. And thank you all so much for being here this evening. What a beautiful place to have a party, right?" Xander gestured toward the scenery and looked around the room until he found Natalie's eyes. They were so blue he could see them sparkle all the way from the stage. The crowd gave a roar of applause in approval of the venue. So did Natalie.

"Outstanding, isn't it? Listen, I understand that sometimes these sorts of parties can be, well, a little lame . . ." He smiled at Natalie as she covered her face in embarrassment. "But I really appreciate you all being a part of this first step in what I know will be a successful brand here in San Diego, and the rest of the great state of California. In appreciation of your support, make sure you all get your complimentary bottle of King's Ransom before you leave. It's the least I can do for you all being so welcoming of this Kentucky boy and his bourbon."

The crowd showed their approval with a round of applause and several whistles and cheers. Kyle would later joke that they were only cheering Xander because of the free booze.

Xander continued. "That being said, I need you to know that this would never be possible without my best friend and partner in this venture, Kyle Hamilton. Kyle, come on up here and tell these fine folks a little more about our baby here. Just don't tell them any of my deep dark secrets." Xander flashed Kyle a smile as he walked up to the stage. Only Kyle could know the depth of that statement. He returned the tongue-in-cheek statement with a wink as he took the microphone from Xander and gave him a hug.

"Your secrets are safe with me," Kyle joked. "Unless of course one of those beautiful girls in the white dresses ties me up and makes me spill my guts!"

The crowd laughed, and Xander just shook his head and smiled at his half-crazy friend. He made his way offstage, and Natalie caught his eye, gesturing for him to meet her at the back bar. In the background, Kyle told the crowd the story of how King's Ransom had come about. Xander shook hands and exchanged hellos as he moved through the crowd. When he finally made it to the back bar, he was greeted by the most gorgeous woman he had ever laid eyes on.

"Ugh, I feel like such an idiot. I didn't mean your party was lame, I just meant that most—"

"Don't worry about it, really," Xander interrupted. "I know what you meant."

"So, Alexander."

"Call me Xander."

"So . . . Xander, a Kentucky boy without much of an accent but a whole lot of style? It's been a while since I've been in the South, but isn't that sort of a rare combination?"

"You'd be surprised. Some of us in Kentucky actually wear shoes, you know."

41

They shared a laugh at his sarcasm, and Natalie gave him a playful punch on the arm.

"Maybe when I bought my place out here in San Diego it knocked a little of that country out of me," Xander finished.

"Oh, so you moved out here?"

"Sort of. I still have a place in Lexington."

"Oh, I love Lexington! My dad took me there once when I was young to the horse races. Keeneland, I think it was called?"

"*You've* been to Keeneland?" Xander asked.

"You sound surprised. I haven't always lived in Hollywood, you know. I'm just a small-town girl from Tennessee at heart."

"Really? Makes sense."

"And just what is that supposed to mean?" Natalie teased.

"Just . . . the way you are. Movie stars, at least the ones I've met, don't seem to have your *approachable* quality. It's refreshing."

"So, you've seen my movies?" Natalie put her hand on her hip.

"Maybe one or two."

Kyle busted in on their conversation at the most inopportune time. "Hey, Xander, there you are. I—Holy shit! Natalie Rockwell?"

Xander smiled at Natalie. "I think maybe my friend has seen a couple of your movies too," he poked fun at Kyle.

"Nice to meet you. I'm Natalie," she said, shaking Kyle's hand.

"Wow, I'm Kyle . . . I love your movies," he said to Natalie, then to Xander, "X, how are you not freaking out right now? You've been talking about how she is your favorite actress for years!" Kyle looked back to Natalie. "Seriously, he *loves* you!"

"Is that right?" Natalie smiled and took a sip of her drink.

Xander gave Kyle an off-color smile. "Wow, that was *real* smooth."

"Oh my God . . . I'm sorry," Kyle said, dropping his head in shame. "What I *meant* to say was, Natalie, there isn't a better man who has ever walked the face of the earth."

"Oh yeah? What about all those *deep dark secrets* you mentioned on stage?"

"Nope, not that drunk. Nice try, though," Kyle joked.

Annie walked up sipping on a Manhattan cocktail. She seemed to Xander to be the same age as Natalie—late twenties. She was tall with long dirty-blonde hair and a tight black dress that hugged her slender but curvaceous figure. Her right arm was almost entirely covered in tattoos—a sleeve of sorts. Right up Kyle's alley.

"Kyle, this is Natalie's friend Annie. Annie, my friend Kyle."

Xander could tell immediately by the look on Kyle's face that he was in love. Not in love in the sense you would think of as romance. In love in the sense that for the rest of the evening the only thing on Kyle's mind would be how to get Annie naked and in bed with him.

Some things never change.

Natalie Rockwell Takes a Chance

The next couple of hours for Natalie were like getting to know someone she had already known for years. She could tell that for Xander the feeling was mutual. It was rare for her to have such amazing conversation with anyone, much less a man she'd just met at a party. She was down from Los Angeles for the weekend visiting Annie, whom she had met on the set of one of Natalie's movies years ago. Annie was an extra then, but the two hit it off and had been almost inseparable ever since. Maybe it was how she met her best friend that left her with an open mind toward Xander. It was either that or the unbelievable amount of charm that fell from his lips. Or maybe just those gorgeous blue eyes?

The two of them talked about anything and everything but mostly surface and childish things such as favorite movies, music, childhood candy, and they even argued about whether or not Mountain Dew was better than Mello Yellow. You know, the important stuff. Xander couldn't fathom how such an intelligent woman could ever believe that Mello Yellow could even come close to being as good as the Dew. Natalie and Xander swapped stories of places they had traveled and shared some secrets from their bucket lists. All the while laughing whenever they would periodically glance over to see Kyle and Annie making out at the bar.

"Shit, Xander, it's late. What time were we supposed to leave for Kentucky?" Kyle ran up and asked in a bit of a panic.

Xander checked his watch, and sure enough, it was already 12:30—thirty minutes past the time he'd told Sam wheels up. He knew before he looked at his phone that she had already messaged or called him at least a dozen times.

He checked, and it had been three texts and four missed calls.

"Can you excuse me while I make a quick phone call?" Xander asked Natalie.

"Of course, go right ahead," she replied.

Xander opened his phone and dialed Sam.

"So, what is so important that you have to get back to Kentucky tonight?" Annie asked while he dialed.

"Let me guess, the Kentucky Derby?" Natalie interjected.

Xander smiled and nodded his head. "Hey, Sam. No, I know. I know I said wheels up at midnight. I'm sorry, we are just having so much fun we lost track of time."

Natalie smiled at Xander's words. "I have always wanted to

45

go to the Derby. It looks like so much fun," Natalie said to Kyle and Annie.

A wry smile came across Kyle's face, and as Xander was listening to Sam bitch through the phone, he knew exactly what his friend was thinking.

"Sam, Samantha . . . I know. I know. Hang on just a second, Sam." Xander hit the mute button on his phone and turned to the girls. "I have an idea. Do you ladies have anything going on tomorrow that you absolutely can't miss?"

"We were just going to relax by the pool at the Marriott, but nothing important. I thought you were going to Kentucky?" Natalie replied.

"We are, but didn't you just say that you always wanted to go to the Derby?"

"Well, yes, but there's no way we could catch a plane before tomorrow morning, and by then we will have missed most of the fun at the Derby with the time change and all. Plus, it has to be impossible to get a Derby ticket at this point," Natalie said.

"But you would go if all that wasn't the case?" Xander asked.

"I mean, in theory, of course! But we don't even have anything to wear or anything, so it's silly to even think about," Natalie went on.

Xander clicked off mute and spoke back into his phone. "Sam? Tell Melanie we will have two more guests joining us on the plane. And, if you don't mind, have her call Don Farrington and let him know Miss Natalie Rockwell and Annie. . . ." Xander looked up from his phone for her last name.

"S-Sanders," Annie replied, shrugging her shoulders in an "is this really happening?" gesture to Natalie. Natalie reciprocated. It took a lot to impress Natalie; she had heard and seen most everything. But this was impressive.

"Sanders. Natalie Rockwell and Annie Sanders will be joining us in the box. Thanks, Sam, we'll see you within the hour," Xander ended the call.

"What exactly just happened?" Natalie asked.

"We're going to the Kentucky Derby," Xander answered.

"Just like that?"

"Just like that," he replied.

Annie chimed in, "This is great and all, but we don't have clothes, makeup, shoes, and aren't we supposed to wear some funky hat to this thing or something?"

Natalie gasped and her face got deadly serious. "Xander, I can't go to the Kentucky Derby without a hat. That's like going bowling in street shoes."

"Don't worry about any of that. I'll give all your sizes to my assistant, Melanie, and she'll have everything ready to go by the time breakfast is on the table in the morning," Xander assured them.

"Sounds like tomorrow is shaping up to be a fairly decent day." Natalie winked at Xander.

"All right then, let's get out of here!" Kyle shouted.

"We Ubered here," Annie said. "Is there any way we have time just to go grab an overnight bag? I don't live too far from here."

"Of course, I'll have our driver swing by your place on the way to the airport," Xander replied.

Natalie turned to Xander, gave him a hug, and then held him at arm's length. "Now, as nice as this gesture is, don't get any ideas about getting me into bed, Mr. King."

"Speak for yourself, Natty," Annie said. Then she grabbed

47

Kyle and planted a long and passionate kiss on his lips. Before it got any more awkward, Annie pulled herself away, grabbed Natalie's hand, and they laughed their way toward the elevator. Just before turning the corner Natalie turned around, continued walking backward, and gave Xander a steel-melting smile.

Kyle turned to Xander with the look of a kid on Christmas morning. "Holy shit, is this really happening? Is Natalie Rockwell really about to get on your G6, fly to Kentucky, and be your date to the Kentucky Derby? X, you are gonna be all over the news now for sure, as if you won't be already when King's Ransom wins tomorrow! You and Natalie Rockwell in the winner's circle at the Kentucky Derby. I swear to God, if I were gay, and if I wasn't about to join the mile-high club with Annie, I would totally let you have your way with me. I would even wear makeup for you," Kyle joked.

"You're sick, you realize that, right?"

Kyle just smiled and shrugged his shoulders. "Oh, wait . . . what does this mean for the other bit of business we have during the race tomorrow?"

"It doesn't mean anything. Nothing changes. Sam is polishing up the details on our target as we speak. I'll look over them on the plane. You'll just need to keep the girls occupied during race eleven," Xander said.

"Not a problem," Kyle said, then paused. "What a crazy weekend." He followed that up with an overzealous hug, driving Xander backward and knocking him into a woman, spilling her drink.

Xander turned and found a beautiful blonde-haired woman dabbing at her sparkling black dress with a napkin. "Ma'am, I am so sorry. My friend here is just a little excitable." He then leaned in and hid his mouth, whispering like he was sharing a secret. "And drunk."

She sat down her drink; a smile grew across her face. "Alexander King."

Xander returned her smile. "Do we know each other?"

"No, you don't know me, but the gentleman on the microphone earlier wasn't shy about telling us all who you are."

"Oh, of course. I'm really sorry about your dress. Can I have it cleaned for you? Miss . . ."

She extended her hand. "Sarah. Sarah Gilbright. And don't worry about the dress, it will be fine. It has seen its share of whiskey spills."

She wasn't happy that she had shared her real name, but she did her best not to let on.

"I know what you mean. Again, I'm sorry. It was very nice meeting you."

"Nice meeting you as well. Good luck with King's Ransom. The bourbon and the horse."

Oh no, had she said too much? It was like she had never been out in the field before.

"A horse racing fan?" Xander asked.

Whew.

"I am," Sarah replied.

"Well, thank you. I hope you have a nice evening."

She smiled. Xander turned away and walked over to Kyle at the elevator.

"Who was that?" Kyle said.

"I don't know. I think she said her name was Sarah."

"She was gorgeous. Did you get her number?"

"No, I didn't get her number, Kyle. Natalie Rockwell, you know, the beautiful, famous movie star awaits me downstairs, and you think I am thinking about getting that woman's number?"

"Um, yeah. Natalie won't be here next time you are in San Diego, but *she* might be. And she is just about the sexiest woman I have ever seen. And did you see the way she was goo-gooing over you?"

"You are out of control."

"Yes. Yes, I am. I'll meet you downstairs." Kyle stepped back and let the door start to close with Xander alone in the elevator.

Xander held his arms out and asked, "Where are you going?"

Kyle smiled. "To get her number for you."

Xander's Head Is in the Clouds

A black Cadillac Escalade pulled up to Landmark Aviation, the private portion of the San Diego International Airport. Champagne in hand, Xander, Kyle, and the two ladies hopped out of the rear passenger door laughing uncontrollably at Natalie's spot-on impersonation of Christopher Walken. Xander grabbed Annie's and Natalie's overnight bags from the back, tipped the driver, and they made their way into the empty airport terminal. Sam, from the plane, had noticed them pulling in and came in from the doors that led out to the tarmac. She walked over to the four of them with a sort of quiet fury in her steps. Xander always found her to be really tightly wound, to the point of annoyance, but it was easily overlooked because she was the very best in the world at what she did and he just couldn't help but love her.

"Well, well, so good of you to make it," Sam started in on Xander. As if she wasn't already hard enough, her deep British accent made her seem all the more angry.

"I know, Sam, I'm really sorry to keep you waiting for over an hour. We honestly just lost track of time."

"Not the first, nor the last time, I'm sure," she snarled, peering straight at Natalie.

"All right, well, we're here now." Xander turned to Annie and Natalie. "Ladies, I think you will find everything you need on the plane, but is there anything I can get for you?"

"I don't really have to go, but maybe I'd better run to the restroom. It's a long flight to Kentucky," Natalie replied.

"That won't be necessary," Sam said as she motioned everyone toward the door. "There is a full restroom on the plane and even room to wash up before you get some sleep. Oh, and of course as always there is pizza if you are hungry. Xander never travels without it."

Annie looked at Natalie with an "impressive" look. Natalie shrugged her shoulders and nodded. "Sounds perfect! Who doesn't love pizza?"

Few things in the world brought happiness to Xander like a fresh, piping-hot, greasy cheese-drenched slice of pizza. Though he loved extravagant things, he was at heart a simple man.

Sam said what Xander was thinking. "Well, darling, if you're trying to win Xander's heart, that was the first good step. Probably the last step in that direction, but it was a good one."

Xander stepped in between Sam and Natalie. "All right. Okay. What do you say, ladies, shall we?" He held out his arm and Natalie hooked hers around it.

"We shall."

The five of them walked through the airport's sliding doors and out into the cool ocean breeze. With the airport being just off the San Diego Bay, the smell of salt in the air was heavy. As they walked out onto the tarmac, in front of them sat a gorgeous Gulfstream 650, one of the most luxurious private jets on the planet. It was painted jet black with a thick chrome streak running through the center that stretched the entire length of the nearly hundred-foot-long aircraft. Also in chrome, the tail number—N800XK—reflected the lights of the airport that were reaching out to it in the night. And so did the chrome crown just below it. It was a magnificent aircraft. As they approached, two pilots in full uniform stood at the bottom and on both sides of the already lowered stairway into the plane.

"Mr. King." The first pilot stepped forward to greet them.

"Charlie, you know you can call me Xander. Sorry to keep you gentlemen waiting."

"No problem, Xander." The second pilot reached out and shook his hand.

"Hey, Bob. How's Mary?" Xander asked.

"She's great. Thanks for asking. And, I'm sorry if it seems like I'm staring, but, Miss, you look an awful lot like my wife's favorite actress, Natalie Rockwell."

"Good eye, Bob, this *is* Natalie Rockwell and her friend Annie Sanders," Xander told him.

"Pleasure to meet you, Bob, Charlie." Natalie bypassed their hands and gave them both hugs. "You guys gonna keep us safe tonight?"

"Of course, Miss Rockwell," Charlie replied, pointing to the top of the stairs and to the entrance of the plane. "And this is Amy. She'll make sure it's a comfortable trip as well."

"Hi, Amy!" Natalie said, outstretching her arms for a hug as she ran up the stairs. Xander shrugged his shoulders to the pilots and followed everyone onto the plane. Natalie took a selfie with Amy, and Annie took a few pictures of the pilots with the movie star as well.

The sprawling interior of the jet was a masterpiece in and of itself. Xander himself had painstakingly picked out every detail. After walking through a serving area and mini kitchen, the party found that the inside opened up first to four oversize plush white leather chairs, two to the right and two to the left. They all either reclined or swiveled 360 degrees, depending on your mood, and all of them had the same crown that was on the plane's tail stitched in white at the headrest. A specially made, lightweight, dark hardwood floor gave the cabin a more homelike feel. The white walls of the plane were accented by a medium-dark and glossy mahogany. Beyond the chairs on the left side and toward the back of the plane was a two-person couch, and on the right were two chairs separated by a table that would retract into the wall if needed. Beyond that, two more plush white leather couches lined both sides of the plane and butted up against the back wall, all made of the same mahogany that accented the rest of the aircraft. On the left and right side of that wall were two oversize flat screen televisions that showed a colorful map of the current weather in San Diego. A door in the middle of that wall, matching the elegant mahogany that surrounded it, opened up into the full-size bathroom that Sam had alluded to a few moments ago.

"Wow, Xander. How much does it cost to charter a plane like this?" Annie asked.

Natalie shot a nasty look at Annie. Xander could tell that Natalie thought it tacky to ask such a question. He liked that.

"I have no idea really," he replied.

Annie put her hand on her hip. "I find it hard to believe that you don't how much you spend on a whopper like this per flight."

"He doesn't know the cost to charter it because it's his plane," Natalie answered for him.

"How the hell do you know that?" Annie asked.

"Easy, the tail number ends in XK. Not to mention the crown underneath it matches the one on his King's Ransom bourbon bottles."

"And she's observant. What can't you do?" Xander asked with a sexy grin.

"Math," Natalie replied with a chuckle.

"That's what calculators are for anyway," Kyle chimed in.

They got in a quick laugh before the captain asked them to take their seats. Xander turned a chair for Natalie, and then he took the one across from her.

"This okay?" he asked.

"Perfect."

"When you get tired, you can head back to one of the couches and get some sleep."

"Is there anything you can't do, Mr. King?" she asked.

"Not a thing," he joked.

She couldn't help but laugh. Amy asked them all to buckle up, and they settled in for departure. The engines fired up as Kyle stole one last kiss from Annie before they sat down. Natalie just looked at them and then back at Xander with a smile.

As the plane settled at one end of the runway and the captain announced they were ready for takeoff, Xander noticed Natalie looking a little nervous as she clutched at the armrests.

"You okay?"

"What?" Natalie started, and then looked down at her hands squeezing tightly at the arms of the chair. "Oh . . . yeah, you would think I'd never been on a plane before. Just something about it all makes me a little nervous."

"It's because it's so unnatural," he reassured her.

"Yeah! I know, right?"

"It really is. I'm pretty sure the thought of sitting in a large metal tube moving at warp speed through the air at thirty-five thousand feet is enough to make anyone nervous. My mom used to get nervous every time, and we were flying somewhere every month."

"At least I'm not the only one."

"You certainly aren't. Here, try this." Xander folded his hands in his lap and interlocked his fingers. "My mom used to close her eyes, take a deep breath, and envision the perfect takeoff."

Natalie mimicked Xander's movement, hanging onto his every word.

"As soon as the engines would fire up, she would visualize the plane soaring off into a bright blue sky. She would feel the warmth of a nearing sun melting its way through the windows, and she would let the feeling of that wash over her. She said, before she knew it, she would be safe and sound gliding through the air and she would be as relaxed as she could be."

The engines fired up on Xander's G6, and he opened his eyes to find Natalie going through his mother's ritual. She was no longer fidgeting, she was no longer clutching at the armrests, and her body seemed far more relaxed than it had just moments ago. The jet furied down the runway, lifted its nose, and as if guided by perfectly steady hands, it ascended flawlessly into the deep black night sky.

Natalie opened her eyes, a smile on her face.

"Did it work?"

"Like a dream."

"Good. Smooth sailing from here. My mom said it works the same for the landing. She always knew how to make everything better. She loved movies, too, you know."

"Sounds like she and I have a lot in common," Natalie said, smiling.

"You certainly would have."

Natalie caught the past tense in Xander's response but didn't think it was the right time or place to inquire. She left Xander alone with his thoughts. As they continued climbing higher into the darkness, Xander zoned out as he peered through the window at the stars. He missed his mother more than words could ever say. He missed the way she would dance in the kitchen to Madonna as she cooked dinner for the family. The way she laughed when he would do some of his impressions for her. Most of all, he missed the way she always had time for anything and everything he and his sister ever needed. It was going on fourteen years now since the tragedy.

Fourteen years.

Xander couldn't believe how the time had passed. How much his life had changed and how many terrible things he had seen. It was now almost as long ago as he was old when it happened. Contrary to the old adage "time heals all wounds," the pain of losing both his mother and father that day had yet to loosen its grip on him. It continued to drive everything he did, to this day.

"Isn't it breathtaking?" Natalie asked him as she, too, gazed out the window. Xander looked from the window to her, pausing for a moment until she turned to him and looked him in the eyes.

"Yes, absolutely breathtaking."

Natalie smiled, knowing full well he meant her; then she looked back out the window at the seemingly endless rows of stars—so bright up at that altitude where no other lights could diminish their shine. Xander had a feeling that Natalie was really enjoying being on the plane with them. She seemed in real life to be a lot like the characters she played in most of her movies. A rare combination of qualities that he thought only existed in those movies. She was charming, funny, smart, feisty, and she had an infectious laugh. Looking at her now as the moonlight poured in over her iconic and effortlessly beautiful face, he hoped he hadn't made a mistake bringing her along.

She sat with her legs crossed forcing her sundress halfway up her thigh, uncovering a toned, tanned, and gorgeous set of legs. Xander unbuckled his seat belt and popped up to go and get a few blankets and pillows from Amy. He handed a couple to Kyle and Annie, then went to Natalie, took her hand, and nodded for her to come with him. She obliged, unbuckled her seat belt, and rose to join him.

"You saw my eyes getting sleepy?" she asked him as they made their way to the back of the plane.

"Saw you getting a little chilly, too," he replied. "If you need anything, just let me know."

He laid a pillow on the couch for her, and still standing, he gently wrapped a long wool blanket around her. She laid down on the couch and gave him a smile.

"Thank you. I will. Goodnight, Alexander."

"Goodnight, Natalie."

She settled in and before long drifted off to sleep. Xander sat on the couch opposite of her and grabbed his iPad, which Sam had left for him in his briefcase. Before he hung up the phone with her earlier at the launch party, she informed him

58

that she had e-mailed him the file on tomorrow's target. The night had been as good as it gets, and the excitement of his first Derby horse running for the roses tomorrow was a lifetime dream come true. However, the sobering reality that kept his nights sleepless and his days filled with darkness came rushing back to him as he opened the target's file.

Target #43 Erik Kulakov:

–5'8"

-145 lbs.

–43 years old

–Dark brown hair

–Brown eyes

–Louisville, Kentucky

To employers and coworkers, Erik Kulakov is a quiet, to-himself ninth grade biology teacher. To a lot of other people around his neighborhood and especially his students at Shelby High School, he is the dealer of a new and devastating form of heroine called krokodil (crocodile). It is desomorphine, a synthetic opiate many times more powerful than heroine, that is created from a complex chain of mixing and chemical reactions, which the addicts perform several times a day. It has become an epidemic in Russia because of how cheap it is to make and the ease with which one can purchase the needed ingredients. The drug gets its reptilian name because of the effects it has on its users. At first, injections of this drug begin to leave the skin scaly, hence the name crocodile. After the user becomes addicted, the user's skin eventually begins to fall right off the bone, literally causing its users to rot to death in a gruesome and painful way. The reason Erik has been able to do this for over four years now, completely undetected by law enforcement, is because the main ingredient can be found in over-the-counter painkillers.

For years he has been supplying area residents and students with this homemade killer. Over fourteen deaths have been attributed to this at Shelby High alone, the school where Erik still teaches and has taught for years. He preys on the addicted young women, often forcing them to pleasure him in exchange for their next fix. In recent months, we have placed our private investigator on the task, and Erik has become more and more brazen; we have captured evidence of young women leaving his home with baggies in hand and multiple bandages on their bodies. Several of the girls have turned up dead with autopsies showing signs of rape as well as the effects of the drug.

"Is everything okay?" Natalie's sleepy voice snapped Xander out of his trance.

Xander clicked off his iPad and placed it on his lap. "Me? Of course, just catching up on some Derby news," he replied over the steady hum of the jet's engines.

"I didn't mean to interrupt you. You just looked so sad."

"Sad? Hmm, maybe that's just my reading face?"

"Maybe. Well, get some sleep, stud. I need you to show this California girl how to get back to her real-world roots tomorrow," Natalie told him as she tried to lighten his mood. She heard him when he said he wasn't sad, but she could tell there was more to that story.

"Yes I will, *Hollywood*. Thanks for the concern. By the way, if it's *real world* you're looking to get back to, tomorrow will be about as far away from that as you have ever been," Xander replied, sinking to a lying position on the couch. She smiled as she closed her eyes. To Xander, it was as if she could see straight into his soul. He wasn't sure that was a good place for anyone to see, much less an undeserving sweetheart like Natalie had turned out to be. Underneath the glitz and glamour-filled surface, Xander's was a dark world. He had never even thought about bringing someone into that world. But then again, he had never spent the night with Natalie Rockwell, either.

What Goes Up...

"Mr. King." Amy placed her hand on Xander's shoulder. "Mr. King, we're going to be landing in just a few minutes."

"Of course. Thank you, Amy," Xander said as he roused from sleep with a deep breath and sleepy eyes. "I'll wake the others. What time is it?"

"Seven," she replied. "I have coffee in some travel cups for everyone."

"Thank you, Amy. You're the best."

"Good morning, handsome," Natalie said, still lying on the couch. "We almost to Kentucky?"

"Hey, gorgeous." He smiled. "We land in ten. You sleep okay?"

"Like a baby. You know, I wasn't sure how I would feel when I woke up this morning."

"Yeah? What's the verdict?"

"Excited."

Xander smiled as Natalie sat up and Amy handed them both coffee.

"Good morning, you two," Sam said, spinning in her chair. "Big day, boss. You ready for this?"

Natalie assumed of course that she meant a big day at the races. Xander knew she spoke of something else entirely.

"Born ready," he replied. "What about you, Miss Natalie? You ready for your first Kentucky Derby?"

"I am really excited for this!"

"Me too!" Annie chimed in from her seat across from Kyle's, toward the front of the plane.

"You kids have fun last night?" Natalie asked them.

"I sure as hell did," Kyle interrupted. "But I have a feeling today is gonna be even better."

Everyone agreed and buckled up in their seats as the plane began its descent into Lexington. Xander loved the scenery into this airport. As beautiful as his ocean view could be from the back of his home in San Diego, in a completely different way the scenery here was just as spectacular. If not more so. Acres of rolling hills lined with what looked like an endless maze of wooden fence, intertwining with each other as they crisscrossed over the perfectly manicured Kentucky blue grass. As if it wasn't beautiful enough already, the sun had just begun to peek over the horizon, casting a majestic orange glow over the land below. It was just as enchanting to him now as it had been when he was a boy.

Moments later, the plane touched down safely, and as it taxied to its spot at the airfield, everyone gathered their things and said good-bye to the jet's staff. Amy opened the door of the plane and pushed a button to lower the stairway. The cool May morning air filtered in around them. The scent of honeysuckle and freshly mowed grass tickled their noses. Annie clutched her arms in a chill.

"Don't worry, Annie. I just checked the forecast and it's supposed to get to 75 degrees today," Kyle told her.

"It's going to be a perfect day," Natalie said, flashing Xander a grin.

At the bottom of the stairs, one red Ferrari and two black Mercedes sedans with drivers holding open the back doors awaited them. A woman in a fitted black dress jumped out of the front passenger side door of the first Mercedes with a bounce and a smile. Her jet-black, chin-length hair bobbed up and down with each quirky step she took. Xander had always loved her nerdy bangs and black-rimmed reading glasses. He thought, without needing words, they explained so well her infectious personality.

"Xander! How was the San Diego launch?" Melanie asked, running up and hugging him. She gave Kyle the same hero's welcome.

"It went great. Melanie, this is Natalie and her friend Annie."

"I thought Sam was playing a joke on me when she told me the name of Xander's guest for the Derby. I am such a huge fan and it is such an honor!" Melanie exclaimed. Natalie bypassed her outstretched hand and went in for a hug. Melanie's face lit up as she mouthed "oh my god!" to Xander over Natalie's shoulder. Melanie extended the same hug to Annie.

"The honor is mine, and I love your hair, girl! Ugh, I wish I could pull that look off," Natalie replied. She had a way of making everyone around her feel good about themselves. Xander couldn't help but smile.

"Oh good! You're sweet! I knew it. I told my mom I just knew you would be the nicest person," Melanie said. Natalie gave Xander a smile, which he quickly returned.

"Okay, good lord . . . I'll see all of you at the house," Sam said from her Ferrari. Xander could tell she was over this Natalie situation. She hated complications, and had warned Xander many times that that was all a love interest was. He knew she was right, of course, but that had never stopped him before.

Just a few minutes after leaving the airport, Ron made a right from Versailles Road and in front of them was a large gated entryway. The two harpsichord-shaped wrought iron gates were held in place by two grayish-colored stone columns. In the middle of the iron entryway, where the two gates met, was a crown of the same material—the same crown that adorned the tail of Xander's plane. Natalie noticed a plate in the middle of the stone column on the right. Usually this is the place where you would find the name of the farm or ranch. Instead of naming his horse farm, however, Xander had chosen the words "Love Like a Prince. Live Like a King."

"That's an interesting choice of words. Are they yours?" she asked Xander.

"The quote? Yes."

"What does it mean exactly?" she asked.

"You tell me."

"Okay." Natalie thought for a moment. "Hmm, I think it means that though you must always strive to achieve your highest level of greatness, you can never let that journey keep you from cherishing what really matters in life. Basically, be all the things a king is, but remember to enjoy life through the unjaded eyes of a prince? That close?"

"Wow, Xander . . . she is good," Melanie said, somewhat in awe.

Planning a Hit Before Breakfast

Melanie pressed the button on the remote, and in a slow inward motion the gate opened to one of the most beautiful things that Natalie had ever seen. It was like a painting. The driveway continued in front of them down a long and perfectly straight path. Massive oak trees lined both sides of the road as far as her eyes could see. She looked to her left, and off in the distance white wooden fencing encased the entire entryway. As if it were planned, three gorgeous Thoroughbred horses frolicked in a field as the yellow glow of the sun shimmered off their brown, sleek-haired backs. As the driver pulled forward inside the gates and Natalie took all of this in, she gasped out loud at its splendor. Xander always loved seeing first timers' reactions to his property. It gave him a sense of pride that no other material thing he owned had ever quite been able to give.

The trees stretched on. In the distance she could see what looked like might finally be their end. The sun was breaking through the open slots in the branches, and as they approached a circular driveway, it shined its rays across a fantastic neoclassical Southern mansion. She knew this term from her research for the role she had played in *Wild Roses*, a film where she'd played the daughter of a racehorse trainer.

We should have filmed here, Natalie thought as she noticed a glistening pond off to the left of the mansion. The driver brought the car to a stop at the front of the house. There was a large gray front door, and over it was a gorgeous circular window that she was sure let a wondrous amount of light into what was undoubtedly a spectacular foyer.

They all walked toward the house as Annie and Natalie continued to marvel at their surroundings.

"Natalie, Annie, I'll show you two to the fitting room where you can pick out your dresses," Melanie said, unlocking the front door. "Jonathan just texted me that breakfast is ready and being served on the patio. Don't worry, we have heaters if you get cold, but the view will warm you right up. You'll be able to shower and get beautified after we eat, so don't worry about any of that right now."

Melanie opened the front door, and sure enough, Natalie's inclination about the grandeur of the foyer was dead-on. Dark hardwood floors greeted them at the doorway. Two winding staircases cascaded down both sides of the room and joined together at the top to form a balcony. It was as if Rhett Butler would be sauntering in from around the corner at any moment. The ceilings must have been twenty-five feet, and a magnificent chandelier pulled everything together from the center of the room.

Xander said, "Okay ladies, you'd better go see if those dresses will work. But don't take long or we might have to start on breakfast without you."

"We'll be there in just a few. I'm starving!" Natalie assured him.

Melanie ushered the girls down a long hallway filled with pictures of Xander and his family. Natalie stopped and admired them along the way. Pictures of a young Xander in baseball uniforms and in family pictures with his mother, father, and sister. *He looks just like his dad,* she thought and wondered if they were still close. Since she had found out on the plane last night that Xander's mother was deceased, she also morbidly wondered if his dad had passed as well. She thought that was probably the case because none of the photos with his father seemed to be recent ones. Xander looked so happy in all of the photos. Not that he didn't seem happy to her now, but there was certainly a sadness in his eyes. Natalie walked on down the hall and noticed a picture of Xander in uniform. She leaned in and noticed that he was being given a medal. The writing on the table banner behind him read "Navy SEALs," and under it, "The only easy day was yesterday, it pays to be a Winner."

"Come on, Natalie," Annie called for her. "Come have a look at these dresses!"

"Do I need to go over everything with you or did you get a chance to look over the file I e-mailed you?" Sam asked Xander as she walked out to the raised patio where Xander and Kyle had just sat down. A large assortment of breakfast foods was spread across the large stone table.

"I'm good, Sam, thank you. I'm not really into planning a hit before breakfast."

Sam ignored him. "So, you know where everything will be waiting for you at the track when it is time to take him out? And

Kyle, you know—"

"I said we're good. Thank you, Sam. Now sit down, relax, and have some breakfast."

"Yeah, relax. Jesus," Kyle chimed in.

"Don't." Sam pointed while locking him in a death stare.

"All right, you two, do I need to separate you?" Xander interrupted their staring contest.

Sam stood from the table and turned to Xander. "I'll be inside tracking the target and making sure everything will be ready for you."

"Thank you, Sam."

Sam walked back inside, but not before shooting Kyle another glare. She would never have involved him in such serious matters, but Xander insisted. It hasn't bit them in the ass, yet.

"Man she is wound tight," Kyle said.

"Thank God. Between me and you goofing around all the time none of this would ever come off without a hitch the way it always does if she wasn't that way." Xander took up for her.

"Yeah, I guess you're right. Hey, speaking of goofing off, Annie was a real shot of life on the plane last night."

"I know, we heard everything. It wasn't awkward at all," Xander said sarcastically.

"Whoops!" Kyle laughed. "Seriously, though, Annie was unbelievable. You think Natalie will actually let you have sex with her?"

"Kyle."

"What? Oh, don't tell me you actually like this one? X? Uh oh, what is that little grin I see?" Kyle teased.

"Honestly, I don't know if it's because I loved her so much in that movie or what it is, but—"

"But what? I was kidding, but holy shit . . . you really like her. Xander King with feelings other than lust? Well, I *never!*" Kyle laughed.

It was true, never before had Kyle seen him do anything other than love them and leave them. It was a defense mechanism for the strong and macho Xander. If he never let anyone get close, there was no way he could lose someone he loved again. It wasn't a conscious decision. But he did understand that he was not the type of man who should ever be in a relationship. Knowing this about himself was what made all the one-night stands so easy. He was doing them all a favor by letting them go. His was not a life fit for love; there just wasn't space for it.

Yet, there she was.

The Darling of the Day

"How'd it go in the barn?" Kyle asked Xander as they stood at the helicopter positioned in the middle of the circular driveway at the front of the mansion. Kyle wore a brown suit with a small tan pinstripe, a white shirt, and a tan tie. Xander had had it fitted just for him, just for this occasion. It hung perfectly on Kyle's six-two athletic figure.

"You know I don't kiss and tell."

After breakfast with Annie and Natalie, Xander took Natalie to see the horses in the stables behind his house. It had been the first time they had any time alone. Xander let her feed one of the foals with a bottle, then managed a kiss at the edge of the barn. A kiss that still left him buzzing.

Xander wore a tailored slim-fit navy-blue suit that carried a faint light-blue pinstripe. He paired it with a white shirt and a navy-blue tie with a matching light-blue stripe that barber-poled down to the tip. Melanie picked it out because she said it made his eyes pop. Xander was okay with that. And the blue did exactly as she said. Xander stood the same height as Kyle but with an even more solid frame. More like one of the hackberry elm trees at the front gate of the property.

The front door opened, and Melanie sashayed out with Annie and Natalie following behind her. Xander smiled to himself at how Natalie had insisted Melanie go to the Derby with them. You could see it all over Melanie's face how happy it made her. Annie and Melanie were beautiful in their Derby getups, and Xander could tell Kyle approved by the nudge he gave him in the ribs at first sight of Annie in that red dress.

Then there was Natalie.

Gorgeous to any man, but to Xander, who was such a fan of the Kentucky Derby, in this outfit she borderlined on overwhelming. It was like a look back in time at how ladies used to dazzle their men in the same tradition. Her lavender dress wrapped tightly around her spectacular frame. The semi-shiny satin began about an inch above her knee, and with thin, almost spaghetti straps, it clung to her upper body, revealing her overly respectable breasts without showing too much skin.

Sexy and classy.

Few women could pull this off. It seemed that most believed showing skin to be the only manner in which a woman could be sexy. Lessons could be learned from the severity of this look on Natalie. She had embraced the tradition of the Derby, and that was clear by the way the curls of her hair fell perfectly from underneath her hat. Her oversize hat that still managed to stay understated by Derby standards. A lavender ribbon wrapped around the base of the khaki-colored hat, a perfect match for the dress. The brim extended out several inches and sturdily flopped with each step she took. Xander almost didn't notice the hat at all because with each step her chest also bounced with the firmness of a woman much younger. Melanie had done a wonderful job selecting their attire, but even she couldn't compete with Mother Nature's triumphs.

"Don't you ladies look outstanding," Xander said to the group. As he helped Melanie and Annie onto the helicopter, he stopped Natalie. "You look stunning."

She gave a curtsy and answered him in the accent of a true Southern belle. "Why, thank you, kind sir, it's nothin' but a li'l hocus pocus." She laughed. He laughed with her and followed her onto the chopper. The five of them strapped in. The rest of the team would travel with Sam by car. They had other business to tend to. The ladies traded their extravagant hats for headphones so they were able to communicate with everyone in the helicopter. The pilot fired up the engine, and three rotor blades began to spin with a grand swooping sound above them.

The captain tapped into everyone's headphones. "If everyone is ready to go, Mr. King, we will get you all on your way."

Xander gave the pilot a thumbs-up, and the pilot announced a travel time of only twenty minutes. Xander noticed that Natalie once again gave the chair a nervous clutch.

"First time in a helicopter?"

She looked down at her hands and gave a nervous laugh. It seemed to be a natural reflex for her, one she didn't even know was happening.

"How'd you guess?" She smiled, and her voice was distorted as it passed through the chopper's comm system.

The helicopter shook for a moment, then began a gentle rise away from the bluegrass below. Xander wasn't all that crazy about helicopters himself; too many of his SEAL team missions had been carried out from them.

At least this time I won't be exiting by squirming down a rope. No rage-crazed terrorists waiting below, either.

Xander glanced around the cabin, and everyone seemed content as the chopper tilted its nose toward Louisville. They leveled off at around nine thousand feet; any higher than that and the cozy unpressurized cabin wouldn't feel so comfortable anymore. Almost as soon as they were up, they were on their way back down. The majestic twin spires on the grandstand at Churchill Downs pointed their peaks toward the bright blue sky. *Severe clear today, son,* his dad would say to him when not a single cloud could be found. He knew his dad was looking down on him today. Proud. His dad always loved going to the track. In hindsight it was probably more about spending time with his son than actually betting on the horses. A billionaire betting pennies on ponies wasn't lost on Xander, even at such a young age. His dad hated losing money.

A crowd of thousands gathered below them. They looked like an army of ants swarming into their hill. The helicopter made its way over row after row of stables until it hovered over a bare patch of grass just off to the side of all the hoopla. Xander couldn't help but judge every landing by its softness, just a habit he and his fellow soldiers became used to because it would help put their minds at ease with each mission they carried out. Even on a day with perfect conditions, it wasn't easy to come to a smooth landing in a helicopter.

"Nice one, Harry," Xander announced with approval. Even Xander was impressed by his pilot's control. The helicopter came to a stop on the grass like your head as it hits the pillow. Immediately, the smell of horses came to the noses of the group, a smell Xander loved. It was most likely a mixture of hay and horseshit, not a combination that would be loved by most. The pilot shut off the engine, and as the rotors slowed their way to a halt, Xander popped the door open and began helping everyone down to the ground. They were greeted with a smile by a Churchill Downs official.

"Mr. King, my name is Rory. I'm in charge of making sure today goes as smoothly for you as it possibly can."

Rory was a lanky young man, couldn't have been a day over twenty-one. His thick combed-over dark hair fluttered in the breeze of the last few turns of the helicopter's rotors. He extended his hand and darted his eyes around the faces of the group with the excitement of someone who had just been told he would be escorting around a movie star all day.

Xander shook his hand. "Rory, call me Xander. This is Natalie, Kyle, Annie, and Melanie."

"Wow, Natalie Rockwell. It is such an honor. You are so beautiful!"

"The honor is mine, Rory, and thank you. Aren't you sweet? It's nice to meet you."

"Mr. King—Xander, your sister and your niece arrived just a bit ago and we have shown them to the owners lounge upstairs. And if you don't mind me saying, I'm a huge fan of King's Ransom, the horse and the bourbon. It's all my friends and I drink," Rory went on. He spoke almost as fast as they could listen. His nerves might have been getting the best of him.

"Thanks, Rory. Glad you all like it. Give Melanie your address later and I'll send you guys a case," Xander told him as they followed Rory toward the stables.

"That's awesome, sir. Thank you! My buddies are so jealous that I get to hang out with you guys today. Anything you need, don't hesitate to ask. Oh, and speaking of King's Ransom, you have about a half an hour before they need you in the media room. Would you like to see him? I went by his stall earlier and he was having a little snack."

"Perfect," Xander replied, then turned to everyone. "Does that sound good to you all?"

Natalie smiled, "I can't wait to meet the man of the hour!"

Kyle and Annie agreed, and they all followed Rory to the entrance of the stables. They entered the metal barnlike structure through the back door so as to avoid the media lurking around front. King's Ransom was the darling of the day. In the weeks leading up to the race, ESPN had done several features of the Kentucky-bred favorite. They even shot a piece at the house before Ransom was moved to Louisville earlier in the week. Gary—Ransom's trainer—thought it would be best to come early and let him acclimate to these surroundings. It also gave him the chance to run some extra furlongs on Churchill's track. The media seemed especially keen on Ransom for several reasons. First off, there was the dizzying amount of cash Xander had laid out two years ago on the untested yearling. Second, he had multiple Derby winners in his lineage. And lastly, he was just a gigantic horse. More freight train than Thoroughbred as his head feverishly bobbed its way down the track over his seven-foot frame. The only thing missing was the warning whistle. His midnight-black coat made him all the more ominous. The media was simply captivated by him.

Rory led them down the dirt-covered walkway, passing stall after stall of beautiful horses. Millions of dollars' worth of horses. Normally, because of the sheer volume of horses parading in and out during the morning, there would be manure land mines to avoid all along this path, but because of the type of people who owned these animals, Churchill had dedicated workers to follow the horses around and make sure all of it barely even touched the ground. It reminded Xander of the summer his dad put him to work on a friend's farm. It wasn't the most fun he had had making money, but he loved the horses. It was the chicken shit that really ruined his day.

"This is so exciting, Xander. Thanks for being a little crazy and inviting us along," Annie said from the back of the pack. The ladies walked gingerly along the path in an attempt to keep from kicking up dust on their pretty shoes.

"Absolutely, Annie, I love bringing first timers. Lets me live it a little for the first time again myself. It doesn't hurt that y'all are so damn gorgeous, either. You'll make my stock rise." Xander winked at Natalie as she walked beside him.

"You surprise me, Xander," Annie answered. "Most good-looking rich guys are too full of themselves to be romantic souls. Now that I've gotten to know you a little, you seem like you might be all right."

"Aw, Annie, that was sweet. Can y'all believe that we just met last night? Seems like a week ago," Natalie said.

"Did I just hear a *y'all*?" Kyle laughed.

Xander laughed. "I believe you did. She's gonna fit right in today."

Natalie gave another curtsy.

As they approached the end of the stables, the air became a little less stuffy. The main stable door was open, and it let a much-needed breeze blow through. The chatter of voices and snapping cameras reached their ears as they turned the corner to the first stall on the second row.

So much for avoiding the media.

A man in a seersucker suit and a tan straw hat approached them as they neared the commotion.

"You want me to get them out of here, Xander?"

"If you think you can without making a stink." Xander hugged the man, then turned to Natalie. "Not sure how they will react seeing you here, Natalie. I'm sorry, Gary, this is Natalie and Annie. You know K and Melanie. Ladies, this is Gary Trudough, the engine that makes King's Ransom run."

Before they could say hello, one of the members of the media noticed Natalie and drew everyone's attention to her.

"Natalie Rockwell? Is that you?" a woman in a blue dress asked. "Natalie, what are you doing here with Mr. King?"

Natalie stepped to them like a pro. Mainly because she was exactly that. Xander figured she had had swarms of paparazzi following her for most of her adult life. A trip to the grocery store was news in Hollywood when it was Natalie Rockwell.

"Hello, everyone. This is Xander's day," she said. Then she walked over to the stall that read "King's Ransom." "More importantly it is this beautiful boy's day. I'm just a friend lending some support."

"Natalie!" a member of the media shouted. "Natalie, how long have you known Mr. King? Are the two of you *together*?"

Gary stepped in as Natalie smiled and repeated she was only there for friendly support. "Okay, all right. Thank you all for coming over. King's Ransom will be available again in an hour. We will let you know. Thank you." He ushered them toward the exit of the stables.

"Mr. King! Mr. King!" another reporter shouted. "How long have you and Miss Rockwell been a couple?"

Xander just smiled. "The only couple in here you should be worried about is a couple of sad Thoroughbred horses that are going to be watching Ransom's ass as he crosses the finish line in front of them. I'll give you all the details on that at the press conference in fifteen minutes."

The crowd of reporters gave an understanding laugh and made their way out of the stables to give him and his friends some privacy. King's Ransom gave an approving whinny at the peaceful silence they left in their wake.

"I see this isn't your first rodeo with cameras and questions," Xander said to Natalie.

"You have no idea," Annie chimed in. "This girl crosses the street in Beverly Hills and double that group of cameramen would be nipping at her heels."

"True story." Natalie smiled. "You get used to it."

"I'd end up kicking every single one of them in the teeth," Kyle jumped in. "That or take a dump right on the sidewalk in front of them. Really give them something to talk about."

They laughed as Xander nodded his head, knowing full well that was the absolute truth. "Anyway, Natalie, Annie, meet King's Ransom. Ransom, this is Natalie and Annie."

The giant horse let out a breath of air and nodded as if to say hello. His stance was one of gallant confidence, his black eyes a quiet fury.

"He is magnificent, Xander. Wow, you said he was big, but, my God, he's as tall as two of me!" Natalie marveled, admiring the black beauty.

"That's not saying much," Annie joked.

Natalie made a pouty face and stuck her tongue out at Annie. They all shared a laugh.

Rory spoke up. "Xander, I hate to interrupt, but you might

want to start over toward the conference room."

"Of course. Would you be kind enough to show them to where we'll all be spending the day? Maybe get them a bottle of champagne?"

"Absolutely. And there is already a bottle of Veuve Clicquot on ice, chilling as we speak."

"Good man, Rory. All right, you guys, I won't be too long and I'll be right up to the box. Rory, make sure you take care of this pretty lady in my absence," Xander said, kissing Natalie on the hand and handing her off to him.

Natalie sent Xander an air kiss, and with a smile she walked out of the stables along with the rest of the group. Xander made his way out into the Kentucky sunshine behind them. Various colored roses lined the cobblestone walkway beneath his feet on all sides. Sprinkled in were some fully bloomed dogwood trees bursting with their signature white and pink buds that spattered like a painting against the backdrop of the grandstand. The sun began to bake on the shoulders of his suit, and he could feel the warmth all the way to his skin. Sam was waiting ahead at the entrance to the conference area. She looked especially pretty today, but he knew that after years of complimenting her it would fall on deaf ears if he were to say so.

"All right, Xander, everything is set. We have to go with plan B, however, because we couldn't bring in everything we needed for your weapon," Sam told him, all business.

"Sounds good. I told you plan B was more suitable for this son of a bitch anyway. Do we have confirmation that he is here yet?"

"We do. Kulakov arrived alone, twenty minutes ago. He will be easy to spot; he's wearing a rubbish plaid sport coat with a dreadful pair of striped trousers. He looks as if he dressed himself in the bloody dark."

"Okay, Sam." Xander laughed. "Just tip Kyle like we discussed and he will let me know everything is in place when it's time. I'll see you in the winner's circle?"

"I'll see you back at the house when the job is finished. I'll leave the winner's circle for you and Natalie," Sam replied.

"Ooh, what's this? Do I detect some jealousy, Samantha? I didn't know you were so in love with me . . . Humph, all this time . . ."

Sam just turned up her nose and walked away. It was eleven by then, so Xander straightened his tie and walked into the press conference.

This Owner's Box Will Do Just Fine

Natalie took in the scenery on her walk with everyone to the owner's box. Though she thought them gorgeous, she wasn't interested as much in the dogwoods and the roses as she was the dresses and hats. She just loved the grandeur of this day, much more than she had anticipated. It hearkened back to a time she felt was far more romantic than today. Maybe that was the appeal of Xander. She was used to the redundancy of the big city. Redundant in a way that she hadn't even realized until she came here. It sounded silly to her, even as she thought it, because Los Angeles offered so many different things to be considered redundant. But to her, they were all the same things. She had often wondered how many perfectly lit lounges and super fun nightclubs a nearly thirty-year-old woman could stand anyway. She longed for charm. So far, the charm of this day was suiting her just fine. She got to wear a new dress and a fun hat, feed a baby horse, ride a four-wheeler and a helicopter . . . had a kiss. And what a kiss it was. It reminded her of a line from the movie *Hearts in Atlantis* when Anthony Hopkins, as Ted Brautigan, told young Bobby that his kiss with Carol Gerber "would be the kiss against which all others in your life would be judged . . . and left wanting." She feared this to be true of her first kiss with Alexander King. She couldn't imagine another kiss would ever measure up. Natalie smiled at the thought and laughed at her own hopeless romantic plight. It did, however, seem as though Xander at least shared her romantic soul.

They walked up a set of concrete stairs and outside through a short tunnel. The concrete roof of the tunnel gave way to the massive wooden overhang of the classic Churchill grandstand. In front of her sprawled an amazing view of the track. Beyond the dirt track and the white railing lay a gorgeous display of roses, colored and shaped to form the words *The 141st Kentucky Derby*. Beyond that, a colossal video screen that marked the beginning of what she remembered someone calling the infield. There looked to be a carnival of sorts happening inside that grass-covered inner ring of the track. Hot dog stands, bands playing, and swarms of people all came together under the deep blue Kentucky sky. She had heard on several occasions that it always ended up an out-of-control party in there. By the time the actual run for the roses took place in a few hours, as she had been told, half the eighty thousand some-odd people in there wouldn't even know there was a race going on. Bourbon had that effect on people. Natalie had felt those effects far too many times in her life for the idea of the infield to be appealing to her now.

84

No, thanks. This owner's box will do just fine.

"Well, are y'all excited?" Kyle bellowed as he walked them into the box and began to work his way into the champagne. There were ten chairs in the open-air box that could be situated any way anyone saw fit. On the two tables that were fastened to a short wall sat a couple of ice buckets, chilling the champagne. Another couple of buckets held bottles of Xander and Kyle's very own King's Ransom Kentucky straight bourbon whiskey. A few mixers and some extra ice were in a couple of buckets on the ground. The races had yet to begin, but hordes of people had already packed the place full of drinking and laughter.

After meeting Xander's sister, Helen, and his adorable niece, Kaley, Natalie noticed Kyle pouring some champagne, but what really caught her eye was the way Annie was looking at him as he did so. Annie was a lot like Natalie when it came to relationships. There had been some tough ones that had left them scarred enough to be really wary when it came to men. Kyle had an infectious personality, so she could see why Annie was drawn to him. Unfortunately for Natalie, the last couple of guys she had met who'd had such boisterous personalities kept wanting to share it with other women. *Lots* of other women.

"Well, what do you think? A little overwhelming, huh?" Melanie asked.

"It is, but in a good way. I don't really know how to bet, though. I'll probably make a fool of myself," Natalie replied.

"Oh, don't worry about that. Xander will have you up and running in no time! Pardon the pun!" Melanie laughed.

Kyle walked over and handed Natalie a glass of champagne. "Cheers! To a day full of fun with a boxful of fun people!" Natalie clinked Kyle's glass and then took a sip from her own.

"So, tell me," Kyle said, "what exactly are your intentions with

85

my best friend?"

"All above board, I assure you." Natalie smiled. "So, how many times have you had this conversation on Xander's behalf?"

"Um . . . well, zero, I guess. I'm never around a girl long enough to have this conversation."

"It's only been a day."

"Well, it usually doesn't carry over into the next day. Hell, Xander hasn't had a girlfriend since junior high. Don't tell him I said this, but I think he's afraid to get close to anyone since his parents died."

"What happened with that anyway?" she asked, then quickly shook her head. "Never mind. That is far too heavy a subject for a day like today."

"No, it's fine. It was a long time ago. Xander was only fifteen when both his mom and dad were—"

"Hey, what'd I miss?" Xander interrupted as he came up from behind and put his arms around Kyle and Natalie.

"Not a thing yet, buddy!" Kyle answered, handing him some champagne.

"Nothing yet! But I did get to meet your sweet sister and her adorable Miss Kaley," Natalie said.

"Oh, sis is here?"

"She is! She just had to step away to take Kaley to the bathroom."

"Cheers, Xander. To an awesome day at the races," Kyle interjected.

"Cheers." Xander clanged Kyle's glass, then turned to Natalie. "Cheers, gorgeous."

Natalie wrapped her arm around his. "Cheers. How'd the press conference go? I bet you charmed the pants off of 'em."

"Well, fine, I guess. Just not what I expected."

"How so?"

"Well, I thought I was here for a big horse race, but the only thing the media wanted to know was when some movie star and I got together." Xander laughed, giving her arm a squeeze.

"Ugh, I'm so sorry. I should have warned you before letting you bring me here. The last thing I want to do is take away from this day for you."

"Come on now," Xander said, hugging her. "There isn't a thing about today that having you around won't make better."

Natalie raised her glass in excitement. "You are too sweet. Now, teach me how to win some money on these ponies!"

Xander Takes a Bathroom Break

Before he knew it, they had bet their way to the eleventh race. One more race and Ransom would hit the track and run for glory. The box they were in had been surrounded by a steady stream of onlookers since about race three. Once word spread that Natalie Rockwell was there, well, it wasn't long before her fans found her. Her "#Amazing" Derby Instagram posts certainly weren't helping that cause. She had already signed at least a couple hundred programs and snapped probably twice that amount of photos. She took it all in stride. She hadn't complained about any of it, not once. Kyle and Annie were getting more and more promiscuous with each glass of champagne and every toast of whiskey. Xander had had a few himself, but in order to minimize the tabloid fodder he and Natalie restrained their affection to smiles and winks.

And occasionally she would sneak a pinch of his ass.

Sam's intel was to move on the job at the beginning of race eleven. There was, however, a contingency. Throughout the races, Sam would be monitoring the betting, drinking, and bathroom habits of Erik Kulakov. If a variation opened the door for a better time to take him out, she would notify Kyle, who would in turn signal Xander. Xander looked over to Kyle and sure enough, he had thrown his tie over his right shoulder. Xander made sure Melanie and Natalie were preoccupied, then opened his phone and checked the Cyber Dust app.

X – It is exactly 4:32 as I press send. The target will be placing a bet at the lower mezzanine windows in approximately 11 minutes. There is a men's restroom exactly 32 paces to the west. I have made certain the target will need to relieve himself directly after placing his bet. Everything you need will be hidden above the corner tile above the toilet connected to the far wall. Simply place the earpiece inside your ear and I will instruct you to the second of his arrival. You can dispose of all the materials where you found them above the tile. Leave the target on the toilet as if he was using it and I will see to it that everything is cleaned up in a manner so as not to interrupt the running of the Derby. As always, if there are any variations in what I have told you, no matter how small, abort the mission and we will find another time to eliminate the target. No exceptions. This message will automatically disappear without a trace from your phone.

Xander closed out the Dust message Sam sent him, and then it disappeared from traceability. It wasn't exactly like "This message will self-destruct," but it was pretty damn cool.

"Natalie, are you having fun?" Xander asked as he tapped her on the shoulder.

"A blast! It's almost time for the big race, are you getting nervous?"

"I'm good." He smiled. "I do, however, have to run down to do a couple of interviews before the race starts up. When Rory gets back, would you mind telling him that I went down early to use the restroom?"

"Of course, have fun and hurry back!"

"Any tips for a television camera rookie?" he asked.

"Be yourself and keep your chin up. It will make you look thinner on camera. But your handsome face will bring that audience to their knees anyway, so don't worry." She winked.

"Good tip. Good luck on the next race. I'll be right back."

Natalie blew him a kiss, and Kyle gave him a wink as he turned toward the crowded grandstand. His walk toward the target was filled with heavy reflection. Quite the dichotomy this day was. The contrast of emotions was immense, even for someone trained to squelch such feelings. He knew he would be feeling a lot of this, regardless of Natalie; however, she certainly brought a new fold of emotions he never would have dreamed he would be dealing with. She was a special woman, and he knew that what he felt was different. This is exactly why he should have left her in San Diego. But he didn't, and he knew in about twenty minutes he would be extremely happy that he hadn't.

The day had warmed to the seventy-five degrees Kyle had promised. As Xander entered the tunnel toward the stairs, he allowed himself one last thought of Natalie, then one last thought of his horse that was prepping for the biggest horse race in the world.

Then he focused.

He descended the stairs to the mezzanine and found the

window where Kulakov would be betting. Sure enough, there he was, fourth in line. Sam was dead-on, as usual. She was dead-on about the ghastly outfit he wore as well. Xander continued to the men's restroom, thirty-two paces from said betting window. The line into the restroom was always long between races, but Xander didn't worry. He knew Sam had factored this into the timing. The line was three deep outside the door. As he waited, he slowed his heart rate to the optimum level necessary to maximize his cognitive ability. As the line ushered its way in and others continued to make their way out, Xander stepped inside the restroom. He counted eight men inside and made no other move as he patiently waited for Sam.

"Holy shit! What the hell? This is my good suit!" a man shouted from the row of three sinks on the left side of the bathroom. As he was washing his hands, the pipe below the sink had sprung a leak and water was gushing out into the crowded restroom.

"We'd better get out of here," Xander said to the patrons. "I saw maintenance on my way in. I'll run and get him so they can stop the water." He made his way back out as he continued to urge everyone else out as he went. He walked out the door and turned the corner of the wall. With a quick glance, he noticed that Kulakov was next in line to bet. This gave him about two safe minutes. He counted eight men leaving the restroom after him and immediately a large crash from the bar across from him rang out through the mezzanine as a wall of bourbon bottles tumbled to the ground.

Thank you, Sam.

While everyone jerked their heads toward the second distraction Sam had triggered, Xander slipped back inside the restroom. The water on the ground was now above his shoes as

91

it raced toward the overwhelmed drain in the center of the floor. He sloshed his way through water toward the first stall against the wall, just like Sam's message directed. After opening the stall door and closing the lid on the toilet, he hoisted himself to the ceiling and popped in the tile. Per Sam's correspondence there was a small gym bag, a bright-yellow collapsible sign that read, "Sorry for the inconvenience. This restroom is closed," and a two-piece squeegee. Xander used the handicap rail as a shelf for the bag and wasted no time opening it and putting on the janitor suit and hat Sam had provided. It was a hunter-green one-piece suit that zipped up the front. He balanced himself on the toilet seat and slid into the janitor's uniform. It was plenty big enough to put on over and conceal his suit. At the bottom of the bag he found a pair of gloves; he put them on and then took out the earpiece and slid it inside his right ear. There was also a three-inch piece of chrome pipe that would stop the water at the sink and a metal tube that housed the syringe Xander would use to kill Kulakov. He stepped down from the seat, slid the cased syringe down in the uniform's front pocket, and screwed the handle of the squeegee together as he made his way to the sink. The piece of pipe from the bag connected to the sink pipe exactly the way Sam had intended and stopped the water from continuing to run out into the restroom. Using the squeegee, he pushed the remaining bit of water toward another drain that sat under the urinals.

"Twelve seconds," Sam's voice whispered into his ear.

Xander went back to the stall, grabbed the yellow sign, and made his way back outside the restroom. He placed the sign on the floor in front of the door and pulled his hat down lower on his head.

Sam finished the count. "Three . . . two . . . one . . ."

Erik Kulakov rounded the corner at that very moment and stopped short of the yellow sign. He tucked his program under his plaid-covered arm, adjusted his glasses, and read the sign.

"Is the restroom closed?" Kulakov asked Xander in a faint but still detectable Russian accent.

Xander picked up the sign and waved him in. Kulakov walked into the restroom, and as soon as the door shut, Xander replaced the sign in front of the door and walked back inside the restroom. He twisted the lock on the door, ensuring no one else could enter. At the urinal now, his back to Xander, stood a man responsible for the death and destruction of the lives of countless young people in the Louisville area. It amazed Xander that even though he knew these people were awful and disgusting humans, it never got easier to take a life. However, letting more innocent people die at his hands was not acceptable, and he would not let families lose their loved ones to the actions of a monster the way he had so tragically lost his parents years ago.

No one deserves that pain.

Xander stepped toward Kulakov as he urinated. Thoughts of his parents' murder flashed in his head as he wrapped one arm around Kulakov's upper body and pinned him against the urinal. Before Kulakov could react, Xander cupped his free hand around Kulakov's neck, and with a blood choke he squeezed his hand together in a way that compressed both the carotid arteries and the jugular veins, without compressing the airway. This technique causes cerebral ischemia and a temporary hypoxic condition in the brain, essentially starving the brain of blood. When well applied, as it was in that moment, this blood choke leads to unconsciousness in a matter of seconds. If held for more than twelve seconds, it can lead to death. Kulakov struggled inside Xander's grip, but his hold was so tight that he barely even moved. For Xander it was like holding down a four-year-old.

Three . . . four . . . five . . .

Xander counted in his head. At five seconds he felt Kulakov's body slump in his arms. This technique worked the same way as the rear naked choke he had applied many times while training Brazilian jiu-jitsu. Kulakov was unconscious now, but Xander didn't want him to wake up before he had administered the deadly dose of krokodil that awaited him in the syringe. He thought it fitting for this monster to die from the same drug he had killed so many others with. Not to mention it would be better if the press made him out to be a coward who took his own life.

Six . . . seven . . . eight . . .

This choke was perfect for the autopsy as well because there would be no sign of foul play. Xander had practiced this choke a thousand times to ensure there would be no marks on the neck upon release. He let go of the choke at the count of ten and dragged Kulakov's limp body, at the underarms, over to the toilet seat in the designated stall. Upon lifting the top of the seat he placed Kulakov in a seated position and pulled the syringe from his front pocket. Since Kulakov's pants were already down, it was easiest just to use the femoral artery as the injection site. Xander slid the needle in. About three inches down from his genitals on the inner thigh to be exact. He felt the skin give a small pop as he pressed the needle into his dark curly-hair-covered leg. The dark brown liquid krokodil inside the tube of the syringe slowly disappeared as Xander pressed the plunger closer and closer to its base. Sam had loaded enough of a dose to kill two grown men. The krokodil was now coursing through Kulakov's veins, silently killing him as he sat unconscious. Xander retracted the needle once the dose had been fully administered and placed the syringe in Kulakov's cold, dead hand. Xander then began to change out of the maintenance suit.

"Xander, there is a maintenance man moving your sign right now. Whatever you hear outside, just finish what you are doing just as planned." Sam came through over his earpiece. The next sound Xander heard was a shaking of the locked door to the bathroom. Xander didn't pause for a moment as he undressed and replaced everything exactly as he had found it. He knew Sam would take care of any potential problem.

He heard Sam's voice in his earpiece again. "Hello, sir, could you please help me for just a moment? I know you are busy, but I can't find my daughter and I really need you to take me to someone who can help."

Xander knew this was her distracting the maintenance man. He replaced the ceiling tile, then stepped down and around Kulakov's body to the ground. He closed the stall door behind him and walked over to the mirror. He ran his fingers through his hair a couple of times and straightened his tie.

"No worse for the wear," he said aloud.

The same couldn't be said for Erik Kulakov. As savage as killing another human was, Xander knew he was leaving the world a better place. The only thing that scared him about what just happened had nothing to do with the act itself. It was that the very first thing that crossed his mind as he slid the needle into Erik's skin was Natalie. He had no idea what that meant; he just knew that for an assassin it probably wasn't good.

Say Hello to the King

Xander took one last look in the mirror, then made his way out the restroom door.

"There you are, Mr. King." Rory rounded the corner of the wall just as Xander walked out. "I've been looking all over for you. Miss Rockwell said you went down for the interview but you weren't there. Is everything okay?"

The irony of the question was almost enough to make Xander laugh, but he refrained. "Everything is fine, Rory. Let's go get this over with so I can get everyone down to the paddock before we walk out to the track with Ransom."

"Of course. I'll go and get everyone from the box while you do the interview, and we will meet you in the paddock," Rory replied.

Xander followed Rory through the mezzanine. Along the way his eyes found Sam, and he simply gave her a solemn nod.

Rory and Xander walked down another set of stairs and outside through a small concrete tunnel. The crowd swelled now; one television they passed posted a graphic that read "140,000 people in attendance." The sounds of hundreds of conversations and a fair share of drunken laughs filled the air around them on the way to the paddock. So, too, did a waft of beer from the cups around him. A drink sounded real good right about now. A few more strides and Rory dropped Xander off at a makeshift news setup right in front of the paddock where the twenty Thoroughbreds running that day were now being saddled before the big race. Rory introduced Xander to Jonathan Winters of ABC sports, and simultaneously a makeup artist began to paint Xander's face lightly with a brush, preparing him for the bright lights of the camera.

"Okay, Tommy, we ready? Mr. King, I'm Jonathan Winters." A tall, handsome silver-haired man reached out his hand. Xander recognized his tanned and withered face from years of seeing it on sportscasts all over the world.

"Absolutely. Nice to meet you," Xander replied.

The light of the camera fired up, and Tommy gave Jonathan a three count and pointed to them both.

"Thanks a lot, Bob. I am here with King's Ransom owner, Alexander King. Mr. King, what an exciting day this must be for you and your team."

"You have no idea, Jonathan. We are all extremely excited to see Ransom do his best out there today."

"Can you give us a rundown of what your day has been like leading up to the big moment?"

"Just like any other day, I suppose." Xander and Jonathan laughed at the sarcasm. "No, just trying to enjoy a great day of racing with family and friends. Ready for Ransom to take it

97

home."

Oh, and I just murdered someone in the bathroom of the mezzanine. What? You don't believe me? He's still there; go have a look for yourself.

"Well, King's Ransom has been the media darling this week, and with his odds coming in right at three to one at the moment, he seems to be the darling of the people's bets as well. How does that make you feel?"

"It's really a great feeling. And he deserves all the attention. He's a hell of a pony."

Out of the corner of his eye he saw Natalie standing with the others just on the other side of the paddock fence. She was attracting quite a bit of attention herself. She noticed him looking, and she smiled and gave him a thumbs-up

"Speaking of darlings, Mr. King, our field reporter, Kristen Wilkes, is barking in my ear to get the scoop on a media darling of a different sort, Natalie Rockwell. We've been told that the movie star came with you today, and everyone is wondering if you are a couple?" Jonathan pressed.

"Natalie *is* a darling, that is for sure, but she is just here to support King's Ransom's run for the roses. She's become a wonderful friend."

"A friend, I see. Well, there you have it, Kristen. One last question, Mr. King, what does today mean to you knowing that your father was such a big racing fan?"

A flood of emotions raced all through Xander. He wanted to punch Jonathan in the throat for asking such an emotional question. He didn't let it get the best of him, however. Xander took a deep breath and pulled himself together.

"Pops would have loved to throw about ten bucks on Ransom." Xander forced a chuckle. "Today is a proud day for all of us involved. It means a lot that all of my team's hard work got us here where they can enjoy such a momentous occasion. I'm just ready to get in there and give Ransom a little pep talk before he eats these other ponies alive."

"And we will let you go do that. Thanks for your time, Mr. King. Good luck today, and hopefully we will see you in the winner's circle! Back to you in the studio, Bob."

Tommy shut the camera off, and Jonathan thanked Xander again for the interview. Xander nodded and turned his attention toward the paddock where Gary had just walked in with Ransom and was readying the saddle for Jose. Jose was like a child standing next to Ransom. It really was astonishing how small jockeys were. Before he had settled on the name King's Ransom, Xander had toyed with the idea of a more satirical name, maybe something like Midget Taxi? Mud in Your Eye? Or of course there was his personal favorite, Quit Hittin' Me with That Stick.

It was funny to him, at least. He imagined the name would not make it past the Jockey Club. Xander was certain they were far too stuffy to enjoy his sense of humor and approve any of those names—although the name Hoof Hearted did make it past them several years ago. His mom knew how much he loved fart jokes, so she let him put five dollars on it. It ended up being a shit horse, finished dead last.

Gary was putting the finishing touches on tightening the left stirrup of the black leather saddle. King's Ransom stood like a giant, even among the other three-year-old colts in the race. The scene was so beautiful around him that Xander felt as if he were in one of the many scenic horse paintings that used to hang in his father's office. They were lodged as firmly in his memory now as the paintings had been surrounded back then by rich dark woods and hunter-green wall paint.

The area of the paddock he was standing in was a circle walkway of weathered gray cobblestone surrounded by bluegrass. Inside of the larger circular area, which constituted the entire paddock, were all the other colts getting fitted for the race. All along the brown wooden fence that separated the participants of the race from the patrons were rows of pink and white dogwoods, dotted at their base with a rainbow of colored roses. One could search the world over and not find a more breathtaking scene. Xander stepped forward and took hold of the silver ring on the black leather halter that snugged under the bottom of Ransom's chin and rubbed his slick black-haired jaw, which felt like velour-covered concrete. The spatter of white that painted the middle of his nose from eye level down to his nostrils was the only color on his face. As Xander gave his nose a rub, Jose, a small Mexican man, walked up to say hello.

"I think he's ready for something big today, señor," Jose said with confidence.

Jose was adorned in the silks that Xander had labored over for days in an attempt to find a color and pattern that best represented his stable.

"And just what makes you so sure he's ready for something big today?" Xander asked.

"He told me so."

"I don't doubt it. I'm going to have a word with him myself before you lead him to glory. You and Gary have your strategy for the race all lined out?"

"Yes, señor, take him to the lead and never look back."

"Works for me, Jose. Have a perfect run." Xander gave Jose a hug and turned to Gary. "How long?"

"Five minutes. Take a minute with him now if you want it,"

100

Gary urged.

Xander nodded and took back the silver ring on Ransom's halter. Gary took Jose over to the fence line and introduced him to Natalie and the group. A large oak tree stood hovering over Xander and Ransom's spot in the paddock. Xander gave the silver ring a gentle tug, and Ransom followed him as he walked over to the trunk of the massive tree for a private moment with his horse. He squared up in front of Ransom and took his head into his hands. He leaned in, letting the horse's head rest over his shoulder as he hugged his neck.

Xander spoke into his ear. "Hey there, bud. Can you believe we made it here? Two years of training and an undefeated race record. I know that you know, none of these ponies can touch you, so this speech is more for me than it is for you. It doesn't really matter to me what happens. Just go out there and ride the wind. You're ready. Just run and let everything else fall into place." He gave the horse a nice hard pat. Xander had imagined this moment since he was a kid watching the races on television. He always loved a line from the movie *Dreamer,* and he borrowed it in that moment as he took King's Ransom's face in his hands and looked deep into his midnight eyes. "You are a great champion. When you ran, the ground shook, the sky opened, and mere mortals parted. Parted the way to victory, where you'll meet me in the winner's circle, where I'll put a blanket of flowers on your back." A jolt of adrenaline shot through him as Ransom gave a deep, growling, and confident whinny.

They were going to win the Kentucky Derby.

"Xander," Gary called to him. "It's time."

Xander walked Ransom back over to his spot and handed him off to Gary. As Gary helped Jose onto Ransom's back,

Xander looked over and saw Kaley on her tiptoes trying to get a look at Ransom over the wooden rail.

"Just one second, Gary," Xander said, walking away and over to Kaley. "You wanna go say hello to the King?"

Kaley's face lit up and she feverishly nodded her head, and Xander reached over the fence and pulled her into the paddock. He cradled her in his arms, and as he was walking back to the horse, he could see that it drew the attention of the television cameras and he was sure they were sharing this moment with the thousands watching at the track, and the millions watching at home. He carried Kaley over to Ransom, and as you might expect, she was reluctant at first to reach her hand toward a mouth that was twice the size of her head. Xander showed her it was okay by rubbing Ransom's nose himself, and she began to warm to the idea. With great deliberation she reached her hand toward his nose, and as soon as her finger grazed him, she jerked back and let out a belly-busting giggle.

"He *cee-ute*." She laughed. "He *cee-ute!*"

"Yes, he is cute, and so are you, you little monkey." Xander gave her little belly a tickle. He turned his attention to the guys. "Go get 'em, Jose. Gary, thanks for all your hard work. I'll see you and Beth in the box in just a bit."

Gary nodded and Jose gave Xander a thumbs-up from high on Ransom's back. It was customary for the owner to walk in with his horse, but Xander left that to Gary. He felt since he was the one who had spent the countless hours putting in the training that it was just the way it should be for Gary to have the moment. Xander turned back to the smiles of his family and friends. They seemed just as excited as he was. Hell, Kyle was visibly giddy. Xander loved it.

"You all ready to go place a bet?" Xander asked with a

smile, the moments in the men's restroom earlier now far from his mind.

"Looks like he'll probably go off at four to one, X. The fucking Derby favorite!" Kyle shouted.

"Mommy, what does *focking* mean?" Kaley asked.

"Gee thanks, Kyle," Helen muttered. "Thought I would be able to wait a little longer before I had to answer that question." Everyone laughed at how cute Kaley sounded as she said it. Helen attempted to answer Kaley. "It just means Kyle is thirsty, but we don't use that word, okay?"

"*Otay*, Mommy." Kaley smiled.

"Sorry." Kyle grimaced.

They made their way back to the owner's box. The crowd continued to grow to standing room only all around them. The grandstand busted at its seams. Only about fifty yards separated Xander's box and the rail of the track. The racehorses were being paraded in. As if King's Ransom's midnight black coat and monstrous frame weren't intimidating enough, he had drawn the sixth position in the gate, which meant his number cloth was black and only the white six would be seen on his side as if it magically floated there somehow. Six was a good draw for a race of twenty horses. It was far enough away from the rail to keep from being pushed there, yet not so far outside that you had to run a longer route to stay in contention. A strong sense of pride washed over Xander as Ransom loped his way toward the starting gate. When his name was announced, the massive crowd exploded in applause and adulation. Xander figured this must be what it is like to watch your child step up to the plate in a Little League baseball game or catch a touchdown pass on the football field.

Xander broke his own train of thought by letting out a

prideful whistle and a few hand-pounding claps. He gave Natalie a nudge with his hip. "I can't believe you matched my bet of ten thousand dollars on Ransom. I appreciate the faith, but that's a lot of money."

"Yeah, and it's gonna turn into a lot more when he runs right by all these other little ponies!" she shouted, raising the Derby's customary mint julep into the air.

Kyle handed Xander one as well. It was tough to beat a cold drink of sweet bourbon whiskey at the races, especially your own whiskey, as you cheered on your own horse while rubbing elbows with the most beautiful woman on the entire planet. The splendor that was Xander's life wasn't lost on him. He realized how good he had it. At least, how good it was here and now, in this moment.

A man standing among an entrapment of roses began to blow an immaculately polished brass horn. Another Kentucky Derby tradition—"My Old Kentucky Home"—and the thousands in attendance who actually were Kentucky natives sang the words along with his horn.

Weep no more my lady
Oh weep no more today
We will sing one song
For my old Kentucky home
For my old Kentucky home far away

Upon the song's end, the trumpet sounded the charge, and they began to load the horses into the starting gate. Xander looked at Natalie, who swelled with excitement. Kyle wrapped his arm around Xander as Annie, Melanie, Helen, and Kaley rose to their feet right along with the tens of thousands of others who were on hand. *The greatest two minutes in sports,* it had been called a thousand times over the years. The biggest race in the world's richest sport, the sport of *kings,* in fact.

Fitting.

The starting gate was on the other side of the track, so Xander and company watched the mega video screen as they loaded King's Ransom into his gate. They could see Jose on the screen, perched high above the ground on Ransom. He gave Ransom an encouraging pat on the back, and the rest of the horses took their spots in the starting gate. A hush fell over the raucous crowd.

Agent Sean Thompson Receives Disturbing News

There was a knock at the door. "Agent Thompson, you have a call on line three."

Agent Sean Thompson was a big son of a bitch who still had "navy" written all over him. Big broad shoulders, classic crew cut, and all the scars to prove it. The part of him that was clearly *ex*-navy—his midsection—wasn't visible from behind the desk. He looked up from his paperwork and gave his secretary, Allison, a nod. He picked up the phone and pressed the blinking red button next to line three. "This is Agent Thompson."

"Hey, Sean, it's Marvin, how the hell have you been, my friend?" a familiar voice said through the phone.

"Buddy, if I was any better I'd be twins! Where in the hell does the Central Idiots Agency got you screwin' things up these days?"

"Sean, you know how it is, here today, gone tomorrow. Today it's Syria. Apparently I shagged the director's daughter without knowing it or something to draw this assignment. Somebody's not happy with me somewhere, I guess." Marvin laughed.

"Christ, Marv, Syria? I'd rather shit swords for a year than spend a day in that hellhole."

"Tell me about it. How's life back in Langley?"

"Well, Virginia ain't the Bahamas, but at least I get to sleep in my own bed at night. What can I do for ya, brother?"

It was good to hear Marv's voice. It had probably been six years or more since they had trained together at Camp Peary. They were unlikely friends. Sean was from the deep South and grew up hunting and fishing. Marv was from New York and had spent his youth playing baseball and racking up a 4.0 GPA all through school. None of that matters much after you go through SEAL training together, though; it had a way of closing those gaps. The Farm at Camp Peary wasn't easy, but CIA training was a walk in the park compared to the Navy SEALs.

"Well, whether you believe it or not, I do get the requests you send to me in those e-mails every month. I just don't respond so there isn't a paper trail. Plus, I never had any information to offer you, so it was pointless. You know what I mean?" Marv asked.

"Of course, no worries. That's an automated thing I set up anyway just to keep a bug in your ear. Does this mean you have something?" Sean's gruff and husky voice seemed eager now.

"Well, I don't want to get your hopes up because it's early. You've been sending those e-mails since we started with the agency about six years ago, and honestly I had forgotten about the specifics really. Until yesterday, that is."

"Spit it out, Marv."

"Right. Yesterday a file came across my desk, another lead on who is controlling the ISIS movement here in Syria. You know, another real bad dude, been around a while, too. Anyway, nothing jumped out at me until I saw at the very end of the file that he had been investigated for some trouble in the States. That normally wouldn't have meant anything to me either except it said it was in 1998. Even that alone wouldn't have triggered anything except this guy, Sanharib Khatib, made his money in oil," Marv explained.

"No shit?"

"Like I said, Sean, it could all be a total coincidence, I just wanted to give you a heads-up in case you wanted to do some research. You can't tell Xander any of this yet, okay, Sean? This guy is a major terrorist target, and we need to know more about his operations before King comes in here cowboy-style and mucks up years of investigation."

"No, no, of course—"

"I'm serious, Sean. Khatib isn't like these other targets we tip Samantha to for Xander. This guy has a damn army surrounding him. One man could never make his way to this guy. He'd die trying," Marv pleaded.

"You must not remember Xander as well as I do."

"I do, Sean. I know he's the baddest motherfucker who probably *ever* came through the SEALs, but it would take a team of ten Xanders to pull off this assassination. Plus, I could be totally off about this being the right guy."

"No, I hear ya. We definitely have to take the time to vet this thing out before he knows. If we should *ever* tell him. I mean, according to you it'd be a death wish. I ain't tryin' to send the X-man off to his death."

"Okay, good. Glad you see it the same way. I was scared even to tell you really because I know how close the two of you are. That's also why I know you would never send him into an impossible situation."

"I'll check it out, Marv. As long as it takes."

"I can't believe we still do this anyway. Director Manning would hang us both for tipping Xander to any of these targets. You know that, right, Sean?"

"Course I know that. But X is my brother, and he's doing good that this damn government would never get around to doin'. If you don't want to keep—"

"Calm down, calm down. That's not what I'm saying. You know I agree with you. Once in a while, though, I can't help but think of the consequences."

"The consequences would be much worse if all these monsters continued to kill and ruin all these lives," Sean went on, starting to get riled up.

"I'm with you, Sean. I'm with you. I'm just saying, if Manning knew, we'd be out of a job and probably thrown in prison. Shit is getting real. I heard through the grapevine that he is putting together a team to watch Xander. Putting Sarah Gilbright in charge of it, I believe."

Sean rubbed his chin as he thought about that name.

"Sarah Gilbright, huh? Why does that name sound familiar, Marv?"

"To me? I have heard amazing things about her work. To you? Probably because she's just about the most beautiful woman I've ever seen."

"That's right! Gilbright. She's that blonde with legs longer than a decade and big . . . well, you know. Hell yeah, I know her, she's hot as a ghost pepper."

109

"Why am I not surprised?" Marv laughed. "Good to hear you haven't changed a bit."

"Not in that department, my friend. Well, that makes me nervous for X-man, but if they are watching him, they must know what he's been up to and be at least somewhat okay with it. Let's just make sure we watch what we say extra good from here on in."

"My thoughts exactly. Listen, I have a meeting I'm running late for. I hope everything is going well for you back there. I haven't seen a pair of legs around here in about two months. Hell, I haven't so much as seen a forearm with all these Muslim women running around wearing tarps for clothes."

"Shit, I'd go plum crazy. No wonder all them terrorists are going bat-shit trying to blow everything up." Sean laughed.

"You're as crazy as ever, my friend. I love it. I'll let you know if I find anything else. Say hey to the guys for me."

"Will do, Marv. Give me your address over there and I'll send you a blowup doll. That'll keep you sane till you make it back home."

"Perfect." Marv laughed. "Take care, Sean."

"You, too, Marv." Sean hung up the phone.

This was the best and worst news Sean had heard in a long time. He and Marv were the only two who knew what happened to Xander's parents. It was always hard for Sean to believe how Xander had made it through it all. It also baffled Sean how Xander's passion for revenge still burned so hot after all these years. They had gone years now without a single lead.

Until today.

Sean picked up the phone, looked at the receiver for a moment, and then hung it back up. He glanced around his office for a moment, looking for a distraction. He could see the blurred movement of his colleagues through the smoked-glass windows that made up the top half of the walls to his left and in front of him. To his right were clear windows, and the green of the park-like setting three floors down was in full bloom now that it was May. The short but wide horizontal bookcase that sat under the fogged windows on his left offered no distraction. The circular clock that hung from one of the two walled panels in the corner in front of him, which had always reminded him of the clocks that hung in every classroom in high school, read 5:45. He turned in his swivel chair, and the map of the world with various plotted points offered no distraction at the moment, either.

"Fuck it." Sean pulled out his government-issued iPhone and scrolled down to Xander's name in his contacts. The phone rang until it went to Xander's voice mail.

"You have reached Xander King. Leave a message and I'll get back to you as soon as possible. Thanks."

Beep.

"Hey, X-man, oh, shit! I just realized it's Saturday and your happy ass is at the Derby! My tired overworked ass is still at the office. I'm turning the tube on now, brother! Good luck. Just give me a shout when you're done celebratin' the big win! Go, Ransom!"

Sean ended the call and grabbed the remote out of the top drawer of his cheap and dated brown lacquer desk. He hit power, and sure enough the horses were being loaded into the starting gate at that very moment. The camera fixated on a big black pony with the number six floating on his side. A graphic at the bottom of the screen flashed up and read "King's Ransom—King Stables—Lexington, Kentucky." Sean turned up the volume, and as soon as he did the camera flashed to

Xander in his owner's box. The commentator pointed out that Xander owned the gigantic Thoroughbred that also happened to be the odds-on favorite.

"Holy shit, there he is! X-man's on TV!" Sean shouted and laughed with excitement. "Wait, is that . . . Natalie Rockwell standing beside him? No way. That handsome son of a bitch has all the damn luck!" Sean laughed hysterically as he slapped his desk.

The door opened. "Is everything all right, Agent Thompson?" Allison came in, showing concern.

"Allison! Get over here and look at my best friend on TV!"

Allison glanced at the television. "That good-looking guy is your best friend? I need to hang out with you more often."

"Sexy son of a bitch, ain't he? Looks like you're too late, though. That's Natalie Rockwell beside him."

"Aw, I just love her," Allison said.

"Me, too. I hear those things are real."

"Good God, really?"

"Sorry, I'm just excited. My buddy's horse is in the Derby," Sean said with a face full of pride.

"That's awesome! Oh look, there they go!" Allison pointed to the television as the bell rang and the gates of the starting block exploded open. Twenty of the finest racehorses on the planet spilled out in a burst onto the dirt track. Sean jumped to his feet, almost knocking over his chair.

"Go, Ransom, go! He's number six! I fed him once about six months ago down in Lexington when I was visiting Xander!" Sean bragged, his barrel chest swelled with pride.

"Number six, you said? Go six!" Allison joined in.

For a moment, the potential importance of the information that Marv had passed along just moments ago faded in the excitement of the race. Sean grew up in Tennessee watching the Derby every year with his mom and dad. They would all gather around the television and pick out which horse they thought was going to win. Sean never had much luck then, but he hoped he was due as his friend's horse took on the very best in the world.

"Oh no! What happened?" Allison screeched.

"Hey!" Sean shouted at the TV. "That's a foul! That number seven just fouled Ransom!" King's Ransom got bumped and then stumbled, falling to the back of the pack before he could regain his stride. "That's a foul, damnit!"

Hearing the commotion from Sean's office, several of his colleagues poured into the room to see what the excitement was about.

"Ronnie, that number seven just fouled Xander's horse! Remember me telling you about Xander?" Sean continued to shout.

"Yeah, I remember. What number is his horse?" Ronnie replied with urgency as he tried to get in on the excitement.

"Six! He's number six!" Allison shouted, beating Sean to the punch.

"Can he get back in it?" Ronnie asked.

"Not likely, damnit! Too many horses to get around. Xander says he closes like a freight train, but that foul put him too far back, I'm afraid. Come on, Ransom!"

The Ground Shook and Mere Mortals Parted

"Come on, Ransom!" Natalie screamed toward the track as King's Ransom fell to the back of the pack.

"Did you see that, X?!" Kyle shouted, throwing his hands up in the air. "Is that legal? Can that seven horse do that?"

"What happened, Xander? Can he come back?" Natalie asked in a panic.

Xander stood stoic. The only thing he cared about was whether or not Ransom was hurt. He knew if he wasn't hurt, this little stumble would mean nothing about halfway through the race. In front of them King's Ransom had got sideswiped and as a result got pinched and pushed to the back of the pack. Like the closing of a door, the crease Jose had tried to lead Ransom through had shut in front of them with the foul. Jose straightened back out, and with just a few strides he had Ransom running straight again, though lots of ground would need to be made up in a serious hurry. At the head of the pack, Heart of a Lion, one of the other favorites in the race, broke loose, resulting in a blistering pace going into the second quarter mile.

"He's okay, he's fine," Xander said, almost too low for anyone to hear over the volume of the now-insane crowd. But Natalie heard him, and with a deep breath she once again started jumping up and down, screaming for Ransom. Melanie's and Kyle's looks turned from nervous to excited again as Xander began to clap his hands.

"Come on, Ransom. You got it, buddy. Time to fly!"

Jose could see that the inside line was far too crowded and he would be forced to steer Ransom to the outside. This wasn't ideal because the farther outside you ran, the farther you had to run. This could cost tenths of a second, and tenths of a second can cost a three-year-old superstar Thoroughbred his only chance at winning the Kentucky Derby. Hooves pounded against the ground around them now in a thunderous roar. Jose caught quite a bit of dirt in his goggles while in the back of the pack, but he peered through the open slots in the plastic lenses and searched for an opening to drive Ransom through. They were halfway through the race, and it was now or never.

A lady in the box beside Xander's had a handheld radio on, and the announcer's voice snuck its way to Xander's ears over the bellows of the excited crowd.

Ladies and gentlemen, we are halfway through the most exciting two minutes in sports, and the favorite, King's Ransom, is in trouble and has his back against the ropes. Heart of a Lion is roaring down the track and Know Man's Land isn't within five lengths of him. This one might be a runaway, folks!

"Come on, Ransom! You can do it!" Natalie shouted into the air. For the first time Xander felt a sting of worry pierce him. Ransom was running out of track.

Coming down the final turn and it is Heart of a Lion continuing to pull away. This might be one of the most impressive runs I have ever seen here at Churchill Downs. He might actually be able to—

The horses were just far enough away now, just before the final turn, where Xander couldn't see exactly what was going on. However, when he heard the announcer from the woman's radio, who was about to utter the words "go wire to wire", pause midsentence, well, it was right then he knew ol' Ransom had just made his move. Xander's heart jumped into his throat and his adrenaline spiked. He grabbed Kyle's shoulder with his right hand and Natalie's with his left. When they looked back at Xander's face, they, too, knew the freight train was coming.

Wait just a minute, folks! It looks like King's Ransom just found a new gear! Down the stretch they come! King's Ransom is tearing down the outside of the stretch now! Heart of a Lion might very well be speeding down the track, but just as Ransom's owner, Xander King, predicted at the press conference this morning, King's Ransom is steaming down the line like an absolute freight train toward the finish line! Will he have enough time? He passes Free as a Bird and Limoncello, making his way into third! Heart of a Lion continues to lead, but King's Ransom is closing at a speed I have never seen in my thirty-five years of calling this heart-pounding run for the roses!

"X! Xander!" Kyle began to scream.

"Go, King, go!" Annie yelled.

"Faster, King's Ransom! Faster!" Melanie shouted at the top of her lungs.

"Go, go, go, go, go!" Natalie pumped her fist and jumped around.

"Go, horsee, go!" Kaley shouted from Helen's bouncing arms.

Xander went calm.

So, too, did Jose.

The noise of the thundering horses faded. The wind from the speed of Ransom's stride whipped past his ears. Just in front of him ran Heart of a Lion, everything else around him a blur. Just beyond Ransom's bobbing head the finish line came into sight.

"Okay, Ransom. Gimme the rest, big boy," Jose whispered into Ransom's ear. There was no way King's Ransom could have heard this over the pandemonium of the crowd and the pounding of the dirt by the other horses around them. Yet, from somewhere deep inside of him, like dropping the clutch on an old Shelby Mustang GT350, Ransom surged forward. He made Heart of a Lion seem as though he were standing still.

Down to the wire now and King's Ransom finds yet another gear! He pulls even now and this is it! They roar across the finish line, and yes, he did it! I can't believe what I just saw!

King's Ransom does it! He blurs past Heart of a Lion and wins the 141st running of the Kentucky Derby! King's Ransom wins the Kentucky Derby! We will see you in the winner's circle, big boy! Unbelievable! What a comeback! What a comeback!

Xander felt numb. The owner's box sat dead straight on the finish line, and even though Xander had seen his horse pass all the others clear as day, he still couldn't feel the win. Everything around him crept along in slow motion. The hordes of race fans screamed and danced, for their favorite horse had taken the win, but Xander couldn't catch up. Natalie and Kyle descended down upon him, throwing their arms around him, screaming and shouting Ransom's praises. He was sure of it, but he couldn't hear a thing. Finally, as Kyle stood in front of him, shaking Xander and screaming hysterically at the top of his lungs, the air around him swooshed with the sound of thousands cheering for his colt.

"He did it! You just won the Kentucky Derby! Hahahaha!" Kyle laughed maniacally.

"We did it! We did it!" Xander finally broke his silence. He grabbed hold of Kyle and held him high in the air. When he dropped him back to his feet, he planted a powerful kiss on Natalie as he squeezed her face in both of his hands. He went on to lay the same kiss on Melanie, Annie, and Helen before he stole Kaley from her arms and danced her around the box. "We won, Kaley! We won!"

"We did it!" Kaley screamed in the cutest little voice.

"That's right, Kaley! We did it!" Xander screamed. He handed Kaley back to his sister just in time to feel Gary's arms wrap around him.

"We did, Xander! We did it!"

Xander turned to him. "No, you did it, Gary! You made

him the best damn horse I've ever seen! Did you see that son of a bitch close!" They jumped up and down in each other's arms as officials from Churchill Downs began to surround them to escort them down to the winner's circle.

"You wanna go see your Derby champion, Mr. King?" Rory smiled. Xander grabbed him and planted the same forceful kiss he had shared with the others right on Rory's lips. Rory laughed and raised both arms above his head and let out a "Woo-hoo!"

Kyle wrapped his arms around Xander from behind and gave him a squeeze. "I love you, Xander. You deserve this. Thanks for letting me be here to celebrate with you."

Xander turned toward him. "You kidding me? It wouldn't mean a thing if you weren't here. I love you!" He followed that up with another big hug. Then he looked over at the clearly exhilarated Natalie.

"What do you think about that, huh, gorgeous?"

"Unbelievable!" She smiled exuberantly. "Just amazing. Now get down there and see that big lug. We'll be right here when you're finished."

"Hell with that. You're coming with!" Xander insisted as he grabbed her hand. "All of you, let's go see the King!"

And with that, they all laughed and high-fived their way trackside. Xander must have stopped a few dozen times to shake hands and take pictures with the crowd; he was loving every second of it. Too much of Xander's life had been spent in the shadows. Even enjoying the money left to him was difficult. Kyle had played a major role in getting him to loosen up and take advantage of the means he was afforded. Only recently had Xander really started indulging in some of his wants. The extra money spent to acquire a great horse like Ransom, the villa in

Tuscany, the toys in the garage, and the quaint little beachfront getaway he had just purchased in St. Thomas all came in just the last couple of years. He had been so focused on ridding the world of the bad people and on revenge that life was passing him by. Kyle's free spirit and propensity to speak his mind had helped teach Xander that he was allowed to enjoy the light of life, in spite of having to dabble so often in its darkness.

This only deepened Xander's love for his friend. Seeing Kyle jumping around in excitement as they enjoyed this momentous occasion chipped even further away at the cold hand that had gripped his heart for so long. The light that Natalie was shining sure wasn't hurting to pull him away from that darkness, either. Bringing someone into the innermost fold of his life, however, wasn't something Xander thought possible. The danger alone, just in being close to Xander, was enough to continue to keep people at arm's length. He knew that, but he felt the pull of Natalie growing stronger by the second. This scared him far more than any sinister prospective target. In Xander's chosen line of work, nothing could be worse than having something to lose. However, he was going to enjoy this moment and these people who had so greatly enriched his life. Standing in that winner's circle now, placing that blanket of roses over his Derby champion, Xander felt a warmth inside that hadn't surfaced in more than fourteen years.

Xander was finding happiness.

You're Never Too Old For a Pizza Party

The sun began to fade over Louisville, and a burnt-orange shadow fell across the empty grandstand at Churchill Downs. Cleaning crews swept their way through the desolate aisles, collecting the thousands of losing tickets thrown to the ground in dejection throughout the day. A few prayers were undoubtedly answered, but for the vast majority it was a day of excess and heartbreak. Most played within their means; some, however, played their bottom dollar. The rest of the night in Louisville would be filled with Derby after-parties, some monstrous in nature, packing hundreds of people into nightclubs across downtown. Others would simply be a few gathered at a friend's home. Xander's bourbon would be the sponsor at a couple of those parties, but he wouldn't be there to indulge in it.

For the most part, the track had gone silent. Another day of history in the record books. The only sounds that lingered were

Xander's small celebratory gathering at King's Ransom's stall. Gary and Jose puffed their cigars and raised one last glass of champagne with those who were leaving on the helicopter to go back to Xander's home in Lexington.

"To one hell of a day and one hell of a horse!" Gary toasted. Xander had just completed his last round of media before meeting up with the group. The first two questions were always the same to the owner of the Kentucky Derby winner.

How does it feel to win the Kentucky Derby? and, *Do you think he can win the Triple Crown?*

The first answer, more rhetorical than anything, Xander breezed through as he gave the standard "it feels fantastic" answer followed by all the "thank-yous" and "this wouldn't be possible withouts" that he could think of on the spot. The second question, the question of the Triple Crown, normally got artfully sidestepped by owners. The Triple Crown consisted of three of the biggest events in horse racing: the Kentucky Derby, followed by the Preakness, and culminating in the finale at the Belmont Stakes. In more than one hundred years of keeping records, only twelve horses had ever won all three races. Even more daunting was the fact that before last year, it hadn't been done since Affirmed did it in 1978. This being the case, most owners gave the standard answer that they believed their horse had as good a chance as any, and all they cared about was whether or not their horse stayed healthy. Whatever happens happens, they would say. So you can imagine the media's surprise when Xander boldly announced in front of the twenty some-odd reporters in the room and to the millions watching around the world that King's Ransom would indeed follow American Pharoah's lead and be only the second horse in over thirty-five years to take all three races to win the Triple Crown.

Xander walked into the stables and over to his favorite people in the world, who had all gathered around Ransom's stall.

"You didn't get much sleep last night. How you holding up?" Xander asked Natalie.

"I'm good. What about you? I can't even imagine how the excitement of today must have worn you out."

If she only knew. Xander almost felt dirty having such a terrible secret between them. If she knew, she would never look at him the same. She didn't deserve to be dragged into this. Xander just couldn't bring himself to bring it up.

"I actually feel pretty damn good myself," he said as he put his arm around her and gave her a playful squeeze. "King's Ransom says you're welcome, by the way."

"Oh, have I not said thank you for all of this? Oh God, Xander, you must think I'm a spoiled brat."

"No, no, you have thanked me plenty for bringing you here. I'm not talking about that. I'm talking about the fact that he won you fifty thousand dollars today, right?"

"What? What do you mean *fifty thousand dollars*?" She looked at him, confused.

"Well, you put ten grand on Ransom, right?"

"Right. And?"

"And ten thousand dollars at five to one, which ended up being the final odds, is fifty thousand dollars!" He smiled.

"Oh my God! In all the excitement I had for you winning, I totally forgot about that!"

"I knew you had. That says something about you, you know? It takes a special person, I don't care how wealthy you are, to forget about fifty grand just because someone you just met was happy they had accomplished something. You're really something special, you know that?"

"Aw, you are just too nice." She playfully pinched his cheek. "I just don't understand how you haven't already been snatched up. But I guess to have all these expensive habits you must have a few more business ventures that keep you away from a full-time gal, huh?"

"You could say that."

"That's just too bad, Alexander King. A girl could get used to someone so sweet." Natalie leaned in and gave him a long, soft kiss on the lips. "Unfortunately, a working girl like myself understands all too well just how hard that is."

"Xander, I hate to interrupt, but the helicopter is ready," Melanie announced. "I'm assuming Natalie and Annie need to get back to California at some point this evening?"

"That's right, I am so sorry. We never even talked about when you needed to get back," Xander said.

"I guess we didn't, did we? Must have been a good couple of days." Natalie winked. Then her face turned to a frown. "We should probably be getting back, though. I'll have my assistant put us on the last flight out, here in Louisville."

"No way, we'll chopper back to Lexington right now, and I'll have Bob and Charlie fly you both home tonight as soon as we get back," Xander insisted.

"Oh no, that's too much, really."

"Not another word, m'lady." He smiled. "Let me just say good-bye to everyone."

Xander walked away, leaving Natalie and Melanie together. After the coast was clear, Melanie broke the silence. "Wow, you *are* good!"

"You think he has a clue?"

"Nope, not at all, he's going to be so surprised to see

everyone at the house. I'll make sure Charlie files the flight plan for the morning and not tonight. Xander will be so happy you two are staying!"

"That won't be necessary, my assistant already booked a flight for us in the morning from the Lexington airport. I won't have Xander paying all that money to fly us home."

"But Xander will—"

"Thank you so much, Melanie, but I insist. I feel like a mooch as it is."

"Oh all right, but he's not gonna be happy about this. You ready to get out of here?"

"Let's do it. Party number two!" Natalie smiled and followed Melanie out to the helicopter.

The rest of the crew followed, and after Xander said good-bye to Jose and Gary, he gave Ransom a big hug and kiss on the nose. The pride swelled inside of him as he walked out of the stables and toward the helicopter. The rotor began to spin and as Xander grabbed hold of the inside of the helicopter with his right hand, he paused for a moment to take a look back at Churchill Downs. Its famous twin spires were now shadows in the orange evening sky. The day had been all he had hoped for and so much more. No longer would the children of Shelby High School be tormented unknowingly by their monster of a teacher. No longer would young girls be trading sexual favors for a drug that was slowly killing them anyway. He took a long, deep breath as he closed his eyes and cleared his mind. After a moment he felt a hand upon his. He looked and found Natalie smiling at him from the helicopter's cabin. It wasn't a "let's get out of here" smile either; instead, she gave him a look letting him know he could take all the time he needed and that she was happy for him. He squeezed her hand and pulled himself inside the chopper.

The flight home simmered in a silent hum, partly because no one had gotten a lot of sleep the night before and also because it was just such a beautiful ride. The sun held on just long enough to dimly light the entire journey. Natalie held on to Xander's hand as she gazed out into the fiery sky. Xander continued to reflect on what an amazing day it had been. He had fulfilled his lifelong dream when he got to lay that blanket of roses across Ransom's back. What a moment. The only thing that could have made it better would have been if his mom and dad could have been there to live it with him. He pulled out his phone to check the time, and when he did he noticed dozens of notifications. He figured it was his loved ones all wishing him a heartfelt congratulations. One number, however, stuck out to him like a sore thumb.

Sean Thompson.

At first he figured his old SEAL buddy just wanted to congratulate him like the others, but directly after that thought, his stomach turned.

What if?

He immediately unlocked his phone and went to his voice mail. His heart rate quickened. He pulled one side of his comm system headphones off and pressed the phone against his ear.

Hey, X-man, oh, shit! I just realized it's Saturday and your happy ass is at the Derby! My tired overworked ass is still at the office. I'm turning the tube on now, brother! Good luck. Just give me a shout when you're done celebratin' the big win! Go, Ransom!

Xander let the air go from his lungs in a long and steady exhale as the tension fell from his shoulders. Natalie squeezed his hand, and he looked over at her. She mouthed the words "Is everything okay?" He smiled and nodded as he squeezed her hand in return. The helicopter hovered over the open spot in the circular driveway of Xander's home, and once again the pilot got the Xander stamp of approval for a soft landing. Some habits die hard.

The helicopter's rotors swung more and more slowly as everyone piled out of the cabin.

"I left my bag inside earlier. Do you mind if I run in and grab it?" Melanie asked.

"Of course not. Hang around for a bit if you want," Xander replied.

Melanie winked at Natalie and ran ahead to make sure everyone was ready, not that the noise of the helicopter landing wasn't alert enough for them. She had been working on pulling this small gathering together for weeks now, and she wanted it to be the perfect end to a perfect day for Xander. So far, all looked great. There wasn't a car in sight, and she skipped her way to the front door.

"Well, X, let's have a drink or two. I'm not ready to be done celebrating yet," Kyle said, patting Xander on the back.

"No doubt. We can after we run the girls to the airport."

"Well, maybe we can have just one more drink. I think the day merits that." Natalie smiled.

They all played along as they walked up to the front entry. Melanie had left the door open, and as Xander walked in, he entered the house to a thunderous "Surprise!" He was taken aback by the shouting, and Kyle had to hold him up from falling back out the doorway.

"Surprise, Xander!" Melanie walked over to him. "Congratulations. I know how much Ransom winning means to you, and this is how much you mean to us. I hope it isn't too

127

much?"

Xander looked around the room, his pulse still trying to slow as he put his hand to his heart and gave a big smile.

"You kidding me? This is great. Thank you, Melanie."

"Thank you, Xander. For everything you do for all of us. We love you." Melanie hugged him again. Natalie could feel her heart being tugged as she saw how much he meant to them. It made him all the more attractive, if that were possible at this point.

Xander's aunts and uncles were there, along with several friends he and Kyle had both grown up with. There was a congratulatory cake all decked out in candles on the kitchen island. A messy but cute icing drawing of King's Ransom puffed out from the center of the white cake. Balloons were tied to chairs, and Melanie had blown up the first photo Xander ever took with Ransom when he bought him at the Keeneland auction two years ago. She had it displayed on the table in a beautiful decorative black wood frame.

Most importantly, however, he eyed boxes of pizza stacked up beside the cake.

Sam walked up and gave him a hug. "Good on you, Xander. You're never too old for a pizza party."

Xander returned the hug.

"Truer words were never spoken. Let's eat!"

Make Love, Not War

"Thanks again, Melanie." Xander hugged Melanie and closed the front door behind her.

He walked back to the kitchen where Kyle, Annie, and Natalie were winding down at the kitchenette table over one final cocktail. It was getting late, but Natalie hadn't shown any signs of needing or wanting to leave. Before he interrupted them, he poured a glass of his bourbon, neat, into his favorite whiskey tumbler. When Xander was trying to wind down, he liked his bourbon undiluted No ice, no mixers. As he poured that beautiful caramel-colored liquor into his glass, he took notice of the way Natalie smiled and laughed at whatever bullshit story Kyle was telling her. It had been an incredibly long two days, but you wouldn't know it by looking at her. He wasn't sure whether it was the bourbon or the testosterone inside him, but he really wanted her to stay. And he really wanted to see, and feel, what was under that lavender dress.

"Get your fine ass over here, Derby champion," Natalie demanded from across the room.

If she'd had a dozen drinks today, she barely seemed like she'd had two. Natalie was sexy regardless, but there is just something about a woman holding a glass of whiskey. Probably how some women feel about a man with money. It's just sexy.

"On my way, gorgeous," Xander replied.

He took a seat beside Natalie. She held a glass of whiskey in one hand and spun a red rose in the other. She stared at the rose and spoke to the table.

"My dad used to drink whiskey. I'll never forget one time my mom had cut some fresh roses from the garden, and when she walked into the kitchen where Dad was pouring a drink, he stopped her and wrapped his arm around her. He said, 'Natalie, honey, roses are for remembering, and the whiskey's to numb the pain.' I never forgot those words. Not because it even made any sense—I don't even know why he said it—but it always stayed with me. My dad wasn't what you would call a romantic, so those words really stood out to me among all the other hard ones."

Xander bent over behind Natalie, wrapped his arms around her, and kissed her on the cheek. "Roses for remembering, and whiskey to numb the pain . . . I love it. It's sad, but beautiful."

She turned to him. "I always thought the exact same thing. Sad, but beautiful." She looked into his eyes for a moment, then dropped them to his lips. Then, with a deep, trance-breaking breath she turned and looked at Kyle.

"Where do you live from here, Kyle?"

"Not too far." He smiled when he realized why she had asked. "Is that a hint?"

"Maybe," Natalie replied as she gave Xander a new kind of

look. This look was impossible to confuse.

"All right! I'm picking up what you're laying down." Kyle laughed encouragingly. "I'm ready to get this little present home and unwrap it myself." He pulled Annie onto his lap and gave her a kiss on the cheek.

"So does this mean you are staying?" Xander asked Natalie.

"That was always the plan. We don't leave till nine tomorrow morning."

Xander couldn't help but smile. "Well, damnit, Kyle, I love you, but get your ass out of here."

Kyle jumped up and gave Xander and Natalie a hug. Annie did the same. Xander walked him out and shut the door behind them. As soon as he latched the lock, his skin began to tingle as if there were an electric current coursing through the room. The light was off in the foyer. When he turned around, the light pouring through the doorway from the kitchen left a shadow that hugged the curves of Natalie's silhouette. She stood waiting, leaning her elbow against the doorway as she twirled her hair in her fingers.

Xander's libido shifted into overdrive, and he walked toward Natalie, wrapped his arms around her, and pulled her close. Natalie let her body collapse into his arms. His body flamed with heat, and on impulse she unbuttoned his white stuffy dress shirt as he pressed his lips into hers. She first took his bottom lip, then the top, and then the bottom. She placed her hands flat upon his firm, muscular chest and in one motion pushed them up and over his shoulders, helping his shirt fall to the ground as she wrapped her arms around him.

Her body begged to be taken.

Xander unzipped the back of her dress, but she stopped him before he could take it down. She released his shoulders and stepped back into the light. She wanted him to see her undress. In a methodically cruel, slow, and deliberate motion she slipped the first strap down over her right shoulder, then the left, never letting her eyes leave his burning gaze. The light behind her cast a glow on his ripped upper body. His chiseled chest gave way to rows of abdominal muscles. His obliques wrapped around his hip bones and pointed symmetrically south like a road map to her desired destination. When she bit her bottom lip at the sight of him, it sent Xander into a fury. He stepped toward her, needing to feel the soft warmth of her skin. She held up a finger to stop him. His chest heaved as he gave Natalie her wish and stayed away. With the same deliberate movement as before, she lowered her dress to her waist, revealing her chest, which he thought even more perfect than she thought of his. Her round and supple bosom danced in front of him as the movement of the dress being taken off shook them from their resting place. She gave Xander a sexy smile as she could clearly see he enjoyed the show. This made the electric current that was running through Xander jump straight to her, and she quivered as it hit her.

She continued dropping the dress below her waist and she rocked her pelvis from side to side, pushing as the dress slid across her hips, finally falling down around her ankles. She stood in front of him, vulnerable, wearing only a white satin thong. Xander could no longer stand idle. He lunged forward and took Natalie in his arms. Her soft chest pressed against his, and she kissed him softly on the mouth as his hands fell to her bottom and gathered her taut, healthy curves with a squeeze that seemed to release a lifetime of stinging sexual tension. Her fingernails dug slightly into the back of his shoulders, and she gently moaned as he held her in his arms. The same arms that seemed nothing short of chiseled stone wrapped in a veil of warm and tender skin. Xander pulled back and held her at arm's length as he peered into her eyes. She had a wildness in those eyes now, as if he were tapping into some animalistic instinct she had hidden from the rest of the world. He scooped her up into his arms, carried her up the winding stairs, and then down the east wing hallway into his bedroom. As if in a dream, the moonlight poured through the windows, casting rays of romantic light onto the cherrywood king bed. Gently, he lowered her onto the soft white comforter on the bed and struck a match to light a candle on the bedside dresser. She sat up, shuffled to the edge of the mattress, and removed his belt as she softly traced her lips along the middle of his chest.

She needed a moment to catch her breath, so she slithered to the middle of the bed and onto her back. She curled her finger at him in a come-hither motion. The warm yellow-orange light from the candle flickered vivaciously upon her skin, further drawing him in to make love to her. He crawled on top of her, letting only 30 percent of his weight rest on her warm and intoxicating body. As he kissed her open mouth, she tingled with desire. She felt as if the ends of her fingertips and toes were on fire. Xander's lips on her skin, the breath from her lungs, and the crackling flame of the candle were the only sounds that filled the room. A room in which the temperature felt like it had risen ten degrees in the few short minutes they had been entangled there.

Natalie wanted more.

"Make love to me," she said to him, out of breath and prickling with pleasure. And they both enjoyed each other like they had never enjoyed another in their lives.

Xander and Natalie lost track of time as they became lost in each other. After a long and passionate back and forth, finally they were spent.

"That," Natalie said, though terribly out of breath, "was the most amazing . . . thing . . . I have *ever* felt. It was perfect." Her breathing was heavy.

"You were perfect," he replied as he ran his hands along her toned, muscular legs. She moved on top of him, and Xander knew at that very moment, everything had changed. As sweet and genuine as Natalie had been over the course of the last two crazy days, she was equally sexy, if not more so. He had met— hell, he had *slept* with—many sexy women in his life. He had been with sweet girls too. Natalie was like some sort of alpha woman, and as she straddled him, chest heaving, skin flushed with pleasure, he had no idea how he was going to tell her who he really was.

Space Invaders

Xander's iPhone chimed, waking him from a deep sleep. Natalie lay peacefully beside him. He smiled at the sight of her there in the glow of the moon and rolled over to his nightstand to keep the phone from chiming again. It lay next to the dwindled but still burning candle, and he picked it up to silence it. The clock on the backlit screen read 5:00 a.m. The notification below it read that he had a text message from an unknown number. He entered the passcode and went to the text.

Someone is in your house.

The floor next to the bed creaked as if someone had stepped into the room. Xander's reflexes were so fast that even before his eyes could fully adjust from the brightness of the phone's screen, he swiped his arm hard to the left, sending the pistol in the masked man's hand flying against the bedroom wall. The gun had gone off just as he had made contact with the intruder's arm. A loud clanging boom filled the room, and Natalie awoke in a panic to the sight of a man in a ski mask standing over them in the fading candlelight in which they had made love just hours ago. Before she could let out her first terrified scream, Xander, wearing only his boxer briefs, planted both hands flat on the mattress back behind his head. He then brought his knees to his chest, and in a flash he catapulted himself to his feet on the bed. Seamlessly he let his momentum carry his right leg in a sweeping motion, and with a twist of his hips Xander fired a Thai kick at the intruder. His leg whipped around his body, and the sound of his foot meeting the side of the masked man's head made a distinct popping sound, the man's body instantly going limp as he collapsed to the floor. Finally, the scream came. Natalie's fear-ridden and paralyzing shriek filled the room with a volume that rivaled the blast of the gunshot.

Xander turned to her, eerily calm, and took her shoulders in his hands.

"Listen to me, Natalie," he said in a smooth and even tone. She screamed again. "I need you to take a deep breath and listen to me now." He calmed her with his soothing demeanor.

She took a long deep breath in through her nose and let it out through her mouth, which quivered as fearful tears swelled inside her eyes. Although nothing about Xander's calmness about what just happened made sense, she took another deep breath and nodded her head.

"I need you to stay calm now. We only have a second. I need you to get up right now, go to the bathroom, and lock the door. Do not, for any reason, *any reason*, no matter what you hear, open that door. Do you understand?"

Natalie's face scrunched in fear as she tried to process why they were still in danger.

"Natalie, look at me, sweetheart. We don't have time. I need you to do—"

The door to the bedroom flew off its hinges and crashed against the inside wall. Xander pushed Natalie off the bed and onto the floor, giving her a moment of cover. He somersaulted backward off the bed, and as soon as his foot hit the carpet, he sprang himself high into the air. He must have covered ten feet as he spun himself and wheeled his leg around his body. At the height of the twisting jump he brought his leg down and around like an ax as he pounded the man entering the room in the neck, sending him to the floor. The now unconscious armed man was dressed the same as the first intruder, all-black tactical gear and a black ski mask that covered everything but his eyes and mouth. There was no question these were professionals. That didn't mean they were good, but they weren't fresh off the street, either. After Xander landed the spinning jump kick, he ended up on his feet in a crouched position with his back to the open doorway to the hall. The gun he had knocked free from his back on the bed moments ago now lay there at his feet. He grabbed it, and as he stood, turning toward the doorway, he heard a gunshot and felt a searing pain burn into his left shoulder. Natalie squealed from her view, peeking from just behind the mattress. She heard Xander's words, *I need you to go right now into the bathroom,* ring in her head, but she was too frightened to move. Somewhere inside her mind she was waiting for the director to yell, "Cut!" but this wasn't make-believe.

This was real.

Unfazed by the grazing bullet wound and knowing more shots were on the way, Xander kicked his legs out in front of him. Two more shots rang out, and they would have landed if Xander hadn't changed his level so quickly. Two bullets whizzed over his head, and as he was on his way to his ass hitting the floor, he fired two shots himself, both landing to the chest of the third and oncoming masked man. When Xander's ass hit the floor, he immediately rolled out of the view of the doorway toward the bed. He could tell by the weight of the enemy's nine-millimeter pistol that it was a fifteen-round clip. Three shots had been fired, so he knew he had twelve to go before he needed to get to one of his many precisely placed weapons he had stashed around his bedroom and the rest of the house. Xander had known this day would come, and he had been preparing for it since the first day he moved in. His preparation, however, was always for his own survival. He yelled to Natalie once again to get to the bathroom. This time she didn't hesitate, but before he could even get the last word out, another man entered the room. Xander shot him in the head, but before death registered, the man squeezed the trigger on his fully automatic AK-47, and as Natalie was racing for the bathroom, bullets went flying her way. They pierced the mattress first, then, as the dead man dropped to his back on the floor, sprayed in a line up the wall and through the ceiling.

Natalie hit the floor.

Xander checked the doorway.

Eleven bullets left.

The doorway was clear, and he bolted over to Natalie and helped her to her feet. "Are you okay? Were you hit?"

"Xander! What the hell is happening? Who are these people? How do you know how to—"

He put his index finger to her lips, quieting her, as a faint humming sound reached their ears. She obliged, choking back sobs, and they stood in silence for a moment as the humming grew louder—closer. Out of nowhere a bright light shined through the two windows that overlooked the back of the house, and two more masked men crashed through them as they swung from a helicopter's rope into the bedroom. Xander had been standing in front of one of the windows and was knocked to the floor as one of the men crashed through. This also kicked the gun out of his hand and sent it flying to the far wall. As his back hit the floor and the glass fell like rain all around him, he used the momentum to go directly into a back somersault and slide to a crouched position. He leaped forward, tackling the man in front of him. Xander wrapped his arms around the man's legs and drove forward while he simultaneously pulled the intruder's pistol from its hip holster. As they both landed on the ground, Xander rolled over from on top of the man and shot the pistol out of the outstretched hand of the second intruder just before the man squeezed the trigger and shot in the direction of Natalie's head. While Natalie was suspended in shock and the man who had tried to shoot her recoiled his arm from the bullet hitting his gun, Xander brought the same elbow that held his gun straight back and drove it through the nose of the man he lay on top of. Blood spattered onto Xander as he shattered the man's nose, and before the intruder who tried to shoot Natalie could recover, Xander shot him right through the temple. Blood spurted through the air like a geyser and landed on Natalie's face before she could turn away from the action. Xander spun into the man he was resting on and jammed the barrel of the gun into his mouth.

"Who are you?" Natalie screamed at Xander, not comprehending what she was seeing from the man she thought she knew.

Xander ignored Natalie as he removed the gun from the intruder's mouth and ripped the black ski mask from his face. It revealed a Middle Eastern man. He had a large nose—now busted—a beige skin tone, and thick dark eyebrows and hair.

"Who sent you? Answer me!" he shouted as he pressed the gun into the frightened man's forehead, just above his obliterated nose.

A thumping crash from somewhere downstairs kept the man from answering.

"How many more are coming?" Xander asked him.

"Fuck you," the man answered in a thick Middle Eastern accent.

Xander put the gun back in his mouth and blew his brains all over the wall behind him. Natalie squealed and took a step back in fear of Xander. He stood and turned toward Natalie, his body plastered in blood, some his own, some from the intruders, a look of madness in his eyes. It was an image that Natalie—no matter how much time passed—would never forget.

"It's gonna be okay. I'm not going to let anything happen to you. I promise," he said, trying to comfort her. After a brief hesitation she stepped back in and put her arms around him. He could feel her shaking. He squeezed her, and as he let her go he handed her the nine-millimeter. "Have you used a gun before?"

She hesitated, her face blank. "Y-yeah, I was trained to use a Glock on the set of *Runaway*. But they were just blanks."

"Perfect, this will feel exactly the same. Stay behind me. I have no idea how many of them may be down there. You won't need the gun unless we get separated. Just keep your cool and relax your hands when you squeeze the trigger."

She nodded. Fear had stolen her ability for words. The sun was beginning to rise, and the first signs of light illuminated the shattered windows of the master bedroom. The helicopter had either left or landed and shut down its rotors. The bedroom looked like a war zone, littered with bodies, bullet holes, and tiny shards of window glass. The cool air filtered in through the broken windows and caused Natalie's mostly naked body to shiver.

"All right, we gotta move. I can't leave you here, they might come back through the window," Xander told her.

She nodded her head with a terrified look on her face as she grabbed his arm with her free hand and extended the gun out in front of her with the other.

"Step around the glass, and . . . try not to shoot me."

Blood continued to trickle from the grazing wound in his shoulder. He bent down and picked up the only fully loaded gun in the room. He stepped over the first body and found one of the few spots on the floor that wasn't covered in broken glass. He pointed it out to Natalie, and she followed him to the doorway. Xander stopped at the doorway and closed his eyes. Natalie watched as Xander focused on any clue as to where the others might be and how many there were. There was a constant calculation running in the mind of a Navy SEAL. Probabilities, positions, exit strategies—you name it, it was being tallied. He heard a familiar creaking sound and knew someone was on the ninth step on their way upstairs. He counted and exactly 1.3 seconds later they made the eleventh step creak. This meant they would be stepping on the fifteenth and final step in exactly 2.6 seconds.

"Stay on my hip," he whispered to Natalie as he placed her free hand there. He stepped out into the hallway, and in a near sprint he moved forward toward the top of the stairs.

2.6 seconds.

He raised his gun head high and shot a man in the temple as he took his first step into the hallway. Xander took one step forward and shot another man in the middle of the stairs, then put two bullets in the chest of a man at the foot of the stairs, then two more in a man at the middle of the foyer.

Out of nowhere, Xander felt a pounding blow to his forearms, and his gun toppled over the banister down to the hardwood floor some twenty feet below. Natalie fell backward into the hallway in fear, and Xander felt two massive hands wrap around his neck. One man had previously made it upstairs, but Xander had somehow missed him during the commotion in the bedroom.

That is, if you could call this a man.

He turned Xander toward him, and with his neck being relentlessly squeezed, he saw what was at least a six-eight, 275-pound monster standing in front of him. Xander grabbed at the man's arms, which felt more like tree trunks, to free himself. Bursts of pain shot through his neck as the man's grip tightened around him like an anaconda. Air wasn't coming to him now, and he felt a sting of panic. This feeling was the very thing he needed to focus. Xander steadied his mind and let his body go limp, becoming dead weight. At first the man's arms lowered as he took on Xander's full weight. Much to the horror of Natalie, however, they then began to rise back up and dangled Xander's 215-pound frame half a foot above the ground. His deep brown eyes held Xander's struggling gaze. Natalie raised her gun but couldn't get a clear shot. She was afraid she would hit Xander.

The man's strength surprised Xander.

But he didn't panic.

He brought his left knee up to his chest, then kicked straight down on the massive man's knee. The man buckled momentarily but then recovered, not dropping Xander.

Weakness.

Xander raised his knee back to his chest and from deep inside himself conjured a little more strength, using it to drive his foot down through the man's groin. The big man buckled again, momentarily dropping Xander but never letting go. Instead, he lifted him right back up and walked him over to the banister. Natalie screamed and shot the gun, but missed. She went to shoot again, but a man who had entered the house upstairs through one of the open bedroom windows came up behind her and knocked the gun out of her hand. Xander, now sitting on the banister, about to be thrown over, saw this out of the corner of his eye and began punching down on the big man's arms as hard as he could.

The other intruder grabbed Natalie by the hair and stood her up. Xander's pounding on the man's arms was useless. The man pushed him out a little more and almost all of Xander's body dangled beyond the banister, hovering over the ground far below. Xander began to rock his hips wildly from left to right. Natalie now had a gun pressed against her head. Her body quivered in fear. Xander let out a grunt of frustration as he noticed her there, only in her underwear, trembling at gunpoint. With one more grunt, Xander used his Brazilian jujitsu black-belt skills and swung his left leg over the big man's face. All in one fluid motion he trapped the man's left arm in between his legs with the man's elbow at his groin. Using that as a hinge, Xander used both arms to pull back the man's arm at the wrist toward his own chest. Acting as a lever, he thrust his hips upward as he continued to pull the arm toward his chest. The big man was forced to fall to his back, and when he did Xander forced his hips upward again, breaking the man's arm in half. The crack echoed in the hallway and out into the open foyer. The massive man shrieked in pain, and the man holding Natalie began to scream and point his gun at Xander. Underneath Xander's leg, which was pressed against the black leather jacket of the monstrous man, he could feel a pistol bulging into his calf. Xander let go of the man's broken arm and put his hands in the air as if to surrender. The man below him writhed in pain, but he held him in place with his legs.

Xander looked into the eyes of the man holding Natalie. "Don't shoot . . . Don't shoot. You got me."

Natalie let out a cry of fear as she thought now they would surely die. "Xander, help! Help me!"

The man put the gun back to Natalie's head. For three inaudible sentences, on every fifth word the gunman took his eye off Xander and looked at Natalie. Xander figured he was saying in Arabic that he was going to shoot the girl. As the gunman started the fourth sentence, Xander dug his bare foot down inside the man's leather jacket and hooked the trigger loop of the pistol with his long second toe and clamped down with his big toe. When the gunman said the fifth word of the sentence and on cue looked at Natalie, Xander used his foothold to flip the gun up out of the man's jacket, back through the air into his hands, and he shot the gunman in the neck before he ever had a chance to look back at Xander. The gunman stood suspended for a moment, then collapsed straight to his back. Natalie dropped to her knees and started to sob hysterically.

The big man finally sat up from underneath Xander, and Xander turned the gun around in his hand and smashed it against the middle of the black ski mask he wore. There was a distinctive pop upon impact as Xander had shattered his second nose of the night. The man's deep voice raised as he growled in pain. Natalie wasn't sure if she sobbed more out of fear or out of the shock of not knowing who this man in front of her was whom she had been falling so hard for. How did he know how to fight like this? There must be some logical explanation for such a great guy being mixed up in what seemed to be an all-out war.

Xander rose to his feet as the big man grasped at his nose with his one good arm and squirmed around in pain. Xander pressed his foot down on the exact spot where he broke the arm in half and pointed the gun down at the man's head. The man screamed in agony as Xander pressed, and so too did Natalie just a few feet away at the top of the stairs.

"Who sent you? Tell me now or I will blow your brains out the back of your head." Again, Xander was eerily calm.

The man didn't answer. All he could manage were more moans of pain. A car door shut outside at the front of the house. Xander stomped the man in the head, knocking him unconscious, then wheeled around and held the gun directly at the already open front door below. Natalie squealed at the thought of more men coming in to try to kill them, and she scooted back into the hallway. Her head went back and forth from the bedroom to the top of the stairway as she held the gun out in front of her.

"Xander!" someone shouted from outside the house. "Xander! You okay?"

Kyle.

He shouted again from outside, then came running in. Xander lowered his gun.

"Kyle." The name rolled out of Xander's mouth in a breath of relief.

"Xander? What the hell? Are you okay?"

"Annie!" Natalie shouted. "Annie, are you there?"

Xander walked over to Natalie as he spoke to Kyle.

"Yeah, we're okay. Hey, don't let Annie see any of this, all right?"

"Yeah, no problem. She's waiting in the car. Who the hell were these guys? Are they all dead?"

"Two are unconscious, nine are dead. Call Sam and let her know. She'll know what to do."

"Will do. You sure you don't need anything? You're bleeding."

"I'm good, but can you bring Natalie's bag up from the spare bedroom and a bottle of water?"

"Of course, be right back."

Xander bent down to Natalie's level, tucked her hair behind her ear, and wiped her tears. Her mascara had bled down the left side of her cheek, but aside from that, she looked no worse for the wear.

"Natalie," he said in a soothing voice, "everything is okay, sweetheart. They're all gone. Are you okay?"

He waited, but nothing came from her. Nothing but a blank stare and more tears. He gently wiped them away from her flushed cheeks. "Natalie, I know you're scared and confused. I'm going to help you up and sit you on the bed in the spare room up here, all right? Kyle is bringing your clothes and some water. Okay, Natalie?"

She nodded her head, still off in space. Although she didn't know what to make of Xander now, as ironic as it sounded, he at least made her feel safe. Xander helped her to her feet and brought her into one of the spare bedrooms and sat her down on the edge of the bed.

"Is there a shower in that bathroom? I'd really like a warm shower," she said.

"Of course. There are towels under the sink, and I will lay

146

your clothes out on the bed and shut the door."

"No!" She grabbed at his arm, frantic. "No, please. Please don't leave me alone in here." Her voice quivered.

"I'll wait right here. I promise I won't move," he assured her. She gave a half-cocked grin and nodded her head. She slinked into the shower, and Xander's heart dropped. He couldn't imagine the fear and shock she was feeling. To Xander, violence and killing had become routine since he joined the military. He couldn't imagine what that looked like through her eyes. Not just one man killed in front of her, but nine. It was a lot, even for Xander.

Kyle knocked at the door as the water started in the bathroom.

"Come in."

"Xander, what the hell? Does this mean word is out about what you've been doing? Is this a retaliation?"

"I'm not sure. All those men are Middle Eastern, so it could mean a lot of things. Do me a favor and grab the box from under my bed. There is some rope and some duct tape in there. Will you tie up the two unconscious men before they wake up?"

"Yeah. And Sam is on the way. We'll figure this out."

"No, I know."

"How the hell did you take all of these guys out? Eleven guys? In the middle of the night?"

Annie shouted from downstairs. "Kyle? What's taking so— ahhhh! Natalie! What the hell is all this?"

"Damn it, Kyle."

"Shit, sorry, Xander. Shit!"

"Go get her. Cover her eyes and bring her in here, then get those men taken care of."

Kyle ran out of the room. Xander went to the door of the

bathroom. The water was still running, and steam had begun to puff out of the cracked door.

Xander stepped inside. "Are you doing all right in here, Natalie?"

Natalie pulled back the shower curtain and peeked around at him. Her eyes weren't as far off in their own world now, and she nodded to him. He walked over and took her in his arms. The water continued to run over Natalie's back. She hadn't even bothered to remove her underwear.

Natalie pulled back and looked into his eyes. "Xander, who are you? What was this? Are you some sort of spy?"

"It's complicated, but yes, something like that. I'm so sorry that I put you in danger. I never would have brought you here if . . . This is the first time anything like this has happened."

"How did you know how to fight and shoot like that? As a Navy SEAL?"

"How did you—"

"I saw the picture in the hallway downstairs of you getting that award," Natalie said, cutting him off. "Does this have something to do with that? Do you work for the government?"

"The less you know, the better. I'm so sorry . . ." Xander's voice trailed off as he held her. Natalie didn't say another word.

"Natalie?" Annie shouted from the bedroom. "Natalie?"

"In here, Annie. Everything is okay." She released her hold on Xander as Annie entered the bathroom. Annie rushed past Xander and threw her arms around Natalie.

"What the hell is going on? There are dead men all over the place. Are you okay?" Annie asked as she looked over Natalie's body, checking for injuries.

"I'm fine, Annie. Xander saved my life."

"Saved your life? Are you kidding me? He is the reason

you were in danger in the first place, isn't he? Is he some sort of criminal or something?"

"No, Annie, nothing like that. He—"

"He what? You still think you know him? Natalie, there are *dead bodies* lying just outside this room. We saw a helicopter leaving as we pulled up."

"Okay, Annie, okay. I honestly don't have . . ." Natalie trailed off as she stared blankly at the wall.

Annie sounded remorseful. "I'm sorry, Natalie . . . here, here's a towel."

Xander took Natalie's clothes out of her bag and laid them out on the bed. "Natalie, I'm going to be right outside in the hall, all right? Your clothes are on the bed."

"Okay. Please don't go far," she answered from the bathroom.

"I won't."

Xander walked into the hall as Kyle finished subduing the two men in his bedroom. Xander took a moment to drag the dead bodies out of sight before Natalie and Annie came downstairs. He went back upstairs and helped Kyle put the two still unconscious men in the master bathroom and locked them in. Kyle stopped and looked around the bedroom, his eyes finding the broken windows.

"They actually came through the windows?"

Xander ran his fingers through his hair. His breath still labored from the close call. He couldn't believe he had put Natalie in such danger.

"I know. Someone went to great pains to plan this. Someone has been watching us."

Sarah Gilbright Considers Getting Her Ass in Gear

Sarah Gilbright sat wringing her hands just outside of Director Manning's office. She'd barely had time to study the agents recommended for the team she was spearheading to watch Xander, and the shit had already hit the fan. Three incidents in a matter of three days. She couldn't be sure about the man in the bathroom at the Kentucky Derby; there were no real signs of foul play, but it just smelled of Xander King. Smooth and flawless. Miguel Juarez, she knew for sure, was Xander's work, due to the description the young blonde girl had given to the officers who took her statement. It was just too obvious, describing her hero as tall, gentle, and *hot*. Sarah couldn't help but smile.

Manning's door flew open.

"What the hell are you smiling about? Something about all of this funny to you?" His face was red and his chest was heaving angry breaths. He was this mad about Juarez and Kulakov, so there was no way she could tell him about the tip she had gotten about the attack on Xander's home in Lexington. She just hoped Xander was okay. She had no idea yet what actually happened, and until she did, she wasn't telling Manning a thing.

"Get your ass in here. You got your team together yet?"

Sarah stood, shaking her head no. She gave her tight white skirt a tug and pulled her purse up over her shoulder.

"Mr. Manning, I haven't even had time to speak with anyone—"

"Well, Xander has had time to kill more nut jobs. Maybe you should consider getting your ass in gear? I told you this was top priority."

"Yes, sir. You are right."

They both entered Manning's office, but neither of them took a seat. It was more shoebox than office really, not much larger than a prison cell. The walls were filled with medals and certificates of accomplishment. Manning picked up a white Styrofoam cup and spit a tobacco-filled wad inside of it. His chin jutted in anger, and his bottom lip bulged with Skoal. Wintergreen. Sarah noticed the small disk of it on his desk. The entire room reeked of it. It was an unmistakable smell; her little brother had picked up the habit on the high school baseball team.

"You're goddamn right, I am. We've got to get our heads around this, Gilbright. Give me the latest on what you've found out about Xander's parents' killer. You do have an update for me, right?"

Sarah cleared her throat.

"I do, but it isn't much. I spoke with the detective who

investigated the crime scene that day. Said there wasn't much more than shell casings and tire marks to go on. He sent me all of his records, and I may have a lead through the Blue Grass Airport. There was a private plane that flew in that morning and for some reason some information is missing. I'm looking into it. But, sir, I can guarantee you Xander has already been through this information. If the plane had anything to do with his parents' murder, the owners of that jet would already be dead."

"Sounds like you better start thinking outside the box. If Xander has been looking for years, he has already sifted through the obvious stuff. We gotta use our connections. Talk to people who knew Xander's daddy. He was good buddies with some higher-ups in the government. Let's exhaust our inside track."

"I understand we can't have someone treating the world like the wild west, Mr. Manning, but aside from that, what is the rush? You said yourself he's doing good things."

"This small-time shit he's doing *doesn't* matter to me. We have got some major problems in Europe and the Middle East right now, and don't even get me started on Russia. We need someone—Xander—who can change the game for us overseas. Someone who can walk in the shadows. And as you know, the only chance we have of him working with us is if we have something he wants. Otherwise, we can forget it."

"I know. I'm on it. I will personally oversee every move he makes."

"I know you will, Gilbright, and I'm going to be real honest with you. That's part of what makes me nervous."

Manning looked her up and down and shook his head. Sarah shifted her purse from one shoulder to the other.

"How do you mean?"

"I've seen the way you light up when you talk about him and—"

"I beg your pardon," she interrupted. Her face went flush.

"Just that. You should see your face right now."

"There's nothing—"

"Listen. All I'm saying is this, it is clear the two of you are good-looking, young, and healthy adults. And I don't care if you use that to get close to him. But you have got to be careful. You can't go falling for this guy."

"Sir, I—"

"That's all. Just keep it professional. Otherwise, you're off of this. You hear me?"

"I hear you."

"Good. Now get the hell out of here and bring me what I need. I want something in forty-eight hours."

"I'll do my best."

"I don't want your best. I want his. So get this done."

Sarah nodded, and as Manning spit once again into his cup, she turned and walked out the door. Her heels clacked against the concrete floor, and her heart thumped inside her chest. She didn't want to be pulled from this assignment. Because something was pulling her toward Xander King.

You Can't Be Goin' All X-Man on Me

The cursor on the empty text line blinked at him as he stared at his phone, contemplating another message to Natalie. He had called a couple of times to no avail, and he hadn't heard from her since he dropped her off at the airport two days ago now. Did she make it back to California safe? Did she hate him?

"Mr. King." A woman in a knee-length black pencil skirt and a satin maroon short-sleeved top got his attention. "Agent Thompson will be right out. Can I get you a coffee or anything?"

"No, thank you."

This was the first time Xander had been to see Sean since he moved to Langley. The CIA lobby reminded him more of an oversize dentist's office instead of a government facility. Well, except for the armed guards and metal detector at the front door, of course. He felt like he was waiting for jury duty or something. The thought of a desk job made Xander's skin crawl. The thought of taking even just one more bullshit order from the government also made him sick to his stomach. He had gotten what he needed out of his time with the SEALs. He had also learned far more about his government's corrupt and vile under-doings as well. Countless missions took countless innocent lives, and the people giving the orders lied to the American people, all the way to the bank. Sean had witnessed the same things as Xander, and that is why he was so willing to help him when he came to him about carrying out his own missions. Xander loved his country as much as a man could, but the government was another story entirely.

"Damnit, X. You are just as good-lookin' as ever, you sorry son of a bitch!" Xander heard Sean's unmistakable country twang from the other side of the lobby. "Get your ass over here!" Sean stood with his arms wide open like a big ol' bear. The desk job had helped add some weight to Sean's midsection, and there was a little less hair on the top of his head.

"What happened to you? Did your hairline get mad at your forehead?" Xander joked as he walked over and gave him a big man-hug.

"Damn, it's good to see ya, Xander. How about that big badass pony o' yours?"

"You saw him, huh? I told you . . . closes like a freight train."

"You ain't a-lyin', X-man, that is one hell of a horse. He gonna win the Preakness in a couple weeks? You say the word and I'm gonna drop a couple thousand on him."

"I'd say that's a good bet, my man," Xander assured him as Sean led him to his office. Sean shut the door behind him and took a seat at his desk. Xander took a seat across from him.

"Well, I don't imagine good news brought you all the way to Langley on a Monday morning after a wild Derby weekend."

"No, I'm sorry to say it didn't."

"Well, let's have it, X-man."

"I can trust you, right, Sean?"

"Trust me? Is that some sorta joke?"

"No, I'm just—listen, someone is after me, Sean. And I need you to help me find out who."

"How do ya know someone's after you?"

"Well, I killed nine men who broke into my house in the middle of the night Saturday. I still have two more of them alive, but they aren't talking. They had a helicopter and automatic weapons; that shit was well orchestrated."

"Nine men? At your place in Lexington?"

"Yep."

"How are you here? Did your security team get them?"

"I don't have a security team, Sean."

"And you wonder why we nicknamed you X-man. You're a goddamn superhero," Sean wondered in amazement. "You gotta quit this stuff, X. All this is gonna catch up to ya."

"Too late. I just need you to help me find out who did this. I know it was the same man who killed Mom and Dad. I know it was, Sean."

"Hang on now, just hang on. Do ya have any idea who might do this? It's not like people associated with all the targets you've taken out aren't trying to find you. You know you don't have any shortage of enemies."

"I don't have any enemies. No one can link me to the people I've taken out. Listen, all I have is that these guys were Middle Eastern."

"Middle Eastern?" There was a hint of shock in Sean's

voice. Xander picked up on it immediately.

"What? What the hell aren't you telling me?"

"There ain't nothin' I ain't tellin' ya."

"Bullshit, this isn't a joke. They almost killed me and someone special to me."

"You're talkin' bout that Natalie Rockwe—" Sean paused. "Sorry. I'm telling you, I don't *know* anything."

"Damnit, Sean!" Xander stood up. "You weren't calling me Saturday about the Derby, were you?" A pause. "Were you?"

"Now, Xander—"

"Did you know my house might get hit?" Xander rounded Sean's desk, grabbed him by the collar, and stood him up. Sean pushed Xander back away from him.

"Are you serious right now? You think I would have let somethin' like that go down? The hell with you then, buddy. You can take your ass right the hell back out the door if that's what you think."

Xander collected himself.

"Well, someone knew it was going to happen. I got a text right before it from an unknown number. It actually saved my life. It said someone was in the house, and then I saw the first gunman. Who the hell would know that? If it wasn't you, who was it? I know you aren't telling me everything."

"Okay, okay. Sit down. Sit." Sean straightened his collar and sat back down. "All right, you're right. When I called you, I had just gotten off the phone with Marv. But I never sent you no text. Did you trace the number?"

"Of course, but Sam said it was from a burner phone. No trace."

"Looks like more people know what you're up to than ya think. Now listen, if I tell you what I know, you gotta promise me you ain't gonna go run and do somethin' stupid. This is high-level government shit and I can't have you goin' and makin' a mess."

"Sean, what the hell is it? What did Marv tell you?"

"Now this don't mean nothin', but since you said those men who came after you are Middle Eastern . . ." Sean paused.

"What? So help me God—"

"All right, all right. Calm down. Marv called and said there was a bad sum bitch over in Syria they was investigatin'. There was a couple of coincidences that caught his eye, and he made me promise until I did some research that I wouldn't tell you about him. Now, I haven't had the chance to research yet, so—"

"What the hell is the intel, Sean? What are the coincidences?" Xander stood up again as he raised his voice. "Does Marv think this might have something to do with my parents' murder?"

"Now, X, there ain't no way of knowing that." Sean held both arms out, pumping his hands backward and forward in a gesture to try to get Xander to pump the brakes.

"But Marv thought enough of it to flag it? Sean, I've been dreaming of this day for fourteen years. My entire adult life has been devoted to this moment and you think you are going to stand here and not tell me what you know?"

The door to the office opened, and the woman in the maroon top poked her head in. "Is everything okay, Agent Thompson?"

"Everything is fine, Allison. Leave us." She shut the door. "All right . . . Okay. You just gotta promise me you'll do the right thing by this information and take the time to vet it all out. You can't be goin' all X-man on me."

"Just give me the intel, Sean. I'm not playing games."

An Aching Sadness in the Pit of His Stomach

Xander walked out of the federal building with a knot in his stomach. He had already texted Sam to begin running checks on a man named Sanharib Khatib. It didn't really matter what the results turned up, though; Marv's fears of telling Xander had been warranted. Regardless of what Sam told him, Xander's next target would be Khatib. And for the first time, he would have words before the assassination was over. Sean tried to give Xander warning that if he attempted to go in by himself that it would be suicide, so just let them do their jobs. That of course fell on deaf ears as Xander was already texting Sam. As far as Xander was concerned, Khatib was a dead man walking.

Xander spent the plane ride back to Lexington confirming Sean's words. Khatib was a bad dude. Sam had already forwarded some files on him, and a lot of the literature was headlined with the words "The Next Bin Laden." Khatib had been the largest purveyor of oil in Syria for more than two decades. The reports followed along his journey of building an army of militants and killing his way to that position of wealth and power. Xander's wheels were already spinning because of the fact his father had made his money in oil himself.

Coincidence number one.

It looked as though recently Khatib had become bored of the oil-stealing business. Lately, he had made headlines more for drugs, arms, and terrorism. It seemed the thing to do in that part of the world was to leave a legacy of hate before you died in a fury of ignorance. Of course, Xander understood the world's hatred of the United States much more than the average citizen. That wasn't his concern in this situation, however, and the more he thumbed through recent documentation of Khatib, the more he wanted to go back in time to learn more about Khatib's life in 2004—the year Xander's parents were brutally murdered in front of him. For some reason, Khatib's involvement in an event on US soil in 2004 was classified to a point that Sam wasn't yet able to get the intel.

Coincidence number two.

Xander closed his laptop and searched himself for reasons not to go after Khatib as he stared out the window into the deep-blue sky. Puffs of white clouds hovered below the plane as a sort of barrier between him and the real world. It always gave him a sense of peace to be so far above the fray. Above the madness of a world charging toward its own demise. As he pondered it, he couldn't find one single reason *not* to rid the world of such a terrible human. Not a single one. The clouds continued along like a cottony pillow, waiting to bounce the plane back up into the sky if it got too low. The sun was warm on Xander's face. He drifted off to sleep and the familiar dream recounting the day his parents died haunted his unconsciousness.

The sun came up on a summer day in Lexington, Kentucky. Xander awoke in his bed with excitement. His mom had promised they would go to King's Island, aka heaven for a fifteen-year-old boy. King's Island was an amusement park in Cincinnati, Ohio. Though the name King's Island was a coincidence, his mom told him it was their family's personal playground. Xander knew that it was actually the movie company Paramount that owned the park. It was on the sign at the entrance of the park, and they had rides there named after some of Paramount's most popular cartoon characters. His mom liked this little fib, so Xander just played along.

He jumped out of bed and put his favorite Jordan sneakers on, the mid-cuts with the black patent leather around the bottom and white throughout the rest of the shoe. He headed downstairs for breakfast, and he could smell the eggs in the skillet as he rounded the corner. His mom always made him his favorite—egg, ham, and cheese sandwiches—on Saturdays, and usually Sundays too.

"You sure you wanna eat all this, Alexander? Just don't be throwing these up on me when we're on The Beast later." His mom laughed as he scarfed the food down the way a refugee would upon receiving his first real meal.

"I won't, Mom," Xander replied, mouth full of sandwich.

Xander's sister sat at the booth watching TV, eating her Pop-Tarts. She was seventeen now, but she didn't love going to King's Island any less. A couple of Mom's sisters walked through the front door, and some of Xander's cousins ran into the kitchen, raring to go. His mom had rented a van, and they would all take the hour-long trip together. This trip to the amusement park was going to be more exciting for Xander, however, because for the first time, his dad had promised to join in on the fun with them.

"You ready to go, little buddy?" His dad walked into the kitchen. "Don't be mad at me when I whoop up on you in the basketball shot game," he said, joking with his son.

"Yeah, right. You know I'm gonna make it before you!" Xander said, full of confidence.

The lighting in the dream changed from bright and sunny to a strange hue of blue, as darkness filled in the corners of what he was reliving. Everything was in slow motion.

They all walked to the front door, and as soon as they stepped outside, an all-black passenger van screeched to a halt, sideways, in front of them. Two men in ski masks jumped out of the van with guns in their hands. Xander saw his dad turn to provide cover for Xander, a look of sheer terror on his face. Blood spattered all over Xander as his dad's body jerked with each bullet that penetrated his body. The sound of his sister's screams was the only thing Xander heard as his dad hit the ground at his feet. He looked to his right and his mom lay motionless in the grass. The men said nothing, and screamed nothing. Once it was done, they simply got back in the van and drove away. Xander stood in shock. His sister sobbed, and his aunts and cousins all ran to his mom and dad. Xander felt cemented to the ground. The sun shining in his eyes forced him to squint, and it all seemed as if he was in some strange movie.

The wheels of the plane screeched against the runway and jolted Xander awake. Every time he had the dream, he always woke up with an aching sadness in the pit of his stomach. On one hand it felt so good to talk to his mom and dad again, but on the other it made the sting of that afternoon pierce his heart as sharply as it had that day. As the plane taxied its way to its space, he took in long deep breaths to slow his pounding heart and wiped the sweat from his forehead with a folded blanket that lay in the seat next to him. His phone vibrated in the pocket of his black jeans as notifications poured in when it once again acquired its signal from the cell towers. Most were from Twitter, but there were also two texts from Kyle and one from Sean.

And one from Natalie.

He unlocked his phone and went straight to Natalie's text.

Thank you for checking on me. I'm okay. Still just so confused and scared. Sleep isn't coming easy. I accept your apology, and I know you want to see me and try to explain. However, I need some time. I do want to talk to you about everything but I'm not ready. I'm shooting a new movie in Paris. I'll be back in the States in a couple of months. If we both still want to, we can talk then. Until then I am going to process how the greatest weekend of my life was also the worst. I need some time away so that my feelings for you don't cloud my judgment when I consider that I don't even know who you are. Please respect this and put your feelings for me aside as you give me this space.

Xander hated that he had put Natalie and himself in this situation. He knew she wanted to be with him, but he knew it was with the Xander who didn't have the ability to kill nine men in ten minutes. She fell for whiskey-and-roses Xander, not terrifying-assassin Xander. The hardest part of this for him was that he was angry at himself for letting it go this far to begin with. This is why for the last twelve years his relationships with women had only been sexual. This past weekend served as a painful reminder that that is exactly how it had to be going

163

forward. It wasn't fair to bring someone into his dangerous life. And it wasn't healthy to let a woman cloud his thoughts that should so reverently be focused on what really mattered.

Revenge.

He snapped out of his text trance and checked Sean's message as he exited the jet. The message was just Sean making sure he wasn't going to do anything stupid. Xander didn't respond. He then scrolled to Kyle's message, an invitation to watch the Lakers game and have some drinks on the Harry's patio in Hamburg. Kyle suggested it would be good for him.

Xander responded. *Sounds good. I gotta get a good long run in first. I'll meet you at Harry's patio at seven.*

Best-Laid Plans

Somewhere off in the distance, a repetitive and obnoxious sound seemed to be coming closer and closer. Xander's eyes opened, and his familiar twelve-foot master bedroom ceiling blurred into clarity as a streak of sunlight poured in through his freshly repaired bedroom windows. The light seemed like a sword piercing through his eye sockets all the way through to the back of his skull. He shut his eyes, hoping that would stop the pain, but he quickly understood that it wasn't the light of the morning causing the pain, it was the tequila from the night before. It wasn't until the fourth attempt to open his mouth that he actually got his jaws to pry apart. His tongue felt like sandpaper, and swallowing still wasn't an option.

The obnoxious noise that woke him started up again. His phone vibrated and rang from the nightstand beside him. It sat there rattling away beside the dried-up candle he had burned when Natalie spent the night. A longing for her came over him for a moment, then was shoved away by the noise of the ringing phone rattling through his head like a relentless alarm clock. He rolled over and picked up his phone to silence it without looking to see who it was. When he rolled once again to his back in an attempt to clear the cobwebs, he noticed a hump in the sheets beside him. He didn't remember the ride home last night, or what had obviously happened once they made it to the bedroom, but he was certain that it was Megan beside him. Right? He lifted the blanket that covered them both, and he could tell by the unbelievable curve of her body that it was indeed her. Kyle was right: she was damn sexy.

Xander took a moment to try to recall all that had taken place the night before. He remembered meeting up with Kyle. He remembered watching the game and enjoying some bourbon. He even remembered telling Kyle about the upcoming mission in Syria. A mission Kyle was less than enthused about, but ready to go along with regardless. After the first shot of tequila, it was as if he had time-traveled to waking up in bed, where he was now, lying beside Megan. Xander vaguely recalled the discussion with Kyle about whether or not to meet up with Kate and Megan. He remembered being reluctant, because he had slept with Megan before, and he didn't want to see her again and lead her on. He glanced over at her in the bed; once again, better judgment had been drowned by liquor. And no doubt, Kyle was the reason that it happened. Sometimes he could be a terrible influence. Xander knew he would pay for this, and he hated that Megan might get her feelings hurt in the process. Xander turned and laid his phone back on the nightstand.

Megan stirred at the movement of the sheets, and surely

from the obnoxious ringing of Xander's phone a moment earlier. "Good morning, sexy. Did you have fun last night?"

"Good morning, Megan. Of course I did. What I remember of it anyway," Xander answered. His voice was deeper than normal. A lot of alcohol the night before always had that effect on him.

"I didn't figure you would remember much. You were sweet, though. Even though you'd had too much to drink to make love to me, you spent at least a half an hour pleasuring me."

"Oh yeah? Nope, don't remember that." Xander's mouth still smacked of dryness as he choked words out. It was rare he ever brought a woman home. It always made everything much more complicated.

"I tried to return the favor, but you were spent." Megan frowned but quickly turned it into a smile as she wrapped her hand around him.

Before Xander could respond, Megan lifted the sheet and nose-dived in the direction of her hand. Xander had every intention of stopping her. He really did.

Just as soon as Megan was finished, Xander's phone rang again. He took a brief moment to savor the deep relaxation Megan had helped him find, then rolled over and silenced the call. It was Sam. He could already hear the voice mail in his head; there was no reason to check it. Her sharp British rant would go something like this: "Xander, this is the third time I've rung you. Ron said he dropped you completely snockered last night. We have so much work to do. I'm coming at nine so we can get working on this, whether you're in bed with another one of your *whores* or not."

"I'm going to jump in the shower. You want to join me?"

167

Megan rolled out of bed and stood over him, just as sexy as she could be. She had the body of a model. Five-foot ten, all legs, a tiny waist, and curves that someone with her lack of body fat just shouldn't have.

"No, thank you. I'm gonna hit the kitchen to get a start on this hangover. You want anything?"

"I'll be down in just a bit. If you make some breakfast, just make a little extra for me." Megan smiled and pranced toward the bathroom.

Xander watched every single sexy step she took.

"Things could be worse," he said out loud to himself with his hands clasped behind his head and a smile on his face. Nothing cured an agonizing heart like the company of a beautiful woman. Well, maybe that and whiskey. The hangovers of both could often be similarly painful.

The room rocked back and forth as Xander sat up in bed. He staggered to the cherrywood armoire in front of him and pulled some white linen pajama pants and a white under tank from their neatly folded stacks. A waft of coffee hit his nose, and at first his stomach rolled. Kyle and Kate were already up and at 'em. The second whiff that hit his nose comforted his stomach. He walked into the bathroom, and as he brushed his teeth he watched Megan's silhouette as she washed herself behind the fogged glass in the shower. He pictured her body standing over him naked before she left for the shower moments ago, and it seemed Xander wasn't quite finished with Megan yet. He dropped his pants, took off his tank, and opened the shower door. Her body glistened as the water cascaded over her, highlighting every bodacious curve. Xander raised his eyebrow and Megan smiled, pulling him into the shower. Xander knew it was a bad idea, but a man only has so much will power.

Xander made his way into the kitchen where he found Kyle and Kate had gotten a jump on breakfast.

"Good morning, Xander." Kate smiled from the kitchen sink. "I would ask if Megan is up yet, but her moaning at the top of her lungs a minute ago kinda gave that away." She winked.

"Oh yeah, she's up." Xander smiled.

"Yes!" Kyle chimed in.

The doorbell rang, and immediately the door opened and someone came in.

"Mommy's here!" Kyle joked.

He knew it was Sam. She walked into the kitchen.

"Oh good, you're already here, Kyle. I'm assuming she is leaving," Sam asked, referencing Kate. "The two of you shared last night, I see."

"Excuse me?" Kate took offense.

Kyle shot Sam a boyish grin. "Don't mind her. She hasn't been laid since the nineties and she likes to take it out on everyone else."

Sam was not amused.

"No one shared anything," Xander told her. "Megan is upstairs. Grab some coffee and let's have a chat."

"I already have coffee, Xander. Some of us have been up for hours. I prefer to prepare for meetings by doing research, not by drowning in whiskey and one-night stands."

"Everyone's different, Sam." Kyle laughed.

Sam of course did not.

"I'll be in the office. Let's get started ASAP, if you don't mind?"

"Okay, Sam. We'll be there in just a bit," Xander replied.

"Is that all I am to you is a one-night stand?" Kate asked Kyle, pouting her bottom lip.

"Don't listen to her. She's just mad cause she's not you right now." Kyle smiled.

Sam just rolled her eyes and left the kitchen in a huff.

As much fun as Xander had taking a break from the darkness in his mind, Sam sured his focus, and now Xander's switch flipped back to reality. The Gatorade and Advil worked its magic on both Kyle's and Xander's hangovers as they took a seat at the desk. Sam had taken the time to put together an entire presentation on Sanharib Khatib. Xander's passion for eliminating the evil of the world was rivaled only by that of Sam. She had seen much of the same sorrows as Xander with her time in MI6. Xander knew of a story where she had been held captive for over a year at one point, and the tough bitch came out of it with her captor's head in her hands. He didn't know if that was true, but he wouldn't put it past her. She had been through more than Xander knew, but she was about as talkative about the past as a tree in the forest. He had tried on several occasions to break through, but most of the stories he knew of her came from people who had known her longer. She was like a dog on a bone when she felt compelled. Because she felt so highly of Xander and his cause, there was nothing more compelling to her than taking down Khatib.

Sam began. "Okay, I have to start out by saying that we still have not connected the dots that Khatib has anything to do with the murder of your parents, Xander. You must know this as we plan. If it comes back that he could not have been involved, we must not proceed with this target."

"Sam, I appreciate that, but Khatib is the target. Regardless of what information we find. That is how we must prepare."

"I agree, Xander, but this man is *far* too dangerous to risk going after if we aren't targeting him to avenge your parents' death. We must let the military deal with him. He has an army."

"If that is the case," Kyle interjected, "then why are we even talking about this? Regardless of vengeance, which I want for you as much as anyone, but if it's impossible, it's impossible."

Sam said, "You're right, Kyle, we shouldn't be doing this. I just know you, Xander. If this is the man responsible for the death of your parents, you will go whether I help you or not. That is why I am saying I am in, but if we find out it's not him, we have to stop. You are skilled enough to pull any job, especially with my help, but this is not a job; this is bloody war."

"Sam." Xander shifted in his seat. "Do you believe Khatib was involved with the murder of my parents?"

"There is no way—"

"Sam, do you *think* this is the guy?"

"I do; the coincidences are astonishing, but—"

"That's the end of it then. Prepare us for success. I don't care if we have to take out an entire army or not. Because I will."

"Then let's get started," Sam said, ending her side of the debate. She then drew their attention to a screen on the wall. She had her laptop connected to a projector, and the presentation she had built on Khatib was now being projected on the screen.

Sam gave the presentation. "Sanharib Khatib, born 1958 in Ramadi, Iraq. His father was one of the richest men in the country and friends of the Hussein family. He built an oil empire that he passed along to his son Sanharib, and Sanharib continued its growth in Iraq until the Gulf War in the early nineties. Because of US military insurgence there, he was forced out of Iraq and he moved his entire operation to Syria. His entire family was killed by US forces, including his wife and two children. Ever since that day he has made it his mission to have revenge on the United States, and it does not matter to him if it is the government or American civilians who feel his wrath. This is where I believe your father comes into play. In 2004 there was a bomb that blew up one of your father's oil tankers. I believe that your father was targeted because of his success in brokering multiple deals with the petroleum companies in the Middle East. This was a massive spike for your father and a lot of Middle Eastern oil companies were edged out as a result. Intel suggests that your father was believed to be on that tanker the day it was bombed, and that is why it was targeted. Two of Khatib's men were captured shortly after the explosion, and while awaiting trial they ended up dead before anything was resolved."

"So it was him. Khatib had my parents murdered at their own house when he found out dad wasn't on that tanker." Xander stood up and paced the room. "Enough background, Sam. What is the plan?"

"All right, thanks to a relationship I have with a former MI6 mate of mine, James Churchill, who is stationed just south of Syria in Israel, we have an unbelievable amount of classified intel. James has been studying and watching Khatib's every move for more than a decade. He's been frustrated that they have yet to take him out and that is why he is cooperating with us. He has insisted that he help in the mission. Xander, he has seen Khatib murder thousands and train young children to carry out his orders for years. He will be a massive help and invaluable to us as we go forward."

"Perfect. As long as it's understood that I am in charge once we hit the ground there, I am fine with it. So, what's the plan?" Xander urged.

Sam pointed to a map she had pulled up. "This is where Khatib has built his compound. A coastal Syrian city, Baniyas. It works well for him because it's on the water, which he enjoys, and it is just south of one of the largest oil refineries in Syria. Obviously, this gives us an opening to go in under the cover of water. It is, however, heavily guarded twenty-four hours a day. We will fly into Rene Mouawad Air Base, less than one mile south of the Syrian border, in Lebanon. It was a tough trick for James to find an airfield close to Syria that we could fly a G6 into without anyone being able to trace it. Since this airport is military, and so infrequently used, he was able to bribe the controller there and they will let us land and leave undocumented as long as we land after midnight and we are gone by sunrise the next morning. This will be an almost impossibly tight schedule. We are currently having a speedboat modified to shorten our time on the water. The boat as it is now will take us two and a half hours of travel time each way. Sunrise is at 5:40 a.m., so obviously that will not work."

"Forty minutes won't be long enough?" Kyle asked.

"No. We will have to scuba in—"

"In the dark?" Kyle interrupted Xander.

"Yes, in the dark."

"Jesus."

173

Xander replied, "Dark water will be the very least of your worries, I promise. Anyway, by the time we scuba in, infiltrate security, find Khatib, and question him—"

"Wait, Xander. You will not be questioning Khatib," Sam interrupted.

"Of course I will. I have to find out what he knows about what happened to my parents. I mean, why else would James come along if he wasn't translating?"

"He's coming along to help take out security."

"Sam, you know I don't need help with that."

"You most certainly will. Khatib keeps a small army at his compound. Forty-five, maybe fifty soldiers."

"Xander, fifty armed gunmen? This is suicide!" Kyle yelped.

"It's not suicide if James and I accompany Xander in taking them out," Sam said, very matter-of-factly. "These men will not have anywhere near our training. Even you, Kyle. Xander's is the only shot better than mine that I have ever come across. Obviously, I only considered any of this because I assumed you were abandoning your rule of not killing anyone outside of the main target. All of these men will have to die if we wish to succeed."

"Of course," Xander answered. "This is a terrorist cell we will be eliminating. All bets are off. The government will just have to thank us later. But I don't need James's gun. He will translate for Khatib until I get answers, that's all. I have never worked with him and I will not have him disrupting my flow. The only reason you are going is because you have been on missions with me before."

"Xander, I love you, but we cannot succeed at this mission without James. There are simply too many of them. And you will not have time for interrogation. You will put a kill shot through Khatib's head and we will immediately return to the jet. If we are documented coming or going at that airport, Khatib's counterparts will *never* rest until you are dead."

"I agree, Sam. We can't be documented, but I will be interrogating Khatib. And James will stay on the boat protecting Kyle until I bring Khatib back for translation. That's final," Xander insisted.

"Xander, James must—"

Xander slammed his fist in frustration down on the desk in front of Sam. "Enough!" Xander jumped to his feet and paced the back of the office.

"Xander," Kyle said calmly, "Sam is just trying to keep you safe."

"K, not right now. I know what I need to make this happen. Sam knows what I am capable of, and the only thing that will jeopardize our safety is an unknown. I do not work with unknowns."

"Xander, I understand your concern," Sam said in a slow and even tone, "and I do understand what you are capable of. However, just you and I alone cannot take out this entire compound. Your entire SEAL team would struggle with it. I don't want you to work with an unknown either, but James is not an unknown to me. He is a hell of an agent, and without him we will fail. We will all die."

"That's enough for today. Just let me know when we leave. I am going to work all week with Kyle on some tactical training to get him ready for everything. Thank you for the time you are putting into this, Sam. Sorry I lost my cool."

"It's all right, Xander. I know what this means to you. It means more to me than you understand as well. That is why if you let me do my job I will see to it that it is flawless. Like it is every bloody time we do this. Have I ever let you down?"

"Never," Xander answered, still clearly frustrated. He opened the office door and walked away.

"Is all of this even possible, Sam?" Kyle asked, lowering his voice so Xander wouldn't hear.

"If he lets me utilize James? Possibly."

Kyle nodded and walked into the kitchen where Xander stood at the sink splashing water on his face.

"You all right?"

"I'm good. Just still a little hungover," Xander answered. He knew Kyle meant if he was okay about the outrageous mission on which they were about to embark.

"Yeah, I know. You rarely go that hard." Kyle let him off the hook.

Mind meld.

One Lucky Girl

This is your captain speaking. We are making our final approach into Paris, France. Looks like it is going to be a beautiful day today. It is currently sixty-five degrees and lots of sunshine. Fasten your seat belts and we will be on the ground in about ten minutes. Thank you once again for flying Delta.

The ping from the 747's intercom and the captain's voice woke Natalie from a deep sleep. This was the first time she had flown first class overseas with the sleeping pods. She was now officially spoiled. As if the private G6 plane ride to Lexington with Xander hadn't already done the trick. It frustrated her that most thoughts throughout the day eventually led her back to *him*. Especially when it was her first thought of the day, and in Paris airspace, no less.

She sat up in her pod and looked around the aircraft's cabin. The overhead lights were still dark, but a glow of morning light filtered in through the cracks in the shades of various passengers' windows. A jolt of excitement shot through her as she pondered what her stay here would be like. Not only was this her first time in Paris, but it had been a lifelong dream to shoot a movie here. And not just any movie—she really felt like this project was going to be special. She loved the script, and she had really connected with her character. Besides, even if it is make-believe, who doesn't want to find love in Paris? She smiled and cracked her window shade to get a glimpse of the city. The plane jostled a bit before she had the chance to get a good look, and that old familiar fear crept in. She looked down at her hands, and they were once again grasping at the armrests as if she were clinging to a rock while dangling over a three-hundred-foot cliff. Then, of course, she thought of Xander. Xander's mother, really. She remembered his mother's trick to relieving flight anxiety, and she let her mind settle on seeing the massive plane land perfectly on the runway below.

Ten minutes later, the 747 did exactly that.

Natalie's driver pulled the car up to Hotel Le Bristol Paris on the corner of rue du Faubourg Saint-Honoré. This normally would mean nothing to Natalie, except her assistant Jamie had told her the hotel sat in the heart of the fashion, design, and art district. Which were some great sell words for Natalie, but Jamie went on to say that this hotel was where they had filmed one of Natalie's favorite movies, *Midnight in Paris.* As if that wasn't enough, the production company had set her up in the Grace Kelly Suite.

The Grace Kelly Suite!

As she stepped out of the car, she took a long, deep, satisfactory breath full of warmth and floral scents from all the nearby flowers. She was filled with excitement at the sight of her home for the next eight weeks.

The bellhop led Natalie into the grand entrance of the lobby, but she hardly got a chance to take it in as he rushed her through in order to avoid a gaggle of paparazzi. Although she had been dealing with this side of the movie business for years, it never ceased to amaze her that they always knew where she was, no matter how far from Hollywood the next movie shoot took her. Good thing she had touched up her makeup in the airport bathroom and changed into a cute Chanel top. They walked straight past the paparazzi with only a smile and a wave from Natalie. To a soundtrack of clicks and clacks from the cameras, the bellhop guided her onto an elevator made of glass-and-wrought-iron and straight to the top floor of the hotel.

Natalie followed the bellman off the elevator and down the hall of the eighteenth-century-designed hotel. They reached room 188, and as the door opened, the first thing she saw was straight through to an open balcony revealing the Eiffel Tower in the distance. She let out a squeal and rushed straight for the balcony. Two long rectangular flowerpots were fastened to the top of the wrought iron railing, and she leaned out over the bar and laughed aloud with joy as she took in the romance of the city. As soon as she shut the door, she turned and skipped around the suite, her feet barely touching the ground. The sudden urge to explore struck her, and after a quick change she headed out to the city.

Natalie took a sip of her vanilla latte. Open markets with troughs of fruits and vegetables, bakeries, storefronts full of art and jewelry all surrounded her and the café. And so far, with the clever instructions from the concierge to slip out the back,

179

she had managed to avoid the all-seeing eye of the paparazzi. Nevertheless, amidst all of the beauty that engulfed her senses, she did have this very strange feeling in the back of her mind that someone was watching her. Was it leftovers from what happened Saturday night at Xander's?

He would be such a great person to share all of this with.

She physically shook her head to try to eradicate thoughts of him from her mind. She took a moment to search her surroundings with a keen eye. What was she even looking for? Someone blatantly staring at her with a menacing scowl? She laughed at herself as she took another sip of her latte.

Laugh all you want, Natalie. You know someone is watching you.

All of a sudden she didn't feel like finishing her drink. She had let her own worrying mind get the best of her. Maybe a nap would do her some good. She paid her bill and started back toward the hotel. A man with a camera noticed her from a block away, and with a heavy French accent he shouted her name. Four other members of the paparazzi rushed in from around the corner, and they began to follow her, shouting her name and snapping picture after picture after picture.

She made it back up to her room, and as soon as she shut the door behind her, she felt comfort rush back to her. She walked through the open French doors into her bedroom and wondered if they still called them French doors in France. Wouldn't they just be doors? She laughed and noticed a tray of chocolate truffles next to her bed, which was covered in white linen. She immediately took the tray of chocolates and dumped them into the nearest wastebasket. She was to be on set in just two short days. Calories were officially off the table for now. She went over to the small patio, and with her phone she snapped a picture of the city as it sprawled out in front of her, wrapping around the Eiffel Tower in the distance. She uploaded the photo for her millions of Instagram followers with the caption, One Lucky Girl #Paris #Amazing. Then a text message came in from her costar and native Parisian, Jean Gerrard. She had worked with Jean before, and in her mother's words, he was a hunk. They did have a lot of chemistry on the set of their last movie, and when she signed on to do the film, Annie asked her if there would be any offscreen hanky-panky. Natalie just laughed at her friend's use of such an old-school term, but later when she had time to think, she wasn't completely closed off to the thought. However, as she opened the text, a vision of Xander's handsome smile worked its way into her mind. She rolled her eyes and went on to the text from Jean.

Hello Natalie. I noticed on the tele that you have arrived in Paris. I am busy tomorrow with a previous commitment, but if you are free Sunday we could brunch then. I would love to show you around the city and maybe buy you dinner that evening?

Natalie texted her reply.

Hey Jean! That's right, just landed today. Paparazzi here isn't much different than in the States, I see. I would love to meet up with you Sunday for brunch! Thank you for the invite!

To which Jean responded, *Perfect. I will come by your hotel at 10 Sunday if that is okay? There is plenty to see right there in your neighborhood and I will make a reservation for that evening at a beautiful little bistro around the corner from there.*

Natalie quickly replied, *Sounds great, Jean! See you then! :)*

After sending her reply, Natalie clicked off her phone and twirled around before landing on the bed. The soft fluff of the comforter enveloped her as she stared up at the ceiling. The light pouring in through the open patio doors began to take on an orange hue as the day began turning to night. A pang of hunger knocked at her stomach, and she rolled over and grabbed the menu from the nightstand. Natalie just loved hotels. Gourmet food brought to your door on a whim and enjoyed in bed while watching a twenty-five-dollar movie on the TV.

Don't mind if I do.

Despite her impulsive trashing of the truffles a moment ago and her plan to swear off calories, she ordered the cheeseburger and fries. Extra cheese, please.

"I'll swear off calories for real tomorrow," Natalie said aloud to herself, as if somehow actually saying it out loud would help it become a reality.

For Old Times' Sake

Sweat hung on the brow of Kyle's face, and as he bounced in front of Xander with his MMA glove–covered hands held defensively out in front of him, it rolled down into his eye. Kyle wiped at his eye, and without hesitation Xander cracked him in the side of his stomach, just under his lower left rib with a stinging right hook.

"Come on, Kyle. You can't lose focus, even for a second," Xander said, disappointed, huffing and puffing.

"I was just getting the sweat out of my eye!"

Xander stopped bouncing. "This isn't going to work," he said as he started to walk away.

"Come on, X. I'm sorry, I know I gotta stay focused. It's just been a long week. It's been a lot."

"I know it has, but you don't think after traveling ten hours by plane, then more than an hour by boat before we pull up to a terrorist's compound full of gun-crazy terrorist pricks that it isn't going to be a lot? I'm just trying to give you what you need."

"I know, X, but I didn't go through SEAL training. I've never done this shit before."

"Which is all the more reason to push you." Xander stood in front of him, covered in sweat with his arms stretched at his sides, palms in the air.

"I get it."

"Do you?"

"I do, I do. Come on, let's do this," Kyle said, starting to bounce again and put his hands back out in front of his face.

"All right, let's go."

Xander stepped back toward him, but instead of putting up his hands he bull-rushed him and wrapped his arms around Kyle's upper thighs for a double-leg takedown. Kyle's training kicked in, and he kicked his feet out behind him, sprawling out to keep Xander from putting him on his back. As he kicked his feet out, he simultaneously pushed his hips downward, landing himself on top of Xander's back.

"Good!" Xander shouted from underneath Kyle.

Kyle pushed down on Xander's back with both hands and spun on top of him to take his back. Xander curled up into a ball on his knees as Kyle tried desperately to sink his "hooks" into Xander by fitting his feet down to the insides of Xander's legs. This would help him control Xander's body and keep him from escaping.

"Nice! Now stretch me out!" Xander barked.

Kyle wrapped his arms under Xander's armpits and pushed forward and outward. At the same time as he forced Xander's legs backward he pushed his own legs back. This put Xander flat on his stomach and vulnerable to a myriad of submissions and strikes as Kyle rode his back.

"That's it! Now finish me!" Xander shouted, excited.

Kyle slid his right hand under Xander's chin and kept going until his arm wrapped around his neck. Kyle grabbed his right hand with his left in a gable grip, as Xander called it, then pulled back as hard as he could. As he did so, he squeezed his right arm like a clamp, bent Xander's head forward and pushed down into him with his hips. After a second of Kyle squeezing with all he had, Xander tapped on his arm and Kyle let loose of the rear naked choke hold. Kyle stood up, and Xander turned over on his back. His face was red and he was short of breath.

"That was really good. Even a trained fighter would have had trouble getting out of that. The way you put all the steps together seamlessly . . . that's how it's done." Xander reached out his arm, and Kyle grabbed his hand, helping him up. "I'm proud of you. You've learned a lot in a really short amount of time."

"Thanks, brother. Felt good."

"Now, let me show you how to take a pistol from a man's hand." Xander smiled.

"Let's do it!" Kyle had a newfound sense of enthusiasm, and Xander's confidence that he could handle himself was getting stronger.

Thank God.

They were leaving for Syria in a matter of hours, and even though Xander would make sure Kyle stayed out on the boat while he did all the fighting, he had to make sure Kyle could defend himself in a pinch. This was war; anything could happen.

"Where's Sam? Shouldn't she be getting some work in?" Kyle asked.

"Yeah, and she will. She is handing off our one remaining

Middle Eastern friend to the feds and then she'll be back."

"One? How the hell will she explain where he came from?"

"Don't know, and I don't ask. That's not my side of the business. She has a lot of contacts that trust her implicitly, so it really isn't that difficult for her."

"Did you ever get anything out of him?"

"No, neither one would talk. Sam killed the big man to try to scare information out of the other one. Didn't work. She decided she would rather see the one left alive suffer in jail for the rest of his life than give him the easy way out. Plus, on the off chance someone would be dumb enough to bail him out of jail, it would lead us right to who is responsible."

"That's smart." Kyle's tone changed. "Does it ever amaze you how easily we talk about killing? I mean, in your wildest dreams, in fifth grade talking about Jordan and Jerry Rice, could you ever have imagined this would be your life?"

"Of course not, but I also would never have imagined my parents getting mowed down right in front of me."

"No, I know, I didn't mean to—"

"It's okay. You know you don't have to be dragged into this life by me, right? You can stop anytime."

"No, I know. What else would I be doing, though? Running a Denny's? At least with you I'm making a difference in the world. I just want you to find some peace, you know?"

"I know. I do too. I really believe that taking out Khatib and avenging what I lost will do it. Whether or not I will continue to target these bastards after this is over, I don't really know. And right now, I don't really care. We have no room for error. We cannot lose focus here."

"No doubt about that. With what Sam told us, it sounds like this is the toughest thing you've ever done."

"There is no question."

"Do you ever get scared? Because I know I will be shitting bricks."

"You know, I really don't. I feel something different. In the SEALs they train the scared out of you. Instead of being scared when most people would be, we learn focus. It's like a subconscious channeling of the fear emotion that we should feel into an extreme focus," Xander explained.

"That is so damn cool. And scary. All of you are like loaded weapons."

"Well, let me show you this gun trick. You never know when some moron will be dumb enough to point one at you at too close a range. After that, let's get some pad work in. We gotta sharpen your boxing skills."

"Why?" Kyle said, teasing. "I can already take you."

Xander smiled and flicked a boxing mitt at Kyle's groin, tagging him perfectly.

Kyle let out a yelp as just the slightest little knock sent his testicles into his throat. "You asshole!" He lunged forward to try to take Xander down, but Xander sprawled and shucked Kyle to the floor.

"I said you've learned a lot; I didn't say you were ready for me." He stood over Kyle, taunting him, who was now flipping him the bird.

"Fuck you. I hope Megan stalks you until you're miserable."

"You're an idiot," Xander replied. "Let's take a break, I'm starving."

"Sounds good."

The two of them toweled off and took the wraps off their hands. They were on their way upstairs from the basement gym, and Melanie was on her way down.

"There you are. Xander, an Agent Thompson is at the door? He's CIA. Is everything okay? Should I say you aren't home?"

"Sean is here? Now?"

"If Sean is a good-looking government agent, then yes, he is here." Melanie smiled.

"You have the hormones of a teenage boy," Xander told her.

Kyle chimed in. "Yeah, Melanie, you need to get some. You know I'm always willing to lend a helping hand."

"Would you two just hump and get it over with?" Xander laughed. "Just don't catch feelings. I have enough to deal with. I don't need that kind of drama."

Melanie smacked Kyle on the ass. "Pretty firm. I'll consider it." She laughed. "Xander, I'll take Agent Thompson to your office. Kyle and I will give you some privacy as we shit talk over lunch."

"Sounds good. Make enough for Sean, if you don't mind. We'll see you in the kitchen in just a bit."

As Agent Sean Thompson waited for Xander in his office, he looked around at the many artifacts that adorned the walls and shelves. In particular, he noticed a nice shiny new trophy on Xander's desk. It was the Kentucky Derby trophy. It stood about two feet tall and was made of solid gold. Atop the cup-like trophy sat a jockey on a horse. The handles on the sides were horseshoes. Sean noticed the only thing engraved on the front was another horseshoe.

"You know, from 1925 to 1998 that horseshoe was always engraved upside down," Xander said as he walked into the office.

"Hey, X-man!" Sean turned and gave Xander a hug. "So, why'd they change it?"

"Well, it has always been a horseman superstition that if you turn a horseshoe upside down, all the luck will fall out. I guess it just took them seventy-four years to get the nerve to correct the original."

"It's a helluva trophy. Is it real?"

"Actually, it is the only trophy in major American sports that is all real gold."

"Shewweee! That thing must be worth a ton!" Sean shouted.

"Not real sure, but I've heard a couple people say $100k. Anyway, what in God's name are you doing here in Lexington?" Xander changed the subject. He didn't like talking about money. His entire life he had been made to feel bad by all who knew him because his dad had money. Xander had been avoiding and downplaying the subject ever since. He sat down behind his desk, and Sean took a seat on the other side.

"Well, first of all, this visit was long overdue. I can't believe I haven't been here in over six months. Plus, I wanted to see the big Derby winner!" Sean answered, skirting the real reason.

"Okay, well, I agree it is overdue, and we can definitely go visit Ransom, but don't bullshit me. Why the hell are you really here, Sean?" Xander asked, very matter-of-fact.

Sean's face took on a much more serious look.

"Buddy, I'm here to talk you outta whatever suicidal, Middle Eastern, dumb-shit plan you're getting ready to screw up."

"Getting ready to screw up? Since when have you known

me to screw up a mission, Sean? I seem to remember covering your ass on more than a few occasions," Xander pointed out.

"Now hold on, X. Don't take it personal. I didn't mean to imply . . . It's just, Marv is up my ass cause I told him I mentioned Khatib to you and we don't want to see you go and get yourself killed, that's all."

"Look, Sean, with all due respect, you have no idea how capable my team and I are."

"I ain't sayin' you're not, X. Just let Marv's team handle it. They've been—"

"They've been what? Watching him? How long do you watch someone murder and take advantage of innocent people, Sean?"

"I get it, but he's got orders."

"Exactly, and I don't. That is the entire point of what I do, why I work for myself. I don't have to wait until Khatib murders someone else's parents. I can do something about it. And I'm going to, whether you and Marv, or Uncle Sam his damn self, like it or not."

Xander was heated. The vein in his neck bulged and his face turned a crimson shade of red. He had reached the breaking point of everyone questioning him on this target and this mission.

"Okay, okay, X. I get it. I get it. You know I do. I just love ya, man, and I want to see you get what you want. I just don't want it to cost you everything. Hell, at least take me with you."

"You?" Xander took a deep breath; the vein and the redness subsided as he let his mouth curl into a hook of a smile. He appreciated his friend trying to help. "Buddy, you in combat now would be like a declawed house cat in the jungle."

Sean paused. A wan smile grew across his face.

"Shit, you're probably right. Five years ago I would have taken real offense to that. But I can get some training in while we figure out if this is the guy or not in the next couple of weeks."

"Next couple of weeks? Sean, we leave at seven o'clock tomorrow morning."

"Tomorrow morning? Xander, we don't know if this guy is even—"

"Sean, we've been over this. We leave at seven, not a second later. Since you're here, you are more than welcome to come along. I can always use another good SEAL. But don't be mistaken; if you go, it has to be because you want to see this scumbag get what he deserves, not because of me."

"Xander." Sean paused. "X . . . I can't let you go alone. It's suicide."

"I'm not going alone. And like I said, if you go, this isn't about me. It's about Khatib," Xander reiterated.

"One for old times' sake, huh?" Sean took a long pause as he traced his eyes around Xander's things displayed around the office. "Hell with it. I'm in. That bastard deserves the wrath of God more than about any other of these terrorist freaks I've come across in a long time. No tellin' how many people we'd save by killin' him." Sean stood up and reached out his hand. Xander took it with force.

"It's settled then. But this stays between us. I'm serious, Sean, between us."

"I'm 'bout sick uh you actin' like you can't trust me. Just wait till I save your ass in Syria, then we'll see who ya trust. Now let's eat. I'm starving. By the way, introduce me again to that pretty little thing that answered your door if she ain't spoken for. Hell, even if she is." Sean smiled.

191

Xander came out from behind his desk, put his arm around Sean, and walked him out of the office. "Let's just worry about lunch for now, big guy."

Someone Doesn't Know as Much as They Think They Know

Xander shut the door of the G6 as Kyle, Sam, and Sean buckled themselves into their seats.

"Six fifty-seven, three minutes to spare, X. You gotta like that." Kyle smiled.

"My watch says seven, so it's definitely time to go. We've got no time for falling behind. Every second will count. If everything goes perfectly, after ten hours in the air and the seven-hour time change, we will be landing right at midnight."

"Where's Amy?" Kyle asked.

"You're gonna have to get your own beer on this trip. I didn't feel like overseas espionage was really gonna be one of Amy's strong suits."

"Shit, wasn't even thinking." He laughed at himself.

Sam chimed in to say, "You're an idiot. And he seems to be

dumbing you down as well, Xander."

"You two, already? Really?" Xander rolled his eyes.

"X-man, looks like we got ourselves a nice little family here. Family of killers, but a family all the same, I reckon." Sean laughed.

Xander agreed and notified the pilot that it was time to leave. It was illegal to fly this plane with only one pilot, but Bob was the only man Xander could trust. That is why Xander had paid for Sam to be certified on the G6 just in case it ever came into question. The engines immediately fired up and Xander took his seat. In just ten short hours they would be landing at a mostly abandoned airstrip in northern Lebanon. Then getting on a boat and riding through the darkness to almost-certain—well, riding into a messed-up situation. Xander was far more worried about Kyle in this endeavor than anything. Kyle was a lot of things, but a killer? Why had he dragged Kyle into all of this anyway? There was just no reason for it, other than the selfish reason of not being lonely. Lonely. Probably the most frightening word in the English language for Xander. He was good at doing his own thing, but the thought of being alone scared him. It was about the only thing that did. It was undoubtedly a by-product of what happened to his parents. It made his relationships with women all the more strange, however. Instead of doing what most would do if they feared being alone—marrying someone safe—Xander did the opposite. Somewhere, subconsciously, he supposed the fear of being left alone was far worse than just being alone. Hence, all the one-night stands. If he never had anyone he really cared about, he never really had anyone to lose.

As the jet rocketed down the runway and the wheels lifted from the ground, he wondered if Natalie could be the girl to change all of that for him. This was the very reason he couldn't be with her, because he knew it would pull his focus from what was important. Even more so now that Xander was responsible for other people's lives. No one stood a chance of surviving if he wasn't at the very top of his game.

Time to focus.

"Did you see this?" Kyle handed Xander his iPad from the seat across from him.

"What is it?"

"The TMZ app, scroll down a little."

Xander swiped his index finger along the surface of the iPad. His heart jumped when he saw a familiar face. So much for time to focus; it was an article about Natalie. The headline read, "America's Sweetheart Still Charming in Paris."

Below the headline was a picture of Natalie strolling down the streets of Paris with the Hotel Le Bristol in the background. Xander immediately handed the iPad back to Kyle.

"Don't you want to read it?"

"No, thanks."

Kyle could tell it was painful for Xander to see her and not be able to reach out to her. He let it go. The jet pulled up into the sky, the massive engines roaring as Bob steered it toward Lebanon.

Xander pulled out his own iPad and began to study intently all the details that Sam and her sources had thus far gathered about the mission. However, before he could completely focus, he pulled out his iPhone and scrolled to the contact Sam had forwarded to him on the car ride over just moments ago.

Xander had a phone call to make.

195

Sarah Gilbright ended the call with Allison Freedman and set her phone down on the console of the rented Toyota Camry. She let a long sigh exit her lungs as she watched Xander's G6 fly off into the glow of the morning sun. Something was going on. Something big. She just didn't know what. There was no flight plan scheduled for Xander's G6 this morning. He may as well have been flying to the moon for all she knew. When she saw Agent Thompson get on the plane with Xander, a massive pit formed in her stomach. Allison, Thompson's secretary, confirmed that he would be out of the office for a couple of days, but she had no idea why. Sean had called it "personal reasons."

Sarah's phone buzzed in her lap. She couldn't believe who was calling her.

"Agent Gilbright," she answered.

"Hello, Sarah. How are you enjoying Lexington?"

"I-I'm sorry? Who is this?"

She knew exactly who it was. His handsome face had filled the locked screen on her iPhone when he called.

"Let's skip the part where you pretend not to know who I am, and the part where you try to tell me you aren't sitting across the street from the airport in that black Toyota Camry. It may be early, Ms. Gilbright, but I don't miss a pretty face like yours when it's around. Did you enjoy my launch party in San Diego last weekend?"

"How did you—"

"Samantha Harrison. You can't get anything by her. Believe me, I've tried."

"But she wasn't even at the King's Ransom launch party." Sarah was trying to regain her composure, but Xander had zapped it.

"No, but she has full access to my phone, to make sure no one is tapping it. Kyle took a picture of me and Natalie Rockwell, and a beautiful blonde just happened to be in the background. A beauty like that is hard to forget, especially out of all the ugly sons of bitches who are your peers at the CIA. Sam recognized you immediately."

"Shit."

Sarah had no other words. This wasn't how she thought this would go. Now, here she was, on the phone with *him*, and she is floundering. An absolute mess.

"Listen, I know you are just doing your job, Sarah. But I need you to send Director Manning a very clear message. Can you do that?"

"Xander, just give me a minute to explain—"

"I really don't have a minute. As you clearly saw, I'm quite busy. Tell Director Manning to back off and to stop sending people to follow me. I made it very clear to him that I have *zero* interest in working with the CIA, the FBI, or any other acronym associated with the United States government."

Sarah knew she had to speak quickly, so she got right to it.

"Director Manning knows you are killing people."

That ought to get his attention.

"Sarah, I appreciate that, I really do, but if I had anything to worry about from Director Manning knowing about my dealings, he would have made it known six months ago when he stumbled upon my handiwork in Texas."

Sarah was losing him. She needed to get his attention, gain his confidence.

"Xander, we think we know who killed your parents."

Xander didn't hesitate. "Once again, Sarah, you are a step behind. Hang around Lexington for a bit; the Bourbon Trail is a

197

blast, but if you're more of a wine girl, head over to Jean Farris. Order the Tempest Reserve, you'll love it. Better yet, wait till I get back and I'll take you there myself. We can share a Brown Betty milk shake: King's Ransom bourbon, Godiva chocolate liqueur, and vanilla ice cream. It's outstanding."

The blip that was Xander's jet finally disappeared from the sky altogether in front of her. Even though Sarah knew Xander was politely yet ever so condescendingly telling her to "f" off, she couldn't help but wonder how amazing that little trip to the winery with him might be.

"Just call me when you land, handsome. I'll be right here." She played back at him.

"Great, now, if you don't mind, I've got some important things to take care of."

"Xander, don't go in there alone. Come back and let the CIA help you with this."

"Good-bye, gorgeous."

Sarah's phone beeped, indicating that she had dropped the call. She immediately scrolled to Director Manning's number.

The phone rang only once.

"Sarah, did you talk to him about what we know?"

"He's two steps ahead of us, sir. He knows we've been watching him and apparently he already knows the intel we gathered about his parents' possible killer."

"That's impossible. No one on his team has access to those files."

"Tell that to Xander. His G6 just took off for Russia just a couple of minutes ago."

"SHIT!" Manning screamed through the phone. Then silence.

Sarah knew Manning would be pissed. This was his one

shot at bringing Xander into the fold. She was just as surprised as Manning that Xander had somehow found out about Vitalii Dragov. It still wasn't clear that it was he who had murdered Xander's parents, but there was too much evidence not to take a closer look. Apparently Xander felt the same way. Or at least that's what she thought, because she had no idea that Xander's plane wasn't going to be traveling anywhere near Russia.

Sarah steeled herself for what Manning might scream next. Fortunately she found him to be very calm.

"Get a team together yesterday and get to Moscow. I need you there before the end of the day. We've got to stop Xander before he starts the next world war."

Sarah agreed and ended the call. She really couldn't believe Xander knew about Dragov. Samantha must really be as good as he says she is. Either way, she knew Xander was in trouble. Dragov *is* the Russian Mafia.

Sarah ran her fingers through her hair and turned on the radio. She needed a second to cool down. She wondered if, since Xander knew about Dragov, he now also knew his father had dealings with him, and she wondered how Xander was taking such unsavory news. Oil was just one of the many streams of revenue Dragov had dallied in to achieve the over eight billion dollars his outfit was reportedly worth. Billion, with a *b*. The only way she could help Xander now was to get to Moscow.

Hopefully, she wouldn't be too late.

It's Time to Get Serious

"Xander," Sam whispered as she tapped him on the shoulder, waking him, "we are an hour out from Lebanon. I just spoke with James and everything is set for us at the airfield. He is in an abandoned hangar where we will be able to park the jet, undetected, except by the controller on duty that we paid off."

Xander sat up and took a swig from his water bottle. "So, we are just supposed to trust that this Lebanese flight controller is just going to keep quiet that an American G6 jet flew into an abandoned airfield and paid to make sure no one else knew about it? He's gonna keep that a secret?"

"Half a million dollars says he will," Sam said with confidence.

"Wow, you surprise me. Risk assessment being your forté and all, I can't believe you would leave a hanging chad like this. I'm afraid you are putting far too much faith in your boy, James."

"Xander, for the last time, I'll ask you, have I *ever* let you down?"

"No, but I know you realize the gravity of this situation. If this unknown decides to leak info to the wrong people, we will be hunted down like dogs. And they won't stop at just me. You know that."

"I do, but what shall we do? Kill the flight controller? That doesn't seem like your style."

"No, you're right, it's not . . . Maybe James can put a tail on him for a few weeks, just to ease our minds?"

"That we can do," Sam assured him.

"Well, now that that is settled," Kyle said, breaking into the conversation, "I wanna know what we are going to do to celebrate after we rid the world of these sons of bitches?"

Xander smiled. "I'm glad you said that, K. Sam's so damn serious all the time." Xander looked at Sam and gave her a playful wink. "Speaking of rubbing off on me, it has been a while since I've played a game of poker."

Kyle perked up in his seat. "I think I like where this is going!"

"And I don't mean just any old game of poker, either. We are going to take a break from this shit after tonight and you and I are going to Vegas and finding the biggest no-limit private game in town."

"X, Vegas sounds amazing! But I can't afford high-roller," Kyle said, dejected.

"Seriously? You think I'm gonna drag you around the world, risking your life, and give you nothing in return?"

"You know I would do it for free."

"Well, hell," Sean said, chiming in, "I won't! I don't play poker but I sure have a mighty big appetite for fast cars!"

"Fast cars, huh?" Xander raised his eyebrow.

"You know I'm just playin', X-man. I'll take a box of Davidoff cigars and some of your whiskey and we can call it even."

"Cheap date, huh? I like it," Xander said.

Sam interrupted the fun. "I hate to be the bitch that you all already think me to be, but it's time to get serious."

"Aw, Sam, we would be happy to have you in Vegas," Xander assured her.

"We would?" Kyle seemed surprised.

"Yeah, we'll give her a hundred bucks for the penny slots and tickets to Donny and Marie." He laughed, full of sarcasm.

"Ha-ha." Sam fake-laughed. "I get it, I'm the boring one. I'll have you know I left a few fractured hearts in my younger years."

"How long ago was that?" Kyle asked. "Thirty years ago?"

"Again, you all are just too funny, aren't you? I'm only thirty-eight, you *ahs-hole*."

The guys laughed as Sam had a hard time swallowing their sense of humor. Though Xander laughed at her, he was sure she wasn't kidding about breaking hearts. She was a beautiful woman. She had just been hardened by the years of suffocating herself with the madness of this world. It had certainly changed her. It was a wonder it hadn't taken its toll on Xander. It probably would have, but Xander had too much of his family in him, all of them so fun loving and goofy. There was never much that would ever bring them down. From a very early age, Xander had always chosen to see the positive side of life. He had no use for negativity. Of course he knew bad things happened; it surrounded every move he made and drove the very things that made up a lot of his life. The bad things—the bad people. He often thought his positive outlook was the driving force behind why he dabbled in all the negativity. The only way you could ever spend your life dispelling the monsters of the world was to have the brazenly positive belief that one person can actually make a difference. And he knew he *had* made a difference, a big difference, regardless of motive.

Xander slid open the window shade and peered out into the blackness beyond the light flashing at the tip of the wing. He looked out beyond the back of the plane and saw a full moon blasting its light for all to see.

This was a problem.

The element of surprise would be everything tonight, and with a moon that bright it would be hard to sneak up on anyone.

I hope it clouds up when we land.

Xander closed the window shade, sat back in his chair, and closed his eyes. Like a star athlete preparing for the big game, Xander visualized how the entire mission would go, in great detail. He went over everything from how the wind would affect his bullets to how cold the water would be when he fell backward from the boat in his wet suit and scuba gear. There would be surprises along the way; this was without question. However, just as his philosophy was in life, so it was in combat: It's not what happens to you that defines you, it's how you react to it.

No one was better at reacting to surprises in the field than Xander. He knew it, Sean knew it from experience, and Sam had seen it many times herself. That is why they all said he was the best. That theory had never been tested more so than it would be tonight.

"All right, it's time to get in our wet suits," Sam said, breaking the silence. "All of your tactical gear, including your weapons, are waterproof, and they will work for you regardless of what situation you find yourself in tonight. Listen, this is very important, if ever there is a moment, even for a split second, that you are unsure, look to Xander. Do not deviate from our plotted plan at any point, no matter what, unless instructed by Xander and Xander alone. In the event that something happens to him, I will become point and lead us through the mission. Is that clear?" Sam made sure she got a definitive response from both Kyle and Sean.

"Boy, you sure picked a feisty one here, brother," Sean said to Xander. "I'm not sure she knows who I am."

"I assure you she does. It's you who doesn't understand who she is," Xander stated clearly. Sam felt a sense of pride. She knew Xander respected her and her skills, but it wasn't often she heard him announce it with that amount of sincerity.

Sean put his hands in the air as if to say, "Whatever you say, boss," and let Sam finish.

Sam went on as she handed them earpieces. "We will be in constant communication; these are also waterproof. However, do not talk over these unless it is an absolute emergency. Any distraction could result in the worst for any of us. Make sense?" Everyone nodded.

Sam continued to make sure everyone was on the same page. The nose of the jet pitched downward, and they began their descent into Lebanon and into the unknown. In the midnight hour, Xander's biggest concern remained for his greenhorn friend. Kyle's experience hadn't so much as included a fistfight, much less full-on combat. He knew Sean would be fine; he'd seen his fair share of the worst of the world. Though it had been a while, Xander knew Sean's training in the SEALs would inevitably kick in. Xander still couldn't fight the chill of nervousness that crept down his spine. He tried to shake it as he slid on his wet suit, but it wasn't going away. He wasn't used to the feeling of imminent pending doom weighing on him. And he didn't much care for the feeling, either.

Instead of opting to change in the bathroom, away from the glaring eyes of men, Sam slipped out of her clothes to her underwear to get into her wet suit. Xander wasn't sure why he hadn't noticed before, but Sam had a fantastic body. Very well-toned muscle, but ample curves in the right places so it could never be mistaken that she was anything but a woman.

Xander laughed to himself as he pulled the cord to zip the back of his suit.

Sean couldn't help himself. "Damn, woman, I ain't seen a body like that in a long time. Thirty-eight? The hell you say, you sure you ain't twenty-eight?"

Sam just laughed as Sean struggled to pull the wet suit over his little desk-job gut.

"Maybe I should have secured a larger size for your suit?"

"Ha-ha. Yuk it up. I see how it is. I offer you a compliment and you rag on me. See if I take a bullet for ya now," Sean replied.

Sam gave him a wink. The captain gave them the five-minute heads-up, and they began equipping themselves with the weapons they had carried on the plane in large black duffel bags. Xander strapped a knife to his right lower leg with a black Velcro sheath. He followed that with a utility belt that held two Glock 19 pistols, two explosive fragmentation grenades, then one smoke and one flash grenade around his waist. With having to put on scuba gear, there wasn't room for his trusty shoulder holster. Twenty-four bullets and a knife would have to do until he could pick up a dead man's rifle. Of course, he had the sniper rifle and a couple of submachine guns they would be leaving on the boat. Kyle was proficient enough now with the machine guns to protect himself on the boat. The silenced sniper rifle would come in handy taking out the visible guards before they swam their way in to shore from the boat. This might be the only time the brightness of the moon could help— picking out the guards in the scope. Everyone else finished strapping on their equipment, all the same setup as Xander. The captain discreetly lit up the seat belt sign.

It was time.

Hammer of Thor

They all took their seats and buckled in. The reality of the moment began to settle in for Kyle. What was he doing? How had he possibly agreed to this? He wasn't Xander. He didn't have the years of training and combat experience that he had. Panic began to swell inside of him. He knew Xander was good. I mean, he took out eleven gunmen at one time without a plan. Hell, he was half-asleep. He would take care of him. Kyle tried to keep his face solemn, but it sure felt like it had burning panic written all over it. He looked over at Xander. Not a care in the world showed on his face.

What the hell? Kyle thought. *Even Sean looks nervous. What the hell is Xander made of? How could he not be afraid?*

"Hey, you okay?" Xander had unbuckled and come over and kneeled beside him. Kyle jumped a little when Xander touched his arm.

"Jesus, you scared me. Not gonna lie, I'm a little on edge."

Xander put his hand on Kyle's shoulder. "Listen, that is

natural. If you don't want to do this, you know I understand. Just stay back with the plane till we get back."

"No, no I-I'll be fine. Just teach me how to control this . . . this panic. Tell me how to focus it."

Xander knew there was no way to *tell* Kyle how to control it. It was just something you had to learn through experience. However, he could see that Kyle was in the early stages of freaking-the-fuck-out, so he had to give him something.

"Here's what I do . . . Remember when you were a kid and you were walking from the on-deck circle to the batter's box?"

"Yeah, okay . . ."

"Remember how nervous and scared you were when the pitcher was throwing straight gas?"

"Okay," Kyle said, playing along.

"Close your eyes," Xander told him. "Feel yourself stepping one foot out of the batter's box and taking a long, deep breath. Then, feel yourself stepping back in with confidence, and when the pitcher throws that fastball right down the middle, you swing and knock it out of the park. Feel what that feels like to overcome that fear, that nervousness."

Kyle's eyes popped open. "Xander, do you not remember me in Little League? I was absolutely terrible at baseball."

Xander smiled and laughed. "I know, but don't you feel better?"

Kyle took a second, and actually he did. He felt a lot better. He shrugged his shoulders and nodded his head. Xander gave him one last pat on the back and got back to his seat.

"All right, as soon as the plane lands we're gonna huddle by the door," Xander said to prepare them. "As soon as the plane stops and we finish getting our gear together, we are immediately going to head for the beach, half a mile through a wooded area that separates it from the airfield. Our boat will be waiting there. It will be run up on the beach. We'll push it into the water and be on our way. That is step one, and that is all we will worry about between now and then. Sam, if James isn't ready, we will be leaving him."

"He'll be ready."

The captain had shut off the exterior lights of the plane miles ago, and he navigated the winged metal tube through the air solely on his instruments. The feeble lights of the airfield off in the distance were all he had to go on. It was a warm night and the air was calm. Xander checked out the window; the ocean steadily rose up toward them, closer and closer and closer, until a flash of land popped into view and the scratch of rubber on the broken pavement screamed up through the bottom of the plane. Xander nodded, and they all unbuckled their belts and made their way to the jet's door. The G6 taxied toward a small light at the end of the airfield parking lot just off the runway. The light was hanging down over an old and tattered rolling vinyl hangar door, about twice the size of Xander's jet. The hangar door began to roll slowly upward, and before the jet's nose made it into the cast of the light, the captain brought the plane to a stop in full dark.

"This is it," Xander told the three of them as he pulled canisters of dark green and black face paint from a bag. "If anyone is having second thoughts of any kind, it's not a problem unless you let us get out there and count on you. Now is the time to pull back if it's going to happen. We good?"

Everyone nodded and gave Xander a fist pound to solidify it. Xander motioned for Sam to step forward. When she did, he took her face in his hands, gave her a kiss on the forehead, and looked into her eyes. "Sam, I just want to thank you for all you do. You are the engine that runs this machine. If there is ever a moment when you are trapped, give me two whoops—*whoop whoop*—and I will come with the hammer of Thor. You are the eyes. I love you, Sam."

He began to paint her face by separating her face into halves. He drew a line in black from the left middle of her forehead, across her nose and down to the right middle of her chin diagonally. He filled in everything to the left of that line with the same black paint. Everything to the right of that line he painted army green. Like she had done it a hundred times, she closed her eyes and let him get the eyelids too. Her entire face was now a camouflaged green and black. Sam looked like the real badass bitch that she was.

"I love you, too, Xander. This will be a success," she replied with confidence. She snatched up the sniper rifle and hit the button dropping the staircase as the cabin door swung open. A warm and muggy waft of air filled the plane. Xander nodded for Sean. Sean walked over, and Xander, grinning, put his hands on his shoulders.

"Brother, here we are. This sure brings back memories, doesn't it?"

"It sure does, X-man." Sean grinned and slapped him on the shoulder. "Save the speech, buddy. It's time to go old school on these motherfuckers." Xander began to paint his face. Sean continued, "I got a lot a pent-up aggression from sittin' my ass behind that desk. I didn't realize how much. I haven't felt this alive in years. No matter what happens, thank you for this."

"No, thank you. There's no one I'd rather have beside me," Xander replied.

"As always, I'll save your dumb ass when you get yourself in trouble." Sean smiled.

"I know you will." Xander smiled back. Sean readied his equipment at the door beside Sam.

Kyle walked over to Xander. There was a clear look of fear in his eyes. Xander took him by the shoulders.

"You all right, my man?"

"I am scared to death, but I'm okay."

"You know there is no shame in staying behind. You can just make sure the plane—"

"I'm ready." Kyle steadied his confidence and looked sternly into Xander's eyes.

Pride swelled inside Xander for his friend's courage. He nodded to Kyle and began to paint his face. "All right. Now listen, at no point do you leave either my or Sam's flank as we make our way to the boat. Once we get the boat to our anchor point in the water outside of the compound, you will stay there with the sniper rifle, with James, as we swim in and extract Khatib."

Xander shot a look at Sam to squelch any words she might have about keeping Khatib alive. She was about to speak but held her tongue as she knew it was no use.

"I will flash a light to the two of you, three times from shore, when we are ready for you to bring the boat in and get us. That is it. At no time, no matter what, do you leave the boat, or James. Got it?"

Kyle looked into Xander's eyes, his face now covered in war paint. He looked a lot like a badass now himself. "Got it."

Xander turned the paint on himself as Kyle made sure he had everything in place.

"Okay, that's it. Sam, lead us to the boat. Everyone move

with stealth, but move with purpose. Even you, fatty." Xander winked at Sean. Sean flipped him off, and as he smiled, his teeth glowed against the dark face paint. Xander walked over to the captain in the cockpit.

"Bob, I can't thank you enough for this."

"Of course, Mr.—Xander."

"Listen, if we aren't back here by 5:35, you fire this bird up and get the hell back to Kentucky. You hear me?"

"Xander, I can't leave—"

"Bob, I'm not asking, that is an order. We will be coming in hot, so fire these engines up at 5:30. You are heading down that runway at 5:35 whether we are on board or not. We have an alternate route if we don't make it back here in time. You are putting all of us in danger if you stay. Is that clear?" Xander asked, very matter-of-fact.

There of course was no alternate route.

"Yes, sir," Bob said confidently, "crystal."

Xander nodded, gave him a pat on the shoulder, and turned back to the cabin. He motioned to his team, and everyone followed Sam down the plane's eight steps and out into the night. The jet engine gave a whine as Bob pulled it forward and toward the open hangar about a football field in front of him. The four of them were encompassed by the darkness. It was all they could do to see the couple of feet in front of them to make sure they were all together. The bright moon that Xander had noticed from the plane earlier was now camouflaged by a patch of clouds that somberly hovered over them. In a light jog they followed closely behind Sam, unsure when even the broken pavement below them would end. They noticed in the darkness, about two hundred feet in front of them, a glow from a flashlight.

212

"It's James," Sam whisper-shouted back to them.

Sean was behind Sam, then Kyle, then Xander. Xander looked back over his shoulder and saw his jet come to a stop inside the hangar. A hint of worry for Bob hit his stomach, but Bob was ex-military so he knew he could handle himself if anything were to go wrong. Xander looked forward and almost tripped over Kyle as they came to a stop to meet up with James.

"Xander," Sam announced. "This is James—"

"Why are we stopping? Let's move!" Xander ignored her introduction. Sam didn't say another word; instead, she turned toward the trees in front of her. James lagged back to jog beside Xander.

"Listen," James started, "I know you—"

"Unless this is about this mission, save it," Xander interrupted him. "I appreciate all your help. Let's stay focused."

"No, of course," James said as they jogged. They had reached the grass and were now just steps away from the tree line. Just enough light from the moon peeked through the clouds now, and Xander could make out some pines swaying to the right in the breeze that had kicked up. The hum of that wind and their footsteps were the only sounds in the night. "I just want you to know it's an honor, sir. Sam has told me all about your service."

Xander gave no response, and they all continued to jog forward as they entered the woods. Fallen branches snapped beneath their feet, and the wind whispered through the trees above them as they moved together methodically in a straight line. Or what seemed to be a straight line. Xander imagined Kyle's mind was playing tricks on him already by this point. Darkness is a scary thing, regardless of the fact that you are tromping through foreign soil on your way to war. The first few

213

times Xander went on a mission like this, he could hardly feel his feet as they moved, the fear was so intense. It's a lonely feeling being in a situation where you know there will be no cavalry coming to save you if something goes wrong. It's especially lonely when the closest experience you had to this was playing paintball in Ben Carter's backyard. This was certainly no whimsical backyard game, and Kyle's gun was most certainly not filled with paintballs. This was, however, very similar to a Black Ops mission. The powers that be gave you a mission to carry out, and once you left, it was as if you never existed. If trouble found you, there was no backup. And if, God forbid, you were captured, well, that was that. The government just pressed a button and you were a ghost. All records erased.

In front of them, the denseness of the trees seemed to be lessening, and the moonlight looked as if it marked an opening. At the front of the line, Xander made out Sam's shadow. She stopped abruptly and threw her fist in the air. Everyone but Kyle knew this meant stop, so he stumbled to the ground as he tripped over Sean's feet. He landed on a bed of tree limbs, and the snap of the branches under his weight popped and echoed into the still of the night. The beach lay ahead of them, as did the reason Sam stopped so abruptly.

Two men with submachine guns were inspecting the speedboat that awaited them. They turned their attention and their automatic weapons toward the sound they heard coming from the thick tree-covered darkness in front of them. Xander held Kyle on the ground so no other sound could be made. The others lowered themselves to a crouching position and awaited Xander's order. Xander looked up at Sam, got her attention, and motioned to his left shoulder. With that, she slid the sniper rifle from her shoulder and took it in her hands. Xander picked up a hand-size rock that sat beside Kyle's left leg. Sam, knowing what was coming next, turned back toward the men and found them in the scope of the silenced rifle. She took a deep breath and waited. Xander chucked the rock about twenty-five yards to their left. Upon landing, it made a large crash through some pine branches, and the two men whipped their heads, and guns, toward the sound of the rock. Two squeezes later and bullets rocketed the fifty yards to the side of their heads and ended the threat with two bloody smacks. Sam threw the rifle back over her shoulder and motioned the team forward as the two dead men dropped in a heap to the sand. Xander gave Kyle a hand, pulling him to his feet, and they followed Sam to the edge of the tree line.

"S-sorry," Kyle whispered.

Xander ignored the apology as they came to a halt when they reached the sand. The clouds had moved on, and the light of the moon glowed across a long stretch of beach surrounded by trees. They could hear the soothing sounds of waves crashing as Sam once again took a knee and pulled her rifle. She peered through the scope, looking for signs of movement. She noticed a military-style jeep at the edge of the eastern tree line. It looked empty. The two men must have been called to check out the mysterious boat on the beach. This meant someone else could very well be watching. They were many, many miles from Khatib's compound, so his being alerted to any of this was not likely. They were, however, getting ready to step right across the border into Syria as soon as they set foot on that beach.

"Looks clear," Sam whispered. "However, we must hurry. Someone will be along shortly if they aren't already here.

Straight to the boat now, then straight into the water. I'll cover."

Xander motioned everyone forward, and as Sam held position, the four men took to the beach toward the modified speedboat. The steady breeze and the waves beating against the sand were the only sounds. Countless stars dotted the dark sky, and the men tromped their way through the thick sand to the boat. Xander circled the all-black speedboat, ensuring they were alone by its side. As he crossed the back, he noticed the modified engine and supposed it would be more than enough to give them the speed they needed to get to the compound and back in good time.

"Whoop whoop!" Sam called from the trees. Just as two shots rang out from the direction of the abandoned jeep, Xander whirled around the side of the boat and yanked Kyle down to the sand by his collar.

"This is it. Stay behind the boat and make sure you know where your bullets are headed." Xander told Kyle in a rush as they sprang back to their feet. Several more shots rang out of the darkness. Sean fired back from the left side of the boat, but it was like shooting into a cave. They were sitting ducks out in the moonlight.

"Keep laying down cover fire!" Xander yelled to Sean, Kyle, and James as he bolted back across the open beach toward Sam in the trees.

Hammer of Thor.

Xander's feet sank into the sand with each forceful stride he took. Bullets were screaming by him now, and one came so close he could actually feel its buzz as it screamed past his head. The buzz of the bullets raised the hair on the back of his neck as he continued to lumber through the thick and unyielding beach. The guys were firing into the darkness that

216

surrounded the jeep, and finally Xander dove into the cover of the pines. He looked back over his shoulder and saw Kyle was cowered down behind the back of the boat waiting for the gunfire to stop. There was no time to feel for his friend. The gunfire continued, and Xander worked his way through the trees toward Sam. He knew the two of them would be able to flank the gunman and end this standoff.

"That's far enough." The sound of a man's voice with a thick Middle Eastern accent cut through the gunfire, sending a shiver down Xander's spine. He dove down behind a tree, and as he rolled to one knee, he could faintly make out two figures standing in the shadows. He didn't have to see to understand that someone was holding a gun to Sam's head. The whock whock of gunfire continued behind them.

"Step out slowly with your hands in the air, or the woman dies," the shadowed man threatened. As dire as this situation seemed, it wasn't the first time the two of them had been in this spot. And the experience of the last time it happened had prepared them for this one. Xander stepped out from behind the tree, slowly, hands high in the air.

"Whooop!" shot out of Sam's mouth as she dropped to her ass onto the ground. Before the gunman could react, Xander pulled his pistol from his hip like he was in an old Western showdown and put two bullets somewhere around the torso area of the only figure left standing. After a moment, he was standing no more. Xander went to Sam and pulled her up from the dirt.

"You okay?"

"Never better. I told you that would bloody work."

"Indeed you did, Sammy. Let's take out the rest of these assholes. We're falling behind schedule."

217

Life's a Beach

Xander and Sam worked their way around the back side of the jeep. The two gunmen still were not visible, but the small spark the bullets they were shooting made as they left their machine guns indicated their position just on the other side of the vehicle. Sam crouched as she moved around the back of the jeep, and Xander scampered toward the front. As he peeked over the hood, he spotted two men firing across the beach toward his team. As he raised his gun, two more shots entered the fray and their guns ceased firing. When Xander looked up again, the moonlight showed Sam in a combat stance with her pistol extended, and the two men lay dead in front of her.

"You're going to have to be much quicker than that, Mr. King, if you wish to keep up."

Sam was in her element. As much as she loved finding and setting up assassination missions for Xander, she was, like he was, a field agent at heart.

Xander whistled to the guys and ordered them to hold their

fire. The two of them secured the perimeter around the jeep and made sure there would be no more surprises. They made their way across the beach toward the boat, and about halfway there Xander caught wind of a scent that made his stomach drop. He stopped dead in his tracks, about twenty yards from the boat.

"What is it?" Sam asked. Xander didn't answer right away. Then the smell hit her as well. "Bollocks, is that—is that gasoline?"

"Shit! X-man, we got a problem."

Sean's voice traveled from behind the boat with the continuous sounds of the ocean. Xander knew immediately what problem he was speaking of. One of the stray bullets from the two gunmen had punctured the gas tank of the boat. They were lucky it didn't blow. He walked around to the back where Sean stood, dumbfounded, staring at the gasoline that was leaking steadily from the back of the speedboat.

"Ah, for God's sake! What the bloody hell are we to do now?" James sounded off, seemingly mesmerized by the draining out of the gasoline. Xander wasn't as enamored, and he quickly pulled himself up inside the boat to begin searching for something to plug the hole.

"Xander?" Kyle called out. Xander didn't answer as he continued to search the inside of the boat. "Hey, X!" He called out a little louder this time.

"Not now. We have to stop this leak or this mission is over."

"Are the bullets in our machine guns bigger than the bullets those guys were shooting?" Kyle asked despite Xander's plea.

Xander stood from his crouched position inside the boat, and the light of the moon revealed his confused and frustrated expression as he peered down at Kyle. "I told you, I have to . .

." Then he paused to consider. "You son of a bitch! And you thought you wouldn't be any help on this mission." A smile came across Xander's face.

"I don't get it," James said.

Xander hopped down out of the boat onto the sand below. "You don't? MacGyver here just saved this mission."

James looked perplexed. Xander gave Kyle a pat on the back as he whirled his machine gun around his shoulder and into his hands. Without saying a word, he ejected a bullet into the air and caught it in his hand. He walked over to the hole in the boat where the gunman's bullet had entered and shoved the tip of his bullet as far into it as he could. He once again took the machine gun into his hands, and using the butt of it like a hammer he gently tapped the back end of the bullet until it wedged itself inside the hole, sealing it, completely stopping the leaking gasoline. He turned back toward the group with a smile on his face and walked over to Kyle for their signature three sideways claps and fist bump.

"Ho-ly shit," rolled out of Sean's mouth. "You sexy sum bitch! Why didn't I think of that?"

"You really think that will hold?" James interjected.

"Do we really have a choice?" Xander answered.

"Of course we do. If we get out there and that thing leaks again, we are dead. All of us."

"James, you are absolutely right. You'd better stay here and wait for us to bring Khatib back."

"Xander, I—"

"Save it. We are leaving. It's up to you whether you stay or go."

"There is no way you can do this without my gun," James replied.

Xander looked around to the others. All of them, including Sam, nodded their commitment to moving on, with or without James and his gun. Xander walked over to James and stood inches from his face, saying nothing. James continued, "Your arrogance will get you killed, or worse, one of your friends killed."

Sean stepped over to them.

"It'll hold, and if it don't, oh well . . ." Sean took some sand in his hand and let it fall out through his fingers slowly as he smiled and added, "Life's a beach, then you die!"

"James, you seem to be the only one worried about it," Xander said, holding his position.

"No, I am just the only one with balls enough to stand up to your madness, apparently." James took a step back. Xander took a step forward.

Sam stepped in.

"That's enough! We don't have time for this! James, are you in or out? Either way, we are going to finish what we came here to do. The bullet will hold. If it doesn't, we will figure out something else. You of all people, James, should understand how important it is to rid the world of Khatib. Forget Xander's reasons, remember all the evil you have seen over the years as you have been watching him. Remember? Remember?"

James didn't answer; he just held Xander's gaze.

"We do need your gun, but we will do this without you if we must," Sam finished.

After another brief silence, James turned away from Xander and pulled a roll of duct tape out of his bag. He held the tape up to show them and made a sort of "I told you, you need me" face. As he applied the tape across the back of the bullet, Xander shouldered his gun.

221

"Okay . . . all right. Way to be a part of the solution instead of a part of the problem."

"Let's git this bad boy in the water!" Sean bellowed as he walked around to the nose of the boat and began to push. Everyone else pitched in.

Xander took position beside Sean and looked him in the eye, a small hook of a smile on his face.

"Life's a beach? Really?"

Sean laughed as he continued to push the boat toward the water.

For the first time, Xander let doubt creep in. James's negativity was already putting a strain on the team. But was he right? Would the bullet hold? Could they do this without his gun? Xander pushed the boat toward the gently crashing waves. He didn't like being unsure of things. Sam usually made certain the odds were entirely slanted in his favor. It had just been impossible to do that for this mission. She had warned him against that from the beginning. He also wasn't used to worrying about others and their survival. It added a monumental amount of stress to the situation, which wasn't good for any of them. Was he making a mistake? Was he leading them to their deaths? The water rushed up around his feet as they forced the boat to the water's edge. With one final straining push, the boat became easier to move, almost weightless as the water helped ease the friction from the sand. Sam pulled herself up first; then the rest of them followed one by one until they were all aboard and the boat began to float out to sea on its own. Kyle took a seat behind the wheel, cranked up the engine, and the craft roared into the night and out over the water. Kyle gave Xander a nod as he pushed the throttle forward and turned the boat north, in the direction of Khatib's compound.

James shouted over the roaring engine, "This is going to be way too loud! We will give ourselves away if we pull up in this thing!"

Sam nudged James over to the next seat and lifted up the cushion, revealing storage. She reached down inside and pulled up the scuba gear. James dropped his head as he shook it in dismay. Xander saw this from the back of the boat and a singe of fury burned through him.

He'd had enough.

"Shut down the engine!" Xander yelled to Kyle.

Kyle looked up, not understanding what he wanted. Not waiting to say it again, Xander sprang to his feet and pulled the throttle down to the off position, lurching the boat forward and sending James to the deck of the boat. Xander turned off the key and angrily furied toward James, a crazed look in his eye.

"Xander! Xander, no!" Sam shouted from the right side of the boat. It was too late. Xander reached down for James, pulled him to his feet by his vest, and then pushed forward, pinning him against the rail of the front of the boat like he was the weight of a small child. With his eyes wild and veins bulging in his neck, he put his nose to James's nose. It was dead quiet.

"If you say one more word, I am going to throw your ass off this boat!"

Even Sean jerked at the volume of Xander's shout. James wanted to protest, but he dared not. He may not have known Xander personally, but he had certainly heard enough stories to understand that this wasn't a man he wanted to mess with. No one moved a muscle. The lapping of water against the idle boat was the only sound in the night. The only light came from the interior rope lights that wrapped around the inside rail of the boat, giving off a soft yellow glow. Just enough so that James couldn't possibly mistake how serious Xander was. He had had enough of the negativity. He stood over James now, huffing with madness, hoping that James would have something to say.

He did not.

"Xander," Sam said softly, trying not to exacerbate the situation.

"X-man." Sean tapped on Xander's arm. "X-man, don't let this weasel strain your focus. We may not need his gun to finish this thing, but we do need a hundred and ten percent of you."

He tapped on Xander's arm again. Xander let go of James's vest, shoving him into the white pleather seat. James sat up and adjusted his vest, embarrassed.

"Let me tell you how this is going to go. You are going to sit your ass in that seat and not say another word. Not one word. When we get to the compound and we anchor down to scuba in, your ass is going to stay right here on this boat and—"

"Stay on the—" James started, but immediately stopped as Xander lunged forward. Sean stepped in and backhanded James across the mouth.

"You just don't know when to shut your damn mouth, do ya, boy?"

James looked as if he would jump at Sean but knew this was a war he couldn't win. Sean sat back down in his seat.

"Can we please get moving?" Sam said. "We are desperately close to having to call this off due to falling so far behind."

Xander wanted to finish James off, but knew she was right. He nodded to Kyle, who then fired the engine back up and pushed the throttle all the way to the max. The bullet patch in the gas tank seemed to be holding . . . for now.

The Time Xander Popped His Cherry

The hum of the boat's motor surrounded the four of them as they skipped along the mostly calm ocean water toward Khatib's compound. Kyle shut off the rope lighting along the boat's rail, and the only light for miles on end was the cast of the moon. Xander took a seat at the front of the boat, and the warm ocean air blew through his hair as he stared out into the darkness. The moonlight projected a mesmerizing shimmer across the water that helped him fall into a trance deep inside his own mind. He was visualizing now. Thinking through to the perfect end at the compound. He had already memorized the blueprint, and visions of moving methodically through the three-level mansion moved across his mind like a silent film. The danger of the moment sent a shiver through his body.

Xander only really worried about the people he brought with him and their safety. He wasn't afraid for himself, never had been. Well, except for his very first mission with the Navy SEALs. He recalled the moment in his barracks when his commanding officer had sent for him.

"King." Petty Officer Carlson had opened Xander's door. "Lieutenant Commander Anderson wants to see you in the mission room."

Xander remembered the goose pimples that covered his body when he heard the words *mission room*. You didn't get called into the mission room unless, well, you were going on a mission.

"Time to pop that cherry, X-man!" Sean had said behind him in the barracks, slapping him on the shoulder.

Sean had already popped his cherry. He had been frustrated that it was just a simple recon mission. Looking back, his frustration had probably just been a front. Xander thought maybe it was a way to seem macho about wanting blood when, in fact, Sean really didn't. Xander hoped he was walking into a simple recon for his first mission, but it couldn't have been further from it. He threw on his sand-colored V-neck T-shirt and started down the hallway of the USS Abraham Lincoln toward the mission room. His boots clacked against the floor and echoed through the empty hallway. In a way, he felt like a death-row inmate walking toward his demise in an awaiting electric chair. And he hadn't even been offered a last meal. Pizza. It would have been Post Corner Pizza. A small family-owned Greek restaurant on the beach in Clearwater, Florida. His parents used to take him and his sister there as kids.

Thoughts of pizza promptly took a hike the moment he walked through the door to the mission room. It was the first time he had seen it. It looked a lot like a mini classroom. There were three long horizontal tables with six chairs each, all facing a one-hundred-inch projection screen on the front wall. It was a lot like Mr. Epling's science class in middle school. Minus the rows of framed dead butterflies entombed and preserved on display all along the walls. Also missing of course was what Mr. Epling affectionately called the black forest, a special section of the classroom that was quartered off as a place where unruly kids were exiled from the population. Xander was very fond of it because he spent the last half of the semester there, alone. Xander had always been a jokester, but before his parents died, he wore it much more outwardly on his sleeve. He had served as the entertainment for his classmates, whether the moment during class called for it or not. Hence his time in the black forest.

The lieutenant stood at a podium just to the left of the big screen, and Xander took his seat along with six other SEAL veterans. He was the rookie on the mission. He knew this was going to come with some inevitable hazing, but it was comforting that he was with men who knew what they were doing. He also knew this meant his wish for a simple recon was going to go ungranted.

The lieutenant cleared his throat and adjusted his sand camo ball cap, his voice deep, his face solemn.

"Good evening, men. A reporter was abducted early this morning by a group of militants just outside of Baghdad. This information is yet to be leaked to the rest of the media, and she will be back in our company before it ever is."

A map flashed up on the big screen, and the lieutenant walked over to it to explain. "The seven of you will be dropped here, just outside of this compound. Our latest intel is that there could be as many as fourteen men inside this compound. You will move in and extract Miss Evelyn Waterston using any means necessary. They will be armed, and they will be happy to put a hole in your head. I suggest you take this action against them before they take it against you. There is no time for any further info. As we gather more it will be pushed to you on the chopper. Men, let's do what SEALs do. As always, there will be no congratulations or thank-yous from the American people, because this never happens. See you all back here with this pretty lady in a few hours." A picture of Evelyn Waterston flashed on the screen. A couple of wolf whistles sounded from the back of the room. She was gorgeous, but the only way Xander could picture her at the moment was teary eyed and hog-tied in the corner of some dark and scary room. The lieutenant terminated the meeting, and the men walked down the hall to the equipment room to suit up. They were leaving immediately.

"You ready for this, rich-boy rookie?" Ron Parsons asked with a punch to Xander's arm. "Don't you go freezing up on me when we get in that place. But don't worry, if you do I'll save your bitch ass," he said as he high-fived Ricky Johnson.

Ricky just laughed and scoffed. "I'll be saving that pretty li'l princess. Then I just might marry the bitch."

"Marry her?" Ron exclaimed.

"Okay, maybe I'll just start by stuffing her turkey. Gobble gobble, rich boy!" Ricky slapped Xander on the ass.

Using air quotes, Ron said to Xander, "You might be the 'best recruit' Lieutenant Anderson has ever seen, but this shit ain't the practice field. We'll see if he thinks so highly of you once he sees you in a *real* combat situation."

Ron laughed as he slipped on his tactical gear. Xander just ignored him. He had been dealing with these types of conversations for the last couple of months now. The rest of the SEALs weren't too happy that Xander had broken nearly every record in SEAL training history. As much as they needed the best of the best, none of them liked it that it wasn't them getting what they considered to be undue acclaim. You don't prove yourself as a SEAL until you hit the field. Xander knew this, so he just kept his mouth shut and continued gearing up.

Sam took a seat beside Xander at the front of the boat. When she touched his arm, breaking his deep daydream trance, Xander jumped.

"Sorry, I didn't mean to interrupt. I just wanted to let you know we are about ten minutes out now."

"Okay, thanks Sam, I'm ready," he replied, semi-shouting over the hum of the boat. Sam gave his arm a squeeze and went back to her seat. Xander went back to his memory.

The SH-60 Seahawk hovered over their drop point just outside of the militant compound. His first mission had begun. Xander remembered how his heart raced as he tried to tap into his training that helped him control his emotions. It wasn't working, yet. The Seahawk lowered to about thirty feet from the ground, and Ron dropped two massive ropes out of the opening on the side of the chopper. Xander walked over to the opening and looked out into the darkness. Ron motioned downward to Xander, who bent over and took the large rope into his hands. He steadied himself at the door's edge, half of his boot in and half hanging out in thin air. He took one last heart-pounding breath and pushed out as he dropped down and shimmied to the ground. He remembered the thump of his feet against the solid dirt road and the pure terror that ran through him as he looked up and watched Ron make his way down. He had never felt so lonely. Even when he got back to his house in Lexington after his parents' funeral, it still wasn't as lonely as seeing that Seahawk lift toward the sky and slip off in the distance. There the seven of them stood, smack-dab in the middle of enemy territory. It was pitch-black, and Xander followed at the back of the pack as they made their way through a back alley surrounded by chain-link fence. The sand-covered concrete below him was cracked and uneven, and on several occasions he came an inch from rolling his ankle. That would have been a real pill. As they made their way to what Xander could now make out as a three-story concrete building, he must have looked back over his shoulder a hundred times along the way. It was pointless, because he wouldn't have been able to see anything if something was there. He wasn't sure what he expected to see anyway. A militant Iraqi with a switchblade? Maybe one with a gun? A man with a flaming skull sitting atop his body?

Get your shit together, King.

They came to a stop just outside the building. Xander felt fear rising up through his bones, and he took two long, deep breaths to slow its persistent advances. As the fear relentlessly crept back up, with John Winters standing just in front of him awaiting instructions, John's head exploded and blood splattered all over Xander's face. Ron dove on top of Xander, and the rest of the men, six now, took cover behind an old abandoned military truck parked just to the left. Xander wanted to scream, but the wind had been taken from his lungs when Ron fell on top of him.

"Pull it together, rich boy," Ron whispered on top of him. "If you don't, you'll end up just like Winters."

Winters. He meant the now faceless Winters whose body lay in a headless heap of particle brains and spewing blood just feet from Xander. Ron stood up and pulled Xander to his feet behind the truck. A metallic acid filled Xander's jowls, and he was sure he was going to projectile vomit all over the crouched team of SEALs beside him.

"X! Pull it together, goddamn it!" Ricky whisper-shouted. "Pull your rifle and find that towel head! Shoot him between the eyes, and you and Derek meet back up with us. We are going in from the back, X!"

His head was spinning; Xander took a hard swallow, fighting back the acidic bile that continued to ooze up into his mouth. He took one more deep breath and thought of the man in the ski mask. The man who had put bullets inside his dad just a few short years ago. Suddenly, the metallic taste in Xander's mouth was gone and focus came like the correct answer to a test question. He spun his rifle from his shoulder into his hands, looked Ricky Johnson in the eye, and nodded. Ricky took Ron, Todd, and Jack with him and headed around to the back of the compound through a hole in the fence that Ron had just cut.

Derek pulled his gun. "Okay, rookie, time to see if that record-breaking shooting translates out here. Don't let me down."

Just as the words left Derek's mouth, another bullet shattered the front windshield of the old work truck and passed right by Derek's head. "Shit, X! Find him!"

For the first time in combat, Xander raised the scope of his M24 rifle to his eye. At first all he found was darkness. He continued to scan in the direction of the bullets when he noticed a spark fly from a balcony across the street as another bullet hit the exterior of the truck. Without hesitation, and as if he had done it a thousand times, Xander took a deep breath and pulled the trigger, sending a bullet straight though the scope of the gun that was firing on them, bursting through the back of the gunman's head. Through the scope Xander could faintly make out the silhouette of a body standing, then dropping out of sight.

"Holy shit, I guess it does translate! Nice shot, rookie!" Derek whisper-shouted from the ground with the pump of a fist.

Before Xander could process his first time taking a life, gunshots rang out from inside the compound. Derek jumped up, motioning for Xander to follow. Xander swung the rifle back over his shoulder and pulled his nine-millimeter pistol from its holster as he and Derek made their way toward the back entrance of the compound. They rounded the corner of a concrete wall and came upon a square-shaped cinder block house with the large wooden door. There was only silence now. Derek tested the door, and it was locked. Gunfire started again, and Derek kicked in the door immediately so the noise of the lock busting would be covered by the shots coming from inside. Lights came on and poured out the door onto the front stoop. Before Xander could turn the corner of the door to follow Derek inside, the unmistakable boom of a twelve-gauge shotgun rang out and Derek's body came flying back out the door like someone had yanked him by a rope. Xander felt his body move seemingly on its own; he changed levels by dropping and sliding on his knees, then fired inside the compound, dropping the Iraqi man holding the shotgun. It was like an out-of-body experience, moving without thought, running purely on reactive instinct. As the man with the shotgun landed in a thud to the floor, Xander rolled forward to his knees into what was the opening of the kitchen, capping two men with guns as they stood ready for his entrance. However, they hadn't been ready at all. And they paid for it with their lives.

The gunfire ceased again, but Xander heard footsteps crossing the floor above him. He moved through the kitchen and made his way to a hallway. It was clear that the rest of the team had gone upstairs. He moved past a couple more dead militants, one of them with a hole where one of his eyes used to be. With his pistol stretched in front of him, Xander found himself at the bottom of the stairway. He could hear more shots coming from upstairs, and his mind told him to go toward them to help. However, something in his gut was pulling him toward the closed door to his right.

You always have to follow orders, but when you are in the heat of battle, it's your gut you really have to pay attention to. He heard the voice of his trainer, Marx, in his head. He turned away from the stairs and reached for the brass knob on the white door. He gave it a jiggle, but it was locked. He had taken one step back toward the stairs, but a nagging feeling pulled at him from his stomach. He imagined himself kicking the door in and shooting two men on the stairs who were waiting to greet him. Xander turned back toward the door, put his boot to it, and sent the door flying off its hinges. Sure enough, it was as if he had seen into the future. He squeezed the trigger twice, dropping the two dark-bearded, towel-headed militants who were indeed waiting on the other side.

It was almost as if Xander had been born with some sort of sixth sense. And that sixth sense was also telling him that Evelyn wasn't far from him now. The stairway below him made a hard right about six steps down. Xander pulled a flash grenade from his belt line, pulled the pin, and banked it off the left wall, and it bounced down the unseen stairs into the room below. Xander repositioned his pistol out in front of him, walked down the six stairs, and just before he turned right to go down the last six into the basement, he heard a pop and a blinding light flashed through the room. He heard at least two groans come from men waiting for him below. Without stopping, he turned the corner and walked right down the last six steps, shooting two men who were covering their eyes on the left wall, then two more who were shading their eyes from the flash at the mouth of a hallway on his right. He continued walking through the damp and half-lit basement, stepping over the dead men and through the smoke of the flash as he entered the hallway. Twenty-five feet in front of him was another closed door, and he walked toward it. However, he made a mistake. He felt a burning sensation on his back and realized he had made the rookie mistake of not checking if the hallway extended to the other side of the room underneath the stairs. Upon this realization, Xander dropped to his back like a sack of potatoes, and without rolling over he shot his gun upside down and behind him, dropping the man with the machine gun before he could exploit Xander's mistake even further. As Xander paused to consider his error, he heard a scream come from behind the door at the end of the hallway. It was a woman.

Evelyn.

Xander popped up to his feet and moved forward toward the door. He could still hear the pop of gunfire coming from the levels above him. He remembered thinking that there must have been a lot more men there than intel expected. He readied himself to kick in the door, but before he could raise his leg, the doorknob turned and the door crept open in front of him.

Xander crouched into ready stance, pistol extended in front of him.

"Let the girl go and I'll let you live!" Xander shouted toward the room in front of him. His voice echoed off the concrete walls that surrounded him, making him jump inside himself. He waited for a response, but all he could hear was a woman's muffled moans, sounding as if she was struggling to get free.

"Last chance, I'm coming in!"

A man with a thick, almost inaudible Middle Eastern accent spoke up. "You come in, she die, you die!"

Xander could tell by the sound of the man that he was frightened, and that he would shoot the first thing that moved through that door, on reflex alone. He also discerned that the man was most likely standing on the left side of the room, along the inside of the same wall the door was on.

"Ten seconds!" Xander shouted. He then tiptoed quietly back into the basement and snatched up one of the bodies of the men he had shot moments ago. He hoisted him up on his shoulder and walked back toward the door.

"Five, four . . ." Xander kept walking. "Three, two . . ." As the number "one" came out of Xander's mouth, he threw the body as far into the room as he could. Just as he had suspected, the man fired immediately into the body. Before the gunman could turn his gun back toward Xander as he walked into the room, Xander popped two bullets in the man's chest, and the man's gun and the girl dropped from his hands to the ground. His body held its stance for a moment, then, like a freshly chopped tree, he toppled, face forward, to the concrete below, with a bone-rattling thump.

Timmberrr, Xander thought.

The woman squealed through her duct-taped mouth and squirmed away from the now dead man who had been holding her at gunpoint. Xander holstered his gun and pulled a knife from a slot in his combat boots.

"It's okay, miss, United States Navy," he told her as he cut her hands free. She ripped the duct tape from her face and threw her arms around him, sobbing. He lifted her to her feet as she continued to cling to him.

"Thank you," she cried. "Thank you so much!"

"Don't thank me yet. Not till I get you out of here. Are you okay to walk?"

"Y-yes, I'm good."

"All right, stay behind me. I'm gonna get you out of here." She hugged him again, and he pressed the com button on his headset. "Blackbird, this is SEAL team seven, do you copy?" Xander waited. Evelyn tried to calm herself, but the tears kept coming. The relief on her face made Xander feel like a hero. What had just happened seemed like such a blur, almost as if there was someone with a controller moving him along in a video game or something. It was so surreal. "Blackbird, I repeat, this is SEAL team seven. Do you read me?" Another pause followed.

"We read you, SEAL team seven, go ahead," a muffled voice finally said back to him through his earpiece.

Xander felt a rush of relief flow through him. "Blackbird, the chicken is in the coop, we await extraction instructions."

The chicken is in the coop? What the hell is "the chicken is in the coop"?

Xander knew the boys were going to have a field day with that one. But so what if they did. He'd gotten the girl.

Call me rich-boy rookie now, he remembered thinking.

"SEAL team seven, be at the extraction point in three minutes," the voice instructed.

"Three minutes, over," Xander replied.

Ron had come on line after that. "Rookie? That you?"

"This is King. I have the girl in the basement. Is it clear to come up?"

"Nice work, King. We'll come to you. Derek?"

That was the first time he had been called anything other than rookie or rich boy. He had won their respect.

"No. Derek is KIA."

"Shit. Hold your position. We're on our way."

Xander turned to Evelyn. "You're gonna be all right, Ms.—"

"Evelyn, and I can't thank you enough soldier—"

"Alexa—Xander, Xander King. Just doing my job, miss."

"Well, thank you, Xander. You saved my life."

Those words had never left Xander. *You saved my life.* He had never before imagined anyone saying that to him, and he certainly hadn't imagined the weight it would carry.

If only I could have saved them.

The memory of his parents' murder flashed before his eyes as he looked at her.

"Well, I'll be damned!" Xander heard Ron's voice from the other room. Xander had taken Evelyn's hand and walked out through the hallway and into the main room in the basement. When they entered the room, the four remaining SEALs were coming down the stairs and Ron was looking around the room at the carnage Xander had left in his wake. "You did all this, rookie? By yourself?"

Xander nodded.

"Well, I'll be a monkey's uncle. If Anderson liked you before, he sure as shit's gonna love you after he hears about all this. You're like a goddamned Rambo or somethin'," Ron said, his mouth agape.

"He's my hero," Evelyn added. She wrapped her arms around him and laid her head against his shoulder.

She called him that several times—her hero—over the next week as she thanked him the best way a woman can thank a man.

Red lace lingerie and all.

Upon Sam's nod, Kyle brought down the engines, and that snapped Xander out of his trance. It was game time.

"I figure we are about half a mile from shore," Sam said.

Xander could hardly see her it was so black. They couldn't risk lights in the boat, just in case someone might be watching the water from the compound. There was a faint view of lights in the distance, but overall it was fairly dark on land as well. Sean pulled the diving gear from under one of the seat cushions, and he, Sam, and Xander fumbled around with the oxygen tanks and goggles. They secured their weapons and began to slip on their flippers.

"Where's my gear?" James asked from the opposite end of the boat. He was rummaging through the storage, but there wasn't any more scuba gear to be found. Sam had only appropriated enough for three, and originally it was for James, but that was before Sean had decided to come along.

239

"I'm sorry, James, there isn't any more," Sam answered.

"What? You said I was going in with you. Sean, is it? Give me your gear."

"Buddy, you're as nutty as squirrel shit if you think I'm gonna sit out here on this boat while my boy goes into enemy territory."

"I'll show you nutty, country boy!" James shouted as he lunged forward at Sean. Somehow in the darkness, Sean's fist found James's mouth, dropping him to the deck of the boat. The boat wobbled in the water as James's weight shook the entire vessel.

"That's enough!" Sam shouted. She realized shouting was a bad idea with the way sound carried over water, so she lowered her voice back down to a whisper. "That's enough. James, Sean has been on many missions with Xander; it makes more sense this way. You man the com system and keep Kyle safe. We will radio when we need you two to come with the boat. Be ready with your gun then. We will certainly need some cover on the way out."

James didn't protest. A cloud floated eastward, giving way once again to the light of the moon. Xander could now see James sitting up and wiping blood from his lip. Sean looked over at Xander and gave him a wink. Xander smirked briefly, and then went back to securing the final strap on his right flipper.

Sam continued. "Kyle, obviously, keep your headset on. When we are finished, or if we need backup, we will call for you. You won't have cover coming in, so you will just have to be quick. I know Xander will hate me saying this, but it must be said . . ."

"Nothing good ever follows a comment like that," Kyle remarked.

"No, it doesn't. You're right. But it can't be avoided. If you haven't heard from us—"

"All right, that's enough, Sam," Xander interrupted. "Kyle, we will see you in one hour."

"Xander, we must have a contingency plan. Kyle must know what to do in case we don't make it out alive," Sam insisted.

"She's right, I won't know what to do unless there's a plan," Kyle said. Xander stood up, giving his full attention to Kyle.

"How long have we been doing this?"

"I know, X, but this is different."

"Kyle, how long?"

"I don't know, four, maybe five years?"

"Okay, and how many times have I missed my mark?"

"N-not once, X. Never."

"That's right, never. I'll call for the boat in one hour. Be ready." Xander didn't flinch as he peered through the darkness into Kyle's eyes. What Xander understood that Sam didn't in that moment was that any amount of doubt, no matter how small, would eat away at Kyle the moment they all left the boat. That hour would seem like a day. If Xander let Sam explain what happens if they all die, the only thing Kyle would think about over every agonizing minute they were gone was death, and failure. Xander knew that logically Sam was right. There was a strong possibility that this wouldn't work, and Kyle wouldn't know what to do, but Xander knew Kyle would come like the cavalry and get himself killed for no reason if he was thinking the worst out on that boat. Xander had seen this firsthand on a number of missions he had been on with rookies. As cruel as it sounded not to have a backup plan, it was actually the best thing for him.

"Xander," Sam started again, "we cannot leave him—"

"Sam, we'll see him in one hour," Xander said to her with a glare. She had known him long enough to understand there was reason for him saying what he was saying to Kyle. She let it go. Xander sat back down, this time with his butt on the railing. He nodded to Sean and Sam, and they joined him in a seated position at the rail. They made some final adjustments to their equipment, secured their mouthpieces, and with a nod to Xander, Sam and Sean dropped backward into the deep darkness of the Mediterranean Sea.

Kyle walked over to Xander, who looked up at him from his seat on the boat's rail. "One hour, right?" he asked, a sound of pleading in his question.

"One hour," Xander answered with confidence as he secured his mouthpiece.

Kyle held out his fist, and Xander gave it a knock just before he fell backward into the water.

Khatib Is Ready: Too Ready

The compound buzzed like a beehive. Normally after midnight there wasn't nearly this much movement, or this many soldiers. It was as if they were preparing for battle. On the third and top floor of the compound, sitting at his desk, rolling a coin along the tops of his fingers, was Sanharib Khatib. It had come to his attention a day ago that he was being targeted by an American rebel. Khatib never even asked his source why a random American might be targeting him. You see, with a man like Khatib there could be a thousand reasons. None of them mattered. Word came that there would be three of them and that one of them just might be one of the most spectacular killers on the planet. This of course didn't frighten Khatib. He had seen far worse in war than any one man could bring down on him.

Still, he prepared. He doubled his security at the compound to what he felt was a ridiculous forty armed men. According to his source, this American should be arriving any moment. He told his men that an example would be made of this American and broadcast for all the Western world to see. He instructed his men to add ten extra security cameras, and they would edit the video after this man was killed to show the world what happens when you mess with ISIS. Khatib, even though his source told him the United States government was not involved, of course still assumed that they indeed were. He would send them a message as well, that if they wanted to shut him down, it would take a lot more than one measly American assassin. He laughed to himself as he thought of Jason Bourne from the American movies. He enjoyed those movies, and it amused him that the Americans believed it could be a reality. Khatib wasn't some soft villain living inside of a make-believe world. He believed himself to be a god. So far, no one had ever been able to prove the contrary to be true.

James walked from the front of the boat to where Kyle was sitting in the captain's chair. Blood still trickled down his lip from its meeting with Sean's fist. He sat down across from Kyle.

James reached out his hand. "I don't believe we were properly introduced. James."

"Kyle." He took James's hand. James gave what Kyle thought to be an overly firm shake.

"I'm not interrupting you, am I?" James asked.

"No, just sitting on pins and needles here really. Watching them drop down and disappear into that dark water is a scary sight."

"Scary indeed, mate. Listen, mind if we have a chat?"

Kyle sensed arrogance in James. He always thought British accents sounded arrogant, so maybe that was all it was. "I don't mind. Have at it, bud."

"Bud." James laughed. "You Americans love that term. Especially you country boys."

"Yeah, I guess it's a lot like you all with your 'blokes' and 'mates.'"

"I suppose you're right. So, bud, how long have you known Xander? Has he always been wound so tightly?"

"You'd be wound tightly, too, if you knew what he's been through," Kyle answered, a bit put off by James's sentiment.

"No disrespect, mate. Apologies."

"We've been friends for almost twenty years."

"Twenty years? Really? That is quite a long time. You must know everything there is to know about him."

"Pretty much. If he's been through it, I've been through it, and vice versa." Kyle sensed a really condescending and awkward tone from James.

"I bet. So, whatever would cause a man to embark on such a mission as tonight? Swimming straight into suicide really."

"Well, James, if I'm being straight with you, it's really none of your business."

"Oh, we're being straight, are we?" James said snarkily.

Kyle sensed a sharp change in James's tone. "What's that supposed to mean?"

"Well, as long as we are being straight, let's pass the time and play a little game. How 'bout it?"

"I'm not really in the mood for games. Why don't we just go back to ignoring each other, my man."

Kyle was on edge now. James stood up and walked toward the front of the boat. With his back turned to Kyle he looked up into the empty sky.

"Come on, old chap, let's play a game called Have You Ever. What do you say, mate?" James turned back to Kyle with both arms palms up and out to his sides. He wore an almost maniacal grin on his weaselly little face. Kyle said nothing. "All right then, I'll go first. Kyle— bud—*have you ever* held a million pounds—dollars—in your hand?"

"No," Kyle answered, almost grunting.

"No, I figured not. I can tell you really don't like this game, and I am bored with you, so I'll just get straight to the point."

Kyle shifted in his seat as a pit formed in his stomach. Xander would have already sniffed out what was coming, but Kyle had not yet learned this part of the game.

"Your dear friend Xander, I'm afraid, he is, as we speak, swimming to his certain death. He, Sam, and that redneck you brought along last minute. I hated to have to do it to Sam; she is quite the piece of ass, I tell you."

Kyle stood up from his seat. "What the hell are you talking about?" The pit in his stomach had turned into the size of a bowling ball.

"Well, you see, the reason I asked you if you'd ever

held a million dollars is because I have. This morning actually, when Sanharib Khatib handed me a briefcase full of money to give him the specifics of what exactly was going down tonight."

"You motherfucker!" Kyle lunged at James, but before he could close the distance between them, James pulled a gun and let out a ghoulish laugh that echoed over the surrounding water. Kyle froze in his tracks as he stared down the barrel of James's pistol.

"Aw, was it something I said, mate?" James grinned a devilish grin as he took a step forward and put the gun just inches from Kyle's forehead.

"You son of a bitch, how could you do this? You've been hunting Khatib for years!" Kyle's voice cracked with fear.

"I'm certain I just told you how. But again, since you've never actually held a million dollars in your hands, you couldn't possibly understand what it feels like. What *freedom* feels like." James preached with delight.

Kyle felt adrenaline begin to course through his veins and somehow the fear was gone.

"You dumb prick, I flew here on a G650 luxury jet. You think I don't know what money feels like? A million dollars wouldn't even pay for the upholstery on that bird, you stupid little shit!"

"Whoa, my friend, I suggest you relax. I'm not afraid to use this gun that I have to your head."

"Then use it. It won't save you," Kyle said forcefully.

"Save me?" James laughed hysterically. "Save me from what? Your dead boyfriend?"

"Sam clearly didn't give you enough information

about who in the hell you were dealing with." Now a maniacal smile came to Kyle's face. James didn't like it. He pressed the gun to Kyle's forehead and his voice raised as he spoke.

"Who *I* am dealing with? Ha! I suppose your pea brain believes that your hero is going to swim up to that compound, take out the forty some-odd armed guards who are ready and waiting patiently for him to pop up out of the water, then call you on that com and tell you everything is roses? Ha!" James laughed a crazy laugh.

Even in the face of madness, Kyle's pulse slowed. His heart rate fell and a calm came over him. His mind flashed to Xander's gym and to the moment Xander had taught him to disarm a man holding a gun too close to him. James, however, was no ordinary gunman. He saw Kyle's movement in his eyes before it even happened and squeezed the trigger of his nine-millimeter pistol. But it was Xander's words teaching Kyle—*move your head first, no matter what*—that saved Kyle's life. Just as the gun clicked and the bullet fired, Kyle jerked his head to the left and the blast caused a terrible ringing inside his ears. The bullet skipped out over the back of the boat into the ocean. He wasn't successful in disarming James, but he had bought himself a moment.

His training kicked in.

Kyle wrapped his right arm around James's still outstretched gun-holding arm and drove his knee as hard as he could into his groin. The gun popped off again, and as the bullet ricocheted off the rail of the boat, James doubled over and let out a grunt of pain. Kyle, still holding James's arm, lowered his leg back to the floor, and as soon as his toe tapped the ground, he drove his knee right back up and smashed it against the bridge of James's nose. The force of impact was so hard that Kyle lost his grip and James crashed violently onto his back. Before James could move it, Kyle front-kicked the gun out of James's hand, and it skipped along the floor of the boat and came to a stop about ten feet from them. Kyle immediately recoiled and went to stomp on James. As he drove the heel of his boot down toward James's head, James rolled and Kyle struck only the weatherproof carpet that covered the fiberglass floor of the boat. Kyle felt James scissor his legs around his own, and before he could adjust, James sent him flying face forward to the floor. The boat rocked back and forth in the water. The fall knocked the wind out of Kyle's lungs as his chest took the brunt of the impact. James rose to his feet, staggering, desperately trying to stop the blood that was now gushing from his shattered nose.

"You prick! You broke my nose!" James continued to grasp at his face, but the blood kept coming. "You broke my nose!"

Kyle gasped for breath as his forehead rested against the floor. He knew James was on his feet now, but until he caught his breath, there was nothing he could do. Kyle looked up and the moonlight sparkled off the shiny nickel plating of James's fallen gun. As he attempted another deep breath, he threw his arm forward, and his fingers landed about a foot short of the handle. Another deep breath and a push of the knees moved his outstretched hand halfway there.

One more. Just one more stretch.

BRADLEY WRIGHT

He gathered his right knee to the level of his hip and dug the toe of his boot into the carpet. His hamstring fired, and just as his body began to lunge forward, the collar of his wet suit jerked violently against his neck and he hung there, suspended, like a rabid dog at the end of his chain. James had caught him, and the next thing Kyle felt was a thump on the back of his head, courtesy of James's elbow. Purple circles inside sparks of pain burst in front of his eyes. He felt his body go limp, but he immediately snapped back into consciousness when James rolled him over onto his back. Kyle caught James's body in between his legs and instinctively wrapped them around him like an anaconda. As soon as Kyle's vision cleared, James's elbow was rocketing down toward his head. In one movement, Kyle moved his head, avoiding the elbow while trapping that same arm with his right hand. Simultaneously, he brought both legs up around James's shoulders. Kyle's right leg bent to the left, across the back of James's neck, while he wrapped his left leg around the foot of his right leg, placing that foot under the bend of his knee. This created a hinge that allowed him to squeeze his legs around James's neck. Xander and Kyle had drilled this move—the triangle choke—at least a hundred times. To set up the finish, and to really shut off the blood from being able to reach James's brain, he made sure James's right arm—the arm that threw the elbow—was pulled tightly across his body. This was crucial in causing the neck to be properly squeezed and thus to prevent the carotid artery from doing its job of delivering oxygenated blood to James's brain.

James struggled and thrashed wildly as Kyle

250

seamlessly applied the proper steps of the choke. It was almost tight enough now. Kyle just needed to set his hips to the side and—James brought his knees to Kyle's ass and struggled his way to his feet. In an act of pure adrenaline-fueled rage he somehow began to lift Kyle off of the ground. Unfortunately for James, Xander had done this to Kyle many times in the gym. Kyle held his body in position as James raised him up over his head. Kyle knew that if he could stay alert after this oncoming slam, if he could just keep his consciousness and hold the choke by maintaining the squeeze around James's neck, he could—

James arched his back, and with a rebel yell and with all his power he jerked his body forward and sent Kyle's body to the floor of the boat, cracking the fiberglass on impact. It wasn't enough. Kyle had managed to keep his head from taking the force of the slam, and in a twist of irony, it actually further secured Kyle's position, doubling the effectiveness of the choke. Kyle wrapped his hands around the back of James's head and pulled it straight down as he thrust his hips upward. This was the final step.

"Ten . . . nine . . . eight . . ." Kyle counted out loud. James still thrashed inside of Kyle's grip, but his movements started to subside.

"Seven . . . six . . . five . . ." Kyle felt James's body go limp. This was where he would let go if he were in a street fight, because the lack of blood flow just brought James to unconsciousness. This was the point where James would wake up no worse for wear, if he let go right now.

"Four . . . three . . . two . . . one." He squeezed even harder. This was the point where someone should be dead. Kyle's arms and legs burned fiercely as he continued to

251

squeeze, James's lifeless body held suspended in his grip. Finally, after a few more seconds, Kyle let go of the hold and James's body tumbled lifelessly between his legs, facedown on the floor of the boat. Kyle took a moment to catch his breath and let the burning pain subside from his exhausted muscles. The air was thick, but quiet. He got up to his feet and gathered James's vest in his hands. James's head fell back and thumped against the floor, blood still dripping from his broken nose. Kyle lifted him up, dragged him to the side of the boat, and tossed his body over the rail into the dark water below.

Kyle Hamilton Saves the Day... For Now

Even with the light shining from the band just above his goggles, Xander could hardly see more than five feet in front of him. All he could do was check the compass on his watch and trust that heading due east, as Sam instructed, would land them where they needed to be. They had been swimming for a bit now, and Xander knew from his incessant internal counting that they should be just yards from the beach and mere meters to the north end of the compound. He slowed his pace and finally came to a stop as Sean and Sam, who were swimming on his heels, gathered around him. They were deep enough so that their headlamps couldn't be seen from the surface. He motioned to them that he was going up to have a look. He shut off his light and started up toward the surface. The water surrounded him in pure dark now, so black it may as well have been oil. A burning fear crept up his spine. He wasn't afraid of what he might see when he surfaced. Xander feared no man. It was what else might be down there in the darkness of the water with him that really frightened him. He could fight a man; he could not, however, fight a monster with rows of knife-sharp teeth and an instinct only to kill. Much to his surprise, as he tried to steady his nerves, it was Natalie's face that came to mind. In the middle of the blackness of the ocean, as he slowly ascended, with only the sound of his oxygen tank and its bubbles, he thought of her. He didn't fight it, because it worked. Thoughts of giant man-eating sharks faded from his mind. As he fluttered his feet back and forth inside his flippers, he focused in on her beautiful smile and her almond-shaped eyes. He would go and surprise her in Paris, he thought. After all of this madness was over. He would take a break from the anger inside of him that would surely be quenched after he squeezed the life out of Sanharib Khatib. His hunger for revenge would finally be satisfied, and he could live his life for other reasons. Perhaps for her?

Suddenly, in the blackness above, a sliver of light became visible. Just above him, at the end of his ascension, he could see the light of the moon. His head reached the surface and after a brief moment of disorientation, shock gripped his body as he saw it wasn't the light of the moon at all.

It was the spotlight from a boat.

A boat floated just a couple of feet from him, and before he could dip back under the surface, he heard a man scream, and after a loud pop he felt a searing pain in his shoulder. When he looked down, he had a small harpoon lodged through the outside of his deltoid muscle, entangled in his wet suit. He couldn't help the scream of pain that leaped out of him, and before he could react, he was being pulled toward the boat. He knew immediately that there was a rat in the group, and he knew immediately that it was James. Horror rolled like thunder through his body as he thought of his best friend alone on the boat with that traitor. Adrenaline shot through his veins as he grabbed the rope attached to the harpoon and gave it a violent tug. Whoever was on the other end of the rope was dragged forward, and Xander heard a splash as slack came to the rope, and he was no longer being pulled.

He looked up but could only make out the silhouette of a small fishing boat through the intense beam of the spotlight shining in his eyes. He saw another shadow move forward on the boat when the man who had fired the harpoon hit the water. The next thing he heard was the unmistakable bang of an M24. A darting splash rose from the water beside his head as the bullet zinged by. He heard a couple more screams from the boat, and he began to swim sideways. He reached for his pistol as two more shots rang out. He felt nothing, so he pulled his pistol up out of the water and fired at the shadow. A wave rolled through at that same moment and pushed his arms upward, forcing his aim off-line. Another shot rang out from the boat, and this time a ping from the harpoon in his arm sounded off and luckily ricocheted the bullet into the water. Xander immediately fired another shot at the shadow. This time there was no wave to throw off his aim, and the shadow on the boat dropped out of sight. That brought about some scrambling on the boat. Out of the corner of his eye he saw the man he had pulled into the water swimming at him, but Xander put a bullet in his head before he could reach him. Just as he was about to dive back under the water and regroup with Sam and Sean, they popped up beside him.

Meanwhile a second boat, a speedboat carrying three armed

men, raced toward them. Xander knew they were in real trouble. He knew Sam and Sean wouldn't be able to process what was happening in time to dive back down, so he began raising his pistol as a last-ditch effort to keep the worst from happening. Before he could lift his gun back out of the water, shots were being fired from the speedboat, and out of his periphery he saw another man on the first boat raise a gun. Bullets darted through the water around them, and Sam let out a scream through her mouthpiece. The boat was right in front of them now, and if Sam had had time to work up some percentages on the probable survival rate, well, it wouldn't have been good.

Wham! A thunderous crash filled the air when out of nowhere another boat smashed into the side of the speedboat carrying the three gunmen. The boat hit so hard, and in just the right spot, that it cut right through the middle, impaling one of the gunmen and sending the other two into the water. Xander moved his pistol immediately to the remaining gunman and shot him straight through the throat. He looked back to the boat that had sped in last minute, but no one was in it now. The impact must have thrown the driver into the water.

"Kyle!" Xander screamed. It was Kyle who had saved them. "Kyle! Ha-ha! Yeah!" Xander whooped.

Sean and Sam were up to speed now, and they began to swim toward their boat to find Kyle. Xander squelched his celebration as he put a bullet into each of the two men who had been thrown from the speedboat when Kyle slammed into it. The spotlight from the first little fishing boat that discovered Xander was now facing the boat Kyle was driving about fifty yards in front of them. It looked to Xander like it may have even run ashore. He could see movement on the beach now, just

256

outside the compound, only a couple hundred feet from where Kyle had in fact crashed the boat onto the beach. However, there was still no sign of Kyle, and a hint of worry fell on his chest. Xander holstered his gun and started swimming feverishly toward the beached boat. He could see three men running down the beach toward it.

Time was running out.

He kicked it into another gear and passed by Sam and Sean. Now, only twenty feet from the boat, he heard the men from the beach screaming; then shots rang out into the night. The three of them swam up and crawled behind the boat to use it for cover. The shots continued, and they removed their diving equipment and prepared for the standoff. However, before they had a chance to glance over the boat to locate the gunmen, they heard a burst of gunshots from inside the boat, and the shouting coming from the men on the beach stopped abruptly. For a moment, silence fell over the night. Sam looked over to Xander and shrugged her shoulders.

"You guys gonna help a brother out up here, or am I going to have to take everyone out myself?" a voice from just above them at the rail of the boat asked them.

Xander looked up.

"You sexy son of a bitch!" he yelled when he saw Kyle's shit-eating grin staring back at him. The three of them popped up, and Kyle jumped over the rail, rifle in hand, and they all hugged and cheered at the reunion.

"How the hell . . . ," Xander started. "James turned on you, didn't he?"

"How'd you know?" Kyle asked.

"What are you talking about?" Sam chimed in.

Xander gave her an "I told you so" look. "How the hell else

do you think they were so ready for us to pop up out of the water tonight, Sam?"

"Not James, he wouldn't—"

Kyle interrupted, "He would, Sam, and he did."

"How'd you get away from him?" Xander asked.

"He started acting funny, then pulled a gun on me. I was going to use the technique you showed me about disarming, but I only got to the first step before he shot at me."

"He shot at you?" Sam broke in, shocked.

"Yeah, Sam, he tried to kill me."

"But you moved your head first, didn't you?" Xander slapped Kyle on the back and smiled with pride.

"I sure as hell did! If I hadn't, I'd be a dead man. Dead. Instead, shit just came together for me and I kneed him in the balls, then shattered his nose with another knee."

"Yes! Fuck that sum bitch!" Sean yelled.

"That put him on his ass and . . . Xander—" Kyle stopped. Shock broke out over his face as he noticed Xander's shoulder. "Xander, you have a harpoon sticking out of your shoulder!"

Xander gave it a yank and pulled it out of his arm.

"It's fine; it was mostly just stuck in the suit."

"I swear to God, sometimes I think you aren't human," Kyle said, shaking his head in awe.

"I'm tellin' you, if he had a cape he'd be a superhero!" Sean announced.

Xander just gave the three of them a smile, still feeling the high of Kyle using what he had taught him to save himself against James.

"Capes are for pussies."

"Boys, I hate to interrupt, but there are more coming. We've got to regroup," Sam said.

A solemn look fell across all of their faces as they once again realized where they were and what lay ahead of them. Sam continued, "Khatib knows we're here, and we need to regroup and get a plan."

"No plan necessary, Sam," Xander said as he wiped his bloody hand on his wet suit. "I have it all worked out. Ready all your weapons and stay behind me. No one moves without my cue."

Sarah's Worried Heart

"No one moves without my cue."

Sarah Gilbright instructed her four-man team from her van parked close to a notorious hangout of Vitalii Dragov's. She already had the sinking suspicion that she wouldn't be giving any instructions to move. Xander's plane wasn't in Moscow, and according to reports from CIA allies, no such plane had landed anywhere in Russia, for that matter.

Sarah was nervous, for more than one reason. She couldn't understand what had gone wrong. Had Xander received the wrong intel on his father's possible killer? Or had the CIA? It wasn't likely that the CIA got it wrong, but the intel also wasn't conclusive. Just information that Xander's father had done some deals with Dragov. She knew that didn't necessarily mean he killed them, but she knew that information would be enough

for Xander to take a closer look. However, Xander wasn't here.
Where is he?

That brought the other reason for nerves: Xander's safety. Could he be somewhere, chasing the wrong information and getting himself into something he can't get out of? Sarah knew he could more than handle himself, but when it's the Wild West, anything can happen. She desperately wanted to be there when something did go down. Another concern was that if he did have the right intel, and found his parents' killer, there would be no bringing him into the CIA fold. Ever.

Snow had begun to fall around the van. Sarah worried that hanging around Dragov's lair for too long would bring unwanted attention. She would give it another—

Sarah's cell phone dinged with an incoming text message. Director Manning's name appeared on her screen. She knew he would want an update, and she sure as hell didn't want to give him this one. The one where the first time she made a move for the CIA, it was the wrong move. She didn't even want to open the text. She looked up from her phone and followed a slow-falling snowflake filled with a ray of morning sunshine, all the way to the ground.

"Where the hell are you, Xander?" she asked the empty van.

"Come again, Agent Gilbright?" one of her team members answered back through her headset, which she apparently had forgotten to mute.

Sarah sat staring at the snow, zoned out with visions of Xander in trouble somewhere out there in the world. Visions of him pinned down and taking heavy fire, all in the name of revenge. A terrible weight pressed on her chest, and a terrible worry filled her heart.

"Agent Gilbright?"

Sarah erased those visions, cleared her throat, and swallowed hard as she nervously tapped her fingers against the steering wheel, biting her lip and shaking her leg.

"Nothing."

A Moment's Hesitation Will Be a Lifetime of Regret

Xander peered around the corner of the boat toward the compound. Approximately one hundred yards in front of him, all of the lights on the three-story concrete structure were lit. It reminded him of a prison. Each level of the compound had a full wraparound concrete walkway, and it now resembled an anthill with countless men carrying guns taking position on various points of the railing. The part of a human being that would panic in a dire situation like this no longer existed inside of Xander. The sheer volume of Black Ops missions the navy had sent their best SEAL on had squeezed that out of him. The still thick and warm air of the summer night seemed to hold them in the water. Their biggest advantage, the element of surprise, was gone now. Xander knew that to regain this element he would have to split off from his friends. That thought left an empty feeling in his stomach for them, especially Kyle, but he couldn't be leaving him in better hands. Sam and Sean were as seasoned as any soldier could be.

"They'll only be expecting three of us," Xander announced.

"No way, X-man. We stay together," Sean said immediately.

"The heat will be on the three of you. Can you handle that?" Xander asked, looking at Sam.

"Of course. It's the only way to recover an element of surprise." Sam understood. "We will be fine. Kyle will stay in the middle of us. We will go in the back from the beach side, so you will have to go around to the front. It is as good as suicide." She looked at Xander with worried eyes.

"I'm not going in the front."

"Then where will you go, X?" Sean asked.

"It's most likely, since according to the blueprints there is no underground level, that he is on the top floor. So the three of you will make your way there."

"But you don't think everything is on those blueprints, do you?" Sam asked.

"Do you?"

"I don't know. But I do know it will be covered in soldiers willing to give their lives for Khatib."

Xander grabbed the bag from the boat and pulled out the last gun left, his SCAR Mk16 which he'd had fitted with a specially adapted silencer. "Good thing this puppy squirts out six hundred and fifty-four rounds per minute then." He grinned at Sam as he loaded and locked it.

Sam didn't return the grin. "Yes, but only a thirty-round clip."

Shouts echoed over the beach as the militant soldiers prepared to defend the devil's house. The rest of them readied their weapons as they crouched behind the boat. The waves crashed beside them and the water grew closer as the tide had begun to move in.

"The tide is gonna pull the boat out any minute now, so we need to make this quick," Xander announced.

"That boat isn't going to start, X. We'd best be thinking of plan B," Kyle said.

Xander knew Kyle was right, and that was especially bad news. Not only did it affect timing to get back to the plane, but it made it much easier to be followed and attacked by Khatib's soldiers. Even with GPS, it would be extremely difficult to make the kind of time on land in a truck that they could make in the water.

One problem at a time.

"Let me worry about that. We could have used their speedboat if you hadn't cracked it in half." Xander winked at Kyle.

Kyle only returned a stone face. The time for humor had passed. The enormity of the task in front of them had settled in, for all of them. "Okay, Sam, you take Sean and Kyle beachside, around back. They will be expecting this, so be ready. I'll wait here until I see you've drawn some attention, then I'll make my own way in. Listen carefully . . ."

Xander's face took on a seriousness that even Kyle had never seen before. "Do. Not. Hesitate. If your instinct tells you to move, then move. If it tells you to shoot, then shoot. A moment's hesitation will be a lifetime of regret. Sam, Sean, I don't need to tell you that you are ten times the soldiers any of Khatib's men will be. Use it. Kyle, believe me when I tell you, though you haven't been through it, you are better trained than any of these men. That, I promise you. Know that, when the doubt creeps in. Let your training take over; let your mind rest. Got it?"

Kyle nodded. Sam and Sean followed with nods of their own. Sam then nodded back to Sean and Kyle, and they followed her to the front of the boat. Xander pulled a grenade from his belt and pulled the pin.

"Bullets only hurt when they hit you," Xander told them as he chucked the grenade toward the front of the compound. Sand, smoke, and fire shot up into the night as the colossal blast of the grenade filled the air. The boom echoed through the silence, and as Khatib's militant monkeys turned their attention to it, Sam, Kyle, and Sean bolted across the beach into the thick brush that would cover their run to the compound. Xander watched them until they disappeared. Worry for them formed like a storm cloud inside his gut. Then a thought that shook him to his core.

What if Khatib isn't the one responsible for my parents' death?

Then, an even more horrifying thought.

So what if he is?

Xander adjusted the strap on his gun. The grip of sadness wrapped its hands around his throat, and he could hardly swallow. Because he couldn't let go of his rage, more of the people he loved might die. And to what end? Revenge?

Xander got to his feet and walked to the edge of the boat. It was too late to call them back now. How could he have been so selfish? How had this thought not sunk in until now? He felt a warm tear roll out of his left eye and down his cheek. Anger stirred inside of him. Not anger with the one he perceived to be his archenemy, but anger at himself for letting *it* win. Xander put his ass in the sand and took a deep breath. It was too late now. These feelings would do nothing to keep his friends safe. Another deep breath. For some strange reason the thought of that text popped into his head. The text from the night his house was invaded. The message from a still unknown source that had saved his life. *Someone is in your house.*

Tat. Tatat-tatat-tatat! Gunfire rang out from the back of the compound, snapping Xander out of his trance. A calm fell over him and all other thoughts left his mind. He sprinted from the cover of the speedboat to the same brush his friends had entered moments ago, but instead of turning right and staying inside of it, he continued through to the other side. He could see lights on at the front of the compound, but the militants' attention had turned to the beach, where Sam and company had begun their assault. There was only one other building close to the compound and it was across the street. It looked abandoned as there wasn't a single light or sign of life coming from it. Gunfire continued behind him, and a growing sense that the dark building might not be empty grew in him as he moved toward it along the brush line.

Sam's voice came to his ear from his comm system. "Xander."

"Go ahead."

"Xander, we are pinned down. There are more than we'd thought. We are taking heavy fire, we can't move forward. We're going to continue a distraction on this end. Use it to get where you need to go. But, Xander, you must hurry!"

Xander had never heard urgency like that in Sam's voice before. She was always cool and collected.

"I'm coming back to you," Xander replied.

"No. *No!* You coming this way will only hurt our chances. There is no penetrating them from this end. We are covered in the brush behind an old truck. They will be on us soon, but we're covered for now. Do *not* come this way."

"Get out of there, Sam. Go back to the boat and wait for me there. Do not let them get you. Pull back, do you hear me, Sam? Pull back!" Xander shouted into his headset.

"It's too late to pull back, Xander. The only way out of this is if we are the only ones left alive. We will never make it back to the plane if we run now. Goddamn it, Xander, just make it quick!"

Xander heard her grunt just before she released the comm button. Seconds later he heard a blast come from the beach, and when he looked past the compound, he saw a mist of smoke and sand rise up in front of the lights of the building. She'd thrown a grenade.

Toughest bitch on the planet.

He ran on through to the end of the brush, and in front of him was a canal. The water running through it didn't look very deep, but he figured he would certainly have to swim the twenty yards to the other side if he indeed listened to his instinct that the abandoned house wasn't abandoned at all. He was just about fifty yards from the compound, as well as from the commotion on the beach just beyond the brush. He surveyed the dark building until a faint red light caught his eye at the back of it. He pulled up his Mk16 and looked through the scope. Sure enough, there was a soldier there, peering around the corner at the commotion, a burning cigarette in his hand. Xander instinctively hurried down the ten-foot incline into the canal and began his swim across. The water was near freezing, but he continued forward. He knew in the basement of that dark building was Khatib.

He could feel it.

"*Xander!*" a cry rang out through the sounds of gunfire. Xander stopped midstroke and waded for a moment in the middle of the canal. The gunfire stopped and silence fell around him.

It couldn't have been. Sam would never blow her cover. Would she? Not unless—

"*Xander!*" This time it was unmistakable. It *was* Sam. The man he'd searched for in his mind and in reality for the last twelve years was only yards from his grasp. The release that Khatib's death would give Xander would be almost too great to measure. He could completely repurpose his life. He could become the man that his parents had always wanted him to be.

But—

Xander turned from the dark compound and swam to the edge of the canal back toward his friends. They needed him. It was bad or Sam would never have given away her position.

She wouldn't scream unless they'd taken her.

He scaled the ten-foot bank and ran back into the brush. He could hear a man shouting but couldn't make out the words. He dashed through the thick, waist-high foliage, and just in front of him was the truck Sam had radioed him from.

There was no sign of them.

The shouting continued, and as he peered over the hood of the truck, his heart fell to his stomach. There on the beach, under the floodlights that beamed from the compound were his three friends lined up beside one another, in the grips of a group of gun-wielding tyrants. A man stood shouting at them in another language, waving his gun in their faces. Xander raised his rifle for a closer look. Through the scope he could see terror on the faces of his friends. One gunman seemed to be screaming directly at Sean; Xander saw Sean spit in the man's face. The man stopped screaming and wiped the saliva from his face. Xander repositioned his gun, but before the shock of Sean spitting on the man had passed, the man pulled up his gun and squeezed the trigger.

Sean's face disappeared.

Sam's scream rattled Xander's bones and echoed through the night. Instincts were all Xander had at this moment, and he put a bullet in the gunman's head, then one in each of the other men standing beside him. The remaining gunmen holding Sam and Kyle turned them both toward Xander as a meat shield, and then moved them sideways toward the compound's back door and out of Xander's line of sight.

Xander pressed his com button. "Sam, Kyle, if you can hear me, just do whatever they say. Just stay alive. I will find my way to you. Just—"

Static erupted in Xander's ear, and he tore his headset from his ear. The men had broken their coms. Gunmen above the beach on all three floors of the balcony turned their attention to the brush, and bullets began to rain all around Xander as he tucked back down behind the truck. His only chance was the shadows. He knew they would be coming into the brush at any second and he had to move. The only chance he had of saving his friends, and the afterthought of killing Khatib, was to methodically reduce the number of the opposition. The longer he took, the worse the odds became of his friends surviving. He would have to take some chances.

All around him bullets pelted the truck, sounding like a hailstorm on a tin roof. Xander looked down at his utility belt: two frag grenades, one flash grenade, and two smoke. He unclipped one of the smoke grenades and looked around the side mirror of the truck. Four men fired from different levels of the compound above him, and as he raised up a little higher he could see three men, guns pointing out in front of them, running into the brush after him. He pulled the pin on the smoke grenade and tossed it into the middle of the brush, about ten feet in front of him back toward the canal. A hissing sound filled the air and smoke began to rise from the ground like from a fire-filled chimney on a cold winter night. Xander took his gun in his hands and dove outward, belly to the sky. Before the men firing down on him could adjust their aim, Xander shot all four of them dead—one on the bottom walkway, two on the second floor, and one on the top—and then landed flat on his back. The three men in the brush turned the corner of the truck. Xander stayed low and crawled into the smoke cloud he had left for himself a moment ago. Branches cracked and leaves rustled as the men hurried their way through the waist-high thicket toward him. Xander knew they would think he had continued all the way out to the canal, so instead, he held his position right in the middle of the thick white cloud of smoke and crouched to a knee. They were just steps away now and from a sheath he had strapped to the right side of his right leg, he pulled out a knife. Rambo, as he affectionately called it. He took Rambo in his right hand and pulled it up to ready position with the back of the blade to the outside of his forearm. He listened as their footsteps grew closer.

Three . . . two . . . one . . .

The first of the gunmen came running blindly into the smoke. Xander sprang upward, taking the nose of the man's gun in his left hand as he spun into him, sliding the blade of Rambo along his throat. He continued the spin, keeping the gun in his left hand, and 180 degrees later he drove the point of the blade, backhanded, into the Adam's apple of the second man.

Blood spewed from his throat as Xander immediately removed the knife, and with another 180-degree spin back clockwise it found a home in the neck of the third gunman. The momentum of Xander's swing knocked the dying man to his back, and Xander lost a grip on the knife. The sound of the gunman crashing to the ground alerted the others, and they began to regroup at both sides of the compound. They positioned a spotlight from one of the upper levels of the building in Xander's direction. Through the dissipating smoke, Xander could see the olive-skinned, dark bearded man desperately trying to keep his blood from running out of his neck.

"It's no use, you fuck," Xander whispered as he plucked the knife from the man's flesh. More footsteps and shouts started coming from the beach into the brush. Xander wiped the spatters of blood from his face that had sprayed him in the action. He was surrounded now, his only chance the canal.

Sam felt the rope tighten around her wrists. She concentrated on controlling her breathing, because with no vision she tried to tap into her other available senses to get a feel for where Khatib's men were taking them. In case the time came, she might be able to use the scents and audible clues to help her and Kyle find their way out. The burlap sack the men had wrapped around her head was making this a lot more difficult. She had counted thirty-six steps—two right turns—a flight of stairs—and two more right turns since the moment she heard the door shut behind them after walking inside from the beach. Wherever they were now, it was much cooler than the first room that was upstairs. Where they were now was also a cramped space. She could tell because the voices of the men talking sounded very encapsulated. She first faked a stumble to the right. Her shoulder immediately rammed into a concrete wall. The man leading her grunted something and straightened her up. Next, she pretended to trip over her feet to the left. She fell against yet another concrete wall. She was in a hallway. A long hallway at her count. She was no longer in or under the three-story compound on the beach. They were leading her to another location.

They were leading them to Khatib.

"You okay, Kyle?" Sam asked, knowing she would pay for it. But she had to know. The man leading her thumped her on the back of the head with the gun and shouted what she assumed was "shut the hell up" in Arabic.

"Y-yes," Kyle whimpered.

Though the situation seemed disastrous, the fact that they weren't already dead was a stroke of luck, really. She knew with each passing second they kept Kyle and her alive that it was a second closer to Xander spoiling the party. *They'll try to make an example of us,* she thought. She figured there might even be the coordination of a video. She hoped.

Khatib's militants closed in on Xander from both the beach side and the canal side of the compound. It was time to take those chances. He tucked Rambo back down inside the sheath strapped to his leg and bolted toward the edge of the brush in the direction of the canal. He stayed low, moving only his feet below him as he bent over, weaving through the foliage. He once again came to the edge of the ten-foot drop to the canal when a bullet screamed past his head. Two men standing on a walkway—a bridge over the canal—that connected the seemingly abandoned building and the compound were screaming as another was firing a rifle. Xander dropped down to his stomach. He knew they were really closing in on him. God only knew how many men were catching up to him from the beach behind him; three still stood overlooking the canal, and out of the corner of his eye, just before he almost lost an ear from the bullet a second ago, he had spotted at least half a dozen more men coming out of the front door of the compound, headed straight for him.

Fortune favors the bold.

Xander popped to his feet, quick-scoped the man shooting at him on the walkway, killing him. Next, with a massive inhale and two bounding steps he dove headfirst into the canal. It didn't take long for him to reach the bottom, but he felt a small amount of pressure in his ear so he knew it was at least ten feet. He swam from the middle to the far-right side, never leaving the bottom. It was a good thing because as soon as he moved, bullets began thumping through the middle of the small artificial waterway.

A moat? He built a moat? What is this guy, a comic book villain?

Xander knew the darkness of the water would be in his favor, but still he swam feverishly, desperately trying to make it under that walkway the three men were on. If he could make it there, there might just be enough cover to make something happen. The bullets streaming into the water got farther and farther away. Above him as he swam, the moonlight offered little help to see where he was going. However, when that moonlight suddenly became shadowed, he knew he was under that bridge.

Xander slowly made his way to the top. His eyes burned

from the saltwater, and pain shot through the wound in his shoulder with every stroke. He thrashed his bare feet below him to steady himself. He brought his Mk16 up at the same time his eyes raised out of the water. He continued to thrash his feet back and forth to hold himself in place. He saw three men running along the canal, shooting blindly into the water, one pointing to another at where he should shoot, even though he had no idea where Xander had gone. There was a steel beam above Xander's head that ran along the bottom of the walkway, and Xander took hold of it with his left hand, his gun in his right. He kept one eye on the men and worked the other eye along the length of the walkway, looking for a way up.

Or a way in!

His eyes lit up. The moron who had commissioned this little walkway was dumb enough to leave a large storm grate connecting to what Xander hoped was the sewer exit from the compound. There was a chance it was large enough for him. If it was, it was going to be one disgusting entrance, but an entrance all the same. Free of bullets.

Xander let himself slowly back down to the water. Just as he did, one of the men turned Xander's way and raised his gun.

So much for the bullet-free entry.

Xander had never let his gun down, so he shot and killed all three men along the canal. Just as the last one dropped, three more came out of the spot in the brush where he had jumped from into the canal just seconds ago. Xander managed to shoot the first two, but the third rattled off a succession of shots, and one of them ripped right by Xander's hand that held the steel bar; it forced him to let go, plunging him into the water. His Mk16 slipped from his hand as well, and the current of the canal carried it downstream. He was down to two pistols and

Rambo. The gunman continued to fire on him, so he let the current push him behind the walkway and pulled himself out of the canal, crawling the ten feet up the embankment. The two men on the bridge came to his side, and Xander pulled his pistol as he dove behind the concrete railing. This covered him momentarily from the two on the walkway, but it put him directly in front of the gunman who had just knocked him from under the bridge. The man fired and missed. Still flat on the ground, Xander pointed his pistol and squeezed the trigger. The barrel of the gun kicked back and up and over so that Xander saw the man's head jerk back, knocking him off his feet. The shot had hit the man square in the forehead. Before the others could react, Xander shimmied himself along the ground, around the concrete rail, and shot the two men left on the walkway.

Xander was exhausted.

He noticed how quiet it had become, and the lull in men coming out of the woodwork to try to kill him allowed time for the image of Sean being executed to come flooding to his conscience. A heavy sadness fell upon him like a weighted vest. He dropped his forehead to the concrete. His emotions swelled.

"I'm sorry, Sean," he muttered out loud. "I'm sorry." Tears pooled in his eyes.

Use it.

A voice came to his aid. His voice. The voice he had trained to come in at times like these and give him the strength he needed to finish what he started.

Use it, X.

Use the anger.

Save them.

The Most Haunting Image His Eyes Would Ever See

Kyle felt a shove at his lower back, and stars spotted the darkness in his bag-covered eyes as his head slammed into a concrete wall. Dazed, he wiggled a few times until finally he was sitting up with his back against a wall. The purple stars slid back beneath the clouds in his mind, and he began to regain his wits. A thud hit the wall next to him accompanied by a female voice grunting in pain.

Sam.

Where the hell are we, and where the hell is Xander?

Because there was nothing but black in front of his eyes, the execution of Sean played over and over as if on the big screen at the local Cineplex. He tried to do as Xander had taught him and erase the negative from his mind, but shit—this was as bad as it gets. He was stuck in a country full of terrorists, in a room full of gunmen—who were all fully aware that it was their intention to kill them—with his hands tied and a bag over his head. Oh, and none of them even spoke English, so he couldn't even try to charm his way out. The worst part of it all was that he was worried about his best friend. The same friend that got him into this mess. All he cared about, though, was that Xander was okay. As bad as it was in that room, for the moment at least there was no one shooting at him.

"You okay, Sam?"

"I'm okay. Whatever happens, Kyle, don't say a word to them. I will do my best to dangle a carrot for them. Hopefully it will be long enough—" She stopped herself. She couldn't be certain whether or not someone in the room with them spoke English.

"I hear ya." Kyle let her know that he knew she was holding out hope that Xander could save them.

"Long enough for what exactly?" a deep and gravelly Middle Eastern voice asked. Chills simultaneously ran all up and down Kyle's and Sam's spines. "Do tell," he finished.

"Who are you?" Sam asked.

"Who are *you*?" the voice returned. "I'm not sure you are in the position to be demanding answers."

"You already know who I am. I'm sure James filled your ear full of bullshit the moment you filled his pockets."

"Indeed he did, Samantha," Khatib replied. Sam was sure it was him. She shuddered when he said her name. "I am assuming that since you are doing the talking that this is Kyle and not Xander. I am assuming Xander is the one who got his brains blown all over my beach?"

"Yes, you bastard! Your men shot him like a dog!" Sam cried out, selling her pain. Khatib somehow had no idea that

278

there was a fourth among them. Xander was alive! She hated to disrespect Sean with her words, but even though he was dead now, he was still helping them.

A sinister laugh rolled from the terrorist's gut. "So much for *the most spectacular killer that ever lived.*" He continued his laugh. His men, though they couldn't understand what he was saying, joined him in laughter.

"Enough!" he silenced them. "Well, I guess the only thing left to do is make an example of the two of you."

"An example of what exactly?" Sam asked. Her only goal now was to prolong Khatib's inevitable plan.

"An example of what happens to those who try and stop me, stop ISIS. I must thank you, really. This will do wonders not only to build my following but to strike fear in the hearts of those who oppose me." Khatib muttered something else in Arabic, and Kyle and Sam were brought to their feet. He was remarkably well spoken for someone who lived in a bunker, Sam thought.

Kyle felt a tug at his neck, and the next thing he knew white light blasted into his eyes and pain poured inside them as if he had just looked up into a needle storm. He blinked his eyes to try to focus, but he only caught glimpses of a shadowy figure in what seemed to be a small box of a room. Sam cried out in pain beside him. She was desperately trying to adjust her eyes to the light as well. Kyle felt a sharp pain as one of the gunmen drove the butt of his rifle into his stomach. A metallic taste formed in the back of his mouth, and he was sure he would vomit. He gasped for breath, and he felt another sharp pain to the side of his head, and once again purple shooting stars rocketed across his mind's eye. He staggered and fell to his knees. The smell of blood and mildew were almost enough to make him sick. After a moment, the cobwebs began to clear, and when he looked up, he noticed he was staring right into the lens of a camera. Sam was right. The pain seared and his heart dropped into his stomach. He had seen this enough on CNN to know exactly what was going on.

This was his execution video.

Words he couldn't understand and unknown faces swirled around the room. His mind was mostly blank. He thought for a moment he would pass out, but as he started to slump over, one of the terrorists was kind enough to poke the small of Kyle's back with the point of his machine gun. To his left they brought Sam to her knees, and her face held an expression he thought he would never see on her.

Fear.

Her eyes searched around the bright room the same way his had, and it made him wince in pain and squint his eyes as he felt the penetrating needles of light that she too undoubtedly was trying to overcome. Khatib was the master of ceremonies as he stood with another man behind the camera. Every time he spoke, his minions moved into action. The room was hot and damp. The distinct smell of mold filtered through the stench of body odor from the man holding the gun to his shoulder. Although the temperature was hot, it was visually freezing cold. The light-gray cinder block walls and high-output florescent lights reminded him of a hospital room gone wrong.

Khatib barked another order, and moments later Sam, still on her knees, was forced to move over beside Kyle. Her arms were still tied behind her back, just the same as Kyle's. Movement followed more shouting, and for no apparent reason at all, they were removing Sam's ropes from her wrist. What followed would never leave Kyle's memory; it would forever torment him in his dreams. It would be the most haunting image his eyes would ever see. No, they didn't brutally kill her; what happened was far worse. The men shuffled Kyle out of the frame of the camera lens.

Khatib's dark and yellow eyes peered into Kyle's. "This, you arrogant American prick, is what happens when you come for Sanharib Khatib!" His eyes seemed to go black and an almost supernatural evil emanated from his mortal soul.

He shouted something to the two men who were subduing Sam. Immediately they began peeling off her wet suit. The more she fought, the rougher they were, and a third man joined in to help. After a struggle, Sam stood naked. They forced her back down to her knees onto the damp and dirty concrete floor. Two more men joined, and they managed to get her bent over on all fours.

"Stop it! Leave her alone, you sick fuck!" Kyle shouted, doing the best he could to break free from his restraints.

Khatib replied calmly. "Or what? You'll kill me?"

"You're going to pay for this!"

Khatib just laughed as he walked over to Sam. Sam didn't say a word, and she didn't make a sound. It occurred to Kyle that this might not be her first time in a situation like this, because he could see in her face that she wasn't even there. She had traveled somewhere deep inside her own mind and was hiding there. Khatib crouched down, grabbed her by the back of her hair and pulled her face from the ground to look up at him while the men continued to hold her in the sexual position.

"You try to screw Khatib? Well, now it is you that is screwed. And I know you will enjoy it, you filthy whore." Khatib snapped his finger, and one of his men who stood behind Sam stepped up and pulled his hard penis from his robe-like garment. Khatib slammed Sam's head back down to the concrete floor and motioned to the cameraman to make sure he was recording. The man moved in behind Sam and began the act that Kyle knew was one of the worst things that could happen to a woman. Her facial expression didn't change, and she didn't make a sound. Simultaneously, Khatib exposed himself and began to urinate on Sam's back. Kyle had to take his eyes away. He couldn't imagine the horror she was enduring. He would do anything to trade places with her and spare her this nightmare. Khatib filled the room with a long and sinister laugh. The smell of urine wafted to Kyle's nose, and he vomited uncontrollably at the foot of the wall beside him. Khatib gave a solemn speech in Arabic to the camera as he continued his excretion. As horrible as it was what Sam was enduring, Kyle knew that in a matter of moments, none of it would matter. Khatib finished his speech and his degradation, as the man inside of Sam finished as well. They brought her back up to her feet, and her seemingly lifeless body hung in the two men's arms who held her, naked, degraded, before the eye of the camera. Khatib snapped his fingers again, and two men untied Kyle and removed his wet suit. They retied him, arms and legs, and shuffled him over beside Sam.

This was it.

Xander must already be dead.

That morbid thought was the first that passed through Kyle's mind. All but two gunmen moved away from the camera, leaving one man on the right side of Kyle and one on the left side of Sam. On Khatib's command, both men raised long and jagged knives to Sam's and Kyle's throats.

"How long have we been doing this?"

The image of Xander asking Kyle that question on the boat

earlier flashed across Kyle's mind. As he felt the cold steel of the blade press against his throat, a choking swallow of fear made a gulping noise in the silence of the room. He closed his eyes and saw himself on the boat, answering Xander's question—*I don't know, four, maybe five years?* He saw Xander reply to him—*Okay, and how many times have I missed my mark?* Kyle could almost feel his best friend there in that room with him, just like they were back on that boat. Oh, how he wished they were back on that boat. He saw himself answer Xander—*N-not once, X. Never.*

Khatib's voice broke the silence in the room with one final command. "And now, you take your final breath."

Kyle couldn't help but draw in a deep breath through his nose. He thought of Xander's reply—*That's right buddy. Never.*

As the memory of Xander saying that last word—*Never*—fleeted from his memory, he came to the last of his inhale and—

Smoke! he thought as his eyelids flew open, and he propelled himself backward away from the knife. He landed on his back with a breathtaking thud, and sure enough, puffing in through the long hallway was smoke. Khatib shouted, and his men scrambled out of the room through the hallway. The two men holding Sam and Kyle threw them against each other in a pile at the far corner of the room. The men tied their arms to two metal pegs on the wall, preventing them from escaping the room that was now slowly filling with smoke.

Khatib walked over to them. "And now you will burn. You will burn like the trash you are." He spit at the two of them, then put the bags back over their heads, leaving them in darkness. Kyle heard what sounded like a tripod being collapsed, and then he heard something that sounded like a latch. The last thing he heard was a loud thud, as though Khatib had closed an extremely dense and heavy closet door. As the smell of smoke grew stronger, Kyle assumed that Khatib had stashed the camera in some sort of fireproof safe and would return later to retrieve it. He scanned his memory of the room, but he couldn't remember there being any door of that sort, but there had been a lot going on.

"The smoke, Sam! It's Xander! It's Xander! Sam! I'm so sorry they did this to you. But Xander is going to take care of him! Are you okay? Are you still with me?" Kyle shouted as he tried unsuccessfully to wiggle free of his ropes.

"I'm here, and we are alive. That is all that matters," Sam woefully replied, followed by a smoke-induced series of coughs.

Compound Fracture

Flames began to rage and black smoke billowed up into the sky from the partially fire-engulfed compound. As Xander peered through his scope, he still smelled the gasoline on his fingers. He had a perfect view of the front door of the compound that opened out to the walkway over the canal. He would be able to see anyone that exited that door from his spot perched high on the roof of the dark house across the street. When he had tried to investigate the dark house earlier, he had found that not only was it unoccupied but it was a complete and total decoy. A shell, built only to conceal what lay underneath, an underground room. The room where his friends were undoubtedly being tortured. He knew that a tunnel ran underground and the only way to get to that room was through a hidden entrance in the main compound. He had seen this setup before. He'd seen it on a previous mission not far from there in a small town outside of Baghdad, in Iraq.

Just a few moments ago as Xander was searching the premises for something to help him start the fire and get Khatib's attention, he had wondered if where he'd seen this setup before was one of Khatib's previous compounds. Something told him this wasn't the first time he'd had an encounter with this terrorist devil. After Xander had taken out a couple more of Khatib's men, he found a gas can tucked in the bed of a broken-down pickup truck. He carried it with him across the street to the front door of the compound. He looked in through the lone window, and when he saw no one, he knew they were busy with the death of his friends, and he had to hurry. He walked right in the front door into the empty main floor of the compound. The hallway in front of him led straight through to the back door that exited to the beach. Xander could still see the floodlights shining out back, and with a quick search of the main floor, on the tips of his toes, he surmised that those were the only two doors from which you could exit the main floor.

He began to spread gasoline throughout the back room in hopes of forcing everyone out the front door. When the gas was gone, he tossed the can aside. He then took out the last of his frag grenades and rigged it in a way that if the back door was opened it would instantly explode, killing anyone in the immediate vicinity. The basement door faced the front door, so with the back room on fire Xander knew this would increase the chances they would walk right into his bullets as they tried to escape. His biggest problem would be the fire prematurely setting off the grenade, leaving them another door to escape through, but that was a risk he would have to take. He wasn't worried about it blowing up his friends as they tried to escape because he knew once Khatib noticed the smoke filling the secret room, he would only be worried about saving himself. Xander knew Khatib would simply leave Kyle and Sam there to burn. Xander lit a match he found in one of the cabinets of the small kitchen and tossed it into the back of the compound to further encourage the men to run right out the front door in avoiding the fire behind them. He turned away from the igniting flame, walked outside toward the walkway, looked up, and noticed that it would be easy to pick off the remaining terrorists he was funneling through that front door from a perch on the roof across the street. After the grenade blew, of course, he would have to come back down to get his friends and take out whoever was left who tried to make an escape via the beach. Xander had run across the walkway, grabbed the rifle from the dead man who had shot at him earlier, then scaled the outside of the dark house and took his perch.

The fire was pretty well raging now. He figured the smoke had to be about to reach the underground room. Xander steadied his scope on the front door. He had calculated the other option of going in guns blazing and taking out everyone to save his friends. He knew, however, that they would be executed before he could make it to them. With the threat of fire trapping Khatib in the room, he knew that would be the only way to stop the execution, if there was any way at all. The key factor in all of this was of course believing Khatib was dumb enough to think the fire could travel that far down a long concrete hallway. He hoped that in the frightening commotion Khatib would simply leave his friends there, alone in the room, not considering that it couldn't reach them. Xander's biggest concern at that point of course was the smoke. It would just as easily kill Sam and Kyle; it would just take a little longer. Ten minutes to be exact, he computed. Ten minutes from the moment he set the compound on fire, which was now about five minutes ago.

Five minutes.

Xander's internal clock commenced as the front door of the compound finally flung open. He peered through his scope as three men came running out.

POP-POP-POP! With three squeezes of the trigger, three men lay dead. A fourth poked his head out the door, but when he saw his comrades get gunned down, he quickly pulled himself back inside before Xander could end him. Xander heard shouts from inside the house. It was dark, but because of the flames in the room behind them he could see the silhouette of a head looking out a slit in the lone barred window.

Thwock!

Xander shattered the right corner panel of the window and splattered the face that was shadowed behind it. The shadow instantly dropped out of sight within the concrete wall of the compound. This brought a few screams of panic, and finally the barrel of a gun poked through the bottom right of that same window and fired randomly in Xander's direction. A couple of the bullets zinged off the house he was perched on top of, so Xander squeezed the trigger once more and sent a bullet directly through the visible portion of the outstretched gun. A yelp from whomever was holding the gun made its way up to Xander on his perch.

Four minutes.

Xander held his gaze through the scope of the rifle and on the front door. The orange glow of the fire cast a dim light out over the sparkling ocean beyond the compound. It was burning slower than he had expected, but it didn't surprise him all that much because there wasn't a lot that was flammable inside. It was mostly the few pieces of scattered furniture.

Boom!

The grenade finally triggered, and a fantastic blast blew out concrete from the back wall onto the beach. The air was thick with smoke, and another cloud of dust and dirt filled the air with the explosion. If Khatib and his men could get around the fire in the back of the compound, they would have not only cover from Xander's gun but an escape route to boot. Xander shouldered the rifle and made his way down the side of the dark house. If the blast of the grenade took one or two more men with it, Xander figured Khatib had to be running out of resources at this point. As soon as his feet hit the ground, he sprinted across the walkway, up the canal, and back to the area of brush he had jumped in the water from earlier. He high-stepped over the bodies he had gunned down several minutes ago, and as he entered the brush he heard voices coming from the beach. In his haste he had forgotten about the men he had killed with Rambo in the shade of his smoke grenade and tripped over one of their bodies, sending him facedown into a pile of dry and crackly leaved branches. His rifle flew off his shoulder and landed somewhere toward the middle of the thick bushes and shrubs. It, too, made a loud crack that immediately followed the one Xander's body made. The voices coming from the beach stopped immediately. He held his position below the shade of the brush, listening. He could hear the crackling of fire from the compound but not the voices he hoped would resume conversation. Then he heard someone enter the brush. It was a very distinctive crack that these dried-up branches made.

Three minutes.

Xander raised his head slowly, and he soon saw what his ears told him he would see. A man, machine gun in hand, a cloth wrap on his head, and what looked to be a white bathrobe around his body, walked right to the middle of the brush. The man was scouring the brush for the dummy who had just made a loud crashing sound. Fortunately, he was walking more toward the gun Xander lost than toward Xander himself. Xander continued to watch through the foliage, and unfortunately he now also saw something he hadn't expected. Behind the one man stood seven more militants waiting at the brush's edge on the beach. He scanned their fire-lit faces, but there was still no sign of Khatib.

Coward.

The man in the center of the seven snapped his fingers, then pointed, and three of the men went left and three of them went right as they began to form a circle, spreading out around the brush. Xander watched as they didn't quite make their circle wide enough, because he was on the outside looking in. They had made their circle around the gun he dropped. What a stroke of luck it turned out to be that his rifle had fallen so far from him. It was now the focus of their attention, and Xander would easily be able to pick them off before any of them were the wiser.

Xander turned over, lowered himself back down to the dirt on his ass, and leaned back against a shrub. He closed his eyes and took a long, deep breath, focusing himself as the men closed in on what they thought was Xander. Images of his friends gasping for air in a tiny, secluded, smoke-filled room flashed in his head. The seconds were ticking away. A flashback of his father's face as a bullet tore through his shoulder came to mind, and his grip around his utility belt tightened.

Two minutes.

It was time to end this and escape with his friends. He reached for the pistol on his right hip, but it was gone. His stomach didn't drop, however, until he reached for the second pistol on his left hip and it too was missing. He frantically patted down the area directly around him, but he felt only broken branches and sand. He must have lost them somewhere in the shuffle. Eight armed men and Xander had no cover. Only his trusty knife, Rambo, and one smoke and one flash grenade. Xander knew he was good, but this was different. He knew he only had seconds before the man in the brush, in the middle of their gun-toting circle, found out that what they surrounded was only a gun. Xander had been in a lot of dismal situations but none this impossible. He took another deep breath and let his mind go blank.

All of a sudden he heard Sean's voice in his head. It was something Sean had told him long ago as they were riding into a mission together.

X-man, you know what I like most about you? You're a smart sum bitch. A lotta guys can be trained to get real good at killin' people with a gun. But I swear, X-man, I believe you wouldn't even need a damn weapon. Shit, I believe you just might be slick enough to make a fella do it for ya. Yes sir, slick enough to make a man shoot hisself!

Xander looked down at his only resources—smoke and flash grenades. He looked back above the brush at the tight circle the men had formed. That last sentence of Sean's speech echoed in his head.

Slick enough to make a man shoot hisself!

One minute.

Sean, you beautiful son of a bitch, Xander thought as he popped the pin on the smoke grenade and tossed it directly in the middle of the circle of militants. He dropped to the ground, making himself as flat as a pancake. The gunmen were so on edge because of the ease at which Xander had been picking them off that they didn't hesitate long enough to consider their position. Shots rang out into the night from multiple guns as the grenade began to hiss and a continuous stream of bright white smoke wafted upward as if going back home in the sky to live with its family of clouds. It wasn't long before the multiple guns that at first were firing steadily started to decrease in number until finally there was only one rifle left spitting bullets.

One man left standing.

The ill-trained militants had forgotten they were all facing each other in an almost perfect circle. Xander took Rambo in his right hand and the flash grenade in his left. He rose to his feet, and white smoke continued to reach for the sky. Seven men had shot each other to death in their haste to take Xander out. One man stood at the far end of the brush closest to the compound and farthest from Xander. The gunman, at least momentarily, was too shocked to comprehend. Xander took advantage and began to sprint straight for him. Seeing Xander brought a surprised look to his face, but he quickly recovered and fumbled for his gun. Xander still had to close about thirty yards, so he popped the pin on the flash grenade with his thumb and tossed it at the gunman's feet. The man raised his gun toward Xander, and just as he squeezed the trigger, a brilliant bang of light tossed him backward. The bullets meant for Xander sprayed harmlessly up into the air. Xander leaped into the air, one arm covering his eyes to shield them from the flash and the other reared back behind him, ready to swing his knife down toward the gunman. He brought his arm forward and connected with his target. The gunman's flesh parted and his skull caved as Xander drove Rambo right down into the middle of his forehead. Xander stood above the blood-gushing body with madness in his eyes, his chest heaving from the adrenaline that raged inside of him.

Zero.

Xander's internal timer went off, snapping him out of his murderous daze.

For the first time, he had missed his mark.

He reached down and pulled his knife from the dead man's forehead and wheeled around toward the canal. He sprinted around the corner of the compound toward the open front door. As soon as he made it to the doorway, fire roared out toward him and the heat from it sent him reeling backward. He could see inside the house and through to the still open doorway to the basement where now it was obvious they were holding Kyle and Sam because the men had escaped from there when the smoke had forced them out. A thick row of flames separated the front door and that basement door, and they were roughly twenty feet apart. Without hesitation Xander took two steps back as he inhaled a deep breath and ran through the doorway, jumping toward the entrance to the basement. Flames nipped at his heels as he glided through the air and on through the open basement door. Because the doorway led downstairs, he continued to sail over each step all the way down to a bone-jarring crash into the basement wall. Pain bolted throughout his body. The slam had been as violent as a high-speed car crash. The bones in his legs and arms screamed at him to stay down, but his heart wouldn't let him. Xander willed himself to his feet, checked his stability, and found that nothing seemed broken. However, everything was black. The smoke had completely overcome the room, and Xander would have to go in blind.

He began to feel his way along the rough concrete wall. It was hard to focus with the amount of smoke that was around him. He stumbled along, choking, until he found an opening. His breath was still knocked out of him from his crash into the wall, which only exacerbated his problems as he tried desperately not to gasp for air. Coughing wildly, he was able to find the hallway that Sam and Kyle had been forced to walk on their way to the secluded room. Xander's lungs were burning, and he knew that if the smoke was this bad down here for very long, he was already too late.

Xander followed along the wall down the hallway. He tried to cry out for his friends, but he was so overwhelmed by the smoke that the words became trapped in his throat. His entire body yearned for oxygen, and even though there were no flames, he felt as if his insides were on fire. He was closing in on the room now, and he wasn't sure if it was wishful thinking or not, but he sensed the smoke was dissipating. Finally, his hand ran into another wall in front of him, and as he felt around, he found it was a doorway.

"Kyle!" Xander coughed. "Sam!" He dropped to his knees and began to feel around the room. He felt nothing. "Kyle!" he shouted again. He feverishly ran his hands along the hard concrete floor, desperately searching for his friends. They made no sound, and thoughts of the worst began to creep into Xander's mind.

I killed them. I killed my best friends. They're dead because of me! And for what?

Xander's hand ran across something in the smoke-blinded room. Something that was the stark opposite of the rock hard and rough concrete floor.

Bare skin.

"Sam!" Xander cried out as he ran his hands over a naked and lifeless female body. She made no movement at all. He continued to feel around. He felt a stretch of smooth skin turn into the frayed roughness of rope and when he went to pull Rambo from its sheath, it was gone. He remembered that he had it in his hands when he made the leap down into the basement. He must have lost it there. He frantically began to untie the rope. "Kyle! Talk to me, Kyle!" he yelled out, and for a moment he thought he would pass out, the dizziness from the smoke rocking him. The smoke had lessened in the room, but it was still thick enough that he couldn't see.

Kyle didn't answer.

They're both dead. I made it, but I'm too late. They're both—

Just as he got the rope untied and he was finishing that thought, a hand gripped tightly around his arm.

Kyle!

"Kyle! Hang on! I'm getting you guys out of here!" he choked out. A cough came loudly from beside him, and he knew Kyle was trying to speak. "It's okay, you don't have to talk. Just keep your head down!" Xander coughed wildly as he finished those words. His chest burned ravenously, and his head was spinning as he ran his hands along Kyle's arms, which were bound by the rope that secured him to the wall beside Sam. Xander shook his head to try to clear the dizziness, and as he did his survival instincts kicked in. As he ran the escape scenarios, he knew he couldn't carry them both at once. Sam showed no sign of life, so because she was clearly worse off, he would carry her first. Unless, of course—he shuddered—she didn't have a pulse. Before he could run another scenario,

295

however, as he untied the last of Kyle's rope, his left foot slid across an inconsistency in the middle of the concrete floor. He removed the rope from Kyle's arm, freeing him from the wall while simultaneously taking something metal between his toes. A flashing memory of being just outside Baghdad again ran through his mind. He remembered that the similar room they had come across there—the one he thought of earlier—had a trap door in the middle of the floor. An escape hatch. It hit him at that moment that that is exactly why he had yet to see Khatib.

The son of a bitch disappeared through the bottom of the building.

Xander turned and felt for the metal latch with his hands. He grabbed it, turned it counterclockwise, and pulled the concrete hatch up toward him. A rush of smokeless air puffed up through the hole, and Xander took a deep breath and held it in as he turned back toward his dying friends. His hands found Kyle first, his ankle, and Xander pulled him over to the doorway that led underneath the compound. Xander went down the thin metal ladder first and took a deep breath as he pulled Kyle down on top of him. Much to Xander's surprise there were lights down there. Through his watery, smoke-hampered eyes he could make out a lit walkway that resembled a small version of a subway. He laid Kyle's body gently to the ground. Kyle didn't move, but Xander couldn't work on him yet, not until he got Sam out of that room. He shot back up the ladder, and the fresh air from the open doorway had made a clearing in the smoke inside the room. For the first time he saw Sam's naked body slumped over in the corner. His stomach turned in anguish, and he quickly scooped up her limp frame and carried her down the ladder. He laid her down beside Kyle and quickly placed his fingers to her neck.

No pulse.

He began to perform the air-giving portion of CPR. Xander almost jumped out of his skin as Kyle let out a loud cough beside him.

"That's it, Kyle! Cough! Cough till it burns!" Xander shouted. And Kyle continued to do so as Xander once again put his mouth to Sam's and blew air into her lungs.

Nothing.

He put five more puffs of air in her mouth and raised back up to see Kyle was now sitting up, continuing to clear his lungs on his own.

"I'm so sorry, Kyle. I was late. I missed my mark! I promised you I wouldn't, and I did!" Xander shouted as tears formed in his eyes and sadness rushed through his body. He pumped on Sam's chest, hand over hand, but it just wasn't helping.

"Come on, Sam!" he shouted. Then he looked back to Kyle. "This is my fault! Look at her!" he shouted. He lowered his mouth back down to hers, and just before he made contact again, her entire body lurched and a room rattling cough rocketed out of her mouth from her smoke-smothered lungs.

"Sam!" Xander shouted. "Ha-ha! Sam! Kyle, she's alive!" Sam rolled over and a string of gut-wrenching, lung-bursting coughs rolled out of her mouth that shook her entire body. Kyle continued to cough as he got up to his feet. He wobbled a little at first, then regained his balance. Xander stood up, and Kyle threw his arms around him.

Cough! "I knew you"—cough, cough—"would come for us," Kyle managed to say. Sam continued to cough from her knees as Xander kissed Kyle on the forehead and bent down and put his arms around Sam.

297

"I'm sorry, Sam. I'm so sorry. It's gonna be okay. I'm going to get us out of here," Xander said to her. However, with those words came the sobering reality that they were stuck in the middle of nowhere, now only a short time from when their plane was forced to leave the Lebanon landing strip.

"I know you guys are tapped, but Kyle, can you walk? 'Cause if we want to get out of here tonight, we have got to find some transportation now," Xander insisted.

"I-I can walk," Kyle answered softly.

"Okay, it looks like the tunnel leads out that way. Sam, I'm going to put you over my shoulder now, okay?"

Sam couldn't yet find words to answer him, but she managed to nod her head. Xander took her in his arms, but instead of over his shoulder he carried her out in front of him so she would be more comfortable.

She dangled there, exhausted but alive.

Xander Gets a Grip

They rounded the concrete walkway, and in the distance the yellow light of the bulbs that roped along the dirt wall came to an abrupt end. Only darkness lay beyond them. The only sounds in the small tunnel were those of Kyle's boots squeaking and Xander's bare feet slapping against the concrete. Xander still held Sam as she rested in his arms. He looked beyond her body, down to his feet, and they were a bloody mess. His time in the brush had really done a number on them. He felt a sadness for Sam as he looked down at her naked body. She was such a beautiful woman, with a gorgeous figure, and he knew without actually knowing that they had taken advantage of her in that room. He would have been able to smell the urine, but the scent of smoke that still hung so densely around them made it impossible to detect anything else.

"Not far now," Xander whispered to her. "You're gonna be okay, Sam." She didn't respond. Xander looked back over his shoulder at Kyle. He seemed to be walking just fine now. He nodded his head for Kyle to come close. "I'm not sure exactly what's going to be waiting for us at the end of this tunnel. Wait here with Sam and I'll run up ahead and check it out. We don't have any weapons so we really have to be careful."

Kyle nodded. Xander handed Sam over to him and started toward the dark end of the tunnel. If one had a tendency toward claustrophobia, it would really be flaring up at this point. The ceiling was just above Xander's head, and he could reach out on either side of him and touch the dirt wall. As with all phobias, however, it was mind over matter, so Xander of course didn't have a problem. He was far more worried about running into an ambush as he walked out of this little escape route. He figured it at least led to some sort of quick way out—a boat, a car— something. If Khatib went through the trouble of building this thing, he for damn sure would leave something waiting at the end of it to carry his bitch ass away. As Xander drew closer to the darkness, he heard what he thought was the sound of lapping water. Just steps away he saw what he thought was something shimmering in water.

The moon.

He tiptoed to the mouth of the tunnel, and sure enough it was water with the moonlight dancing around on top of it. What he saw next completely shocked him. They had finally caught a break. Xander made sure no one was around to spoil the moment, and then he turned back toward Kyle and Sam in almost a dead sprint. He was so excited he didn't even notice the shooting pains erupting up his legs from his cut and battered feet.

Kyle saw Xander sprinting toward him, and at first he began to backpedal as he couldn't help but think the worst. It was dark, so he had no way of seeing the excitement on

Xander's face, so he thought someone might be chasing him back into the tunnel.

"Jet Skis! There are two Jet Skis!" Xander shouted as he ran. He tried to hold the news until he made it back to them, but he just couldn't stand it any longer. Kyle almost dropped Sam as he instantly started to sob. Xander finally reached them and came to a stop in front of Kyle. He took him in his arms, and with Sam snuggled in between them they shared a long, emotional embrace.

"Get me the hell out of here," Kyle whimpered.

Xander squeezed the back of his neck, then backed away and smiled as he looked into Kyle's teary eyes.

"Buddy, we've got a plane to catch!"

Xander took Sam from Kyle's arms, and they headed back toward the exit of the tunnel. The emotion once again triggered Kyle's cough, and he proceeded to hack and spit most of the way there. They came to the end, and sure enough, to Kyle's delight sat two beautiful, jet-black Jet Skis.

"Will they start?" Kyle asked.

"For sure. Khatib had his choice of escape vehicles. Judging by the size of the empty spot over there in the dock, he is in a speedboat," Xander pointed out.

"So, if he's heading in the same direction we're going, won't we catch him?" Kyle asked.

"Well, yeah, but I don't even care—"

"Xander, if we come up on that motherfucker, you have to end him. There is no other scenario," Kyle interrupted.

"But I—"

"But nothing," Kyle stopped him again. "I'll take Sam with me. Look in that bin and see if there is a weapon or something. And it sure would be nice if there was something in there to cover her up."

Xander nodded, handed Sam back to Kyle, and walked over to a large, rectangular steel bin that had been left ajar, most likely by a hurried terrorist. He opened the lid, and fortunately, there were two black wet suits, a larger one and a smaller one. Xander pulled them out of the bin and held them up as he smiled.

"Looks like they knew we were coming," he said.

Kyle smiled and put Sam down on the small wooden dock beside the water. Xander walked over, and as Kyle put on his suit, Xander gently slid Sam into hers.

"You think she's gonna be all right?" Kyle asked.

"She'll be fine. She's a tough little bitch." Xander smiled. Sam opened her eyes for a moment, then shut them.

"Xander, if you'd seen what they did to her in there."

"I know," Xander answered. Kyle nodded.

"Was there a weapon in there or just the wet suits?"

"No weapon," Xander answered, zipping up Sam's suit and lifting her back up into his arms. "Just an old rope harpoon gun."

Kyle looked at Xander with a grin.

"What?" Xander asked.

Kyle grinned. "Oh, like you haven't killed people with less."

Xander immediately thought of the way he had just killed eight armed men with only a knife. And he'd only had to stab one of them.

"True," he said, smiling. "Let's get out of here. If we don't hurry, it will be all for naught anyway. Bob is leaving with or without us at 5:35. That gives us one hour. We can make it, but we're gonna have to keep the throttle pinned." He turned his attention to Sam. "Sam . . . Sam? I need you to wake up for me, okay?"

Sam rustled a bit, then opened her eyes.

"Are you going to be able to hold on to Kyle on the Jet Ski so we can get you out of here?"

She paused before she answered. "Y-yes . . . yes, I'm fine. I can hold on."

"That a girl." Xander once again scooped her up into his arms and kissed her on the forehead.

Kyle went to the Jet Ski and pushed the start button. Like music to their ears, the engine sang as it idled in the water. Xander sat Sam on the back of the Jet Ski behind Kyle. She wrapped her arms around him.

"I'll be fine," she assured Xander. Xander turned and grabbed the harpoon gun from the bin and jumped on his Jet Ski. Kyle gave him a wink as Xander fired it up, and they both turned their Jet Skis around. Khatib had had a little waterway out to the ocean cut into the land. It was just wide enough for the Jet Skis to idle out of, side by side, toward the light of the moon and the ever-turning tide of the sea. Once they made it to deeper water, Kyle and Xander pulled back the throttle and sped their way down the coastline toward what they hoped would be an awaiting jet.

Forty-five minutes on the Jet Ski made Xander's crotch numb from the constant vibration. Luckily for them the water was calm, so it wasn't a terrible ride. Sam still held strong, and Kyle seemed like he was doing just fine as well. There hadn't been any sign of Khatib. He must have gone north. Xander checked his watch, and it looked like they were going to have about five minutes to spare if they kept their current pace. Just as he started to reflect on what had happened to Sean, he caught a glimpse of something silhouetting against the moonlit horizon out in the distance. At the moment it was still too far away to be sure what it was. Then, out of the corner of his eye, he saw Kyle motioning for him, waving his arm and pointing out in front of him.

Could it be?

Xander motioned for Kyle to fall back behind him, and Xander sped forward toward the shape bobbing up and down just ahead of them now. He felt a spike of adrenaline shoot through him as he noticed it was indeed a boat. He wondered just how much adrenaline he could possibly have left inside his body. Xander drew closer and was now only about a football field away. The moon was strong enough to see that there was just one man on the boat and he was standing at the wheel. About fifty yards later he could see fabric flapping in the wind around the man's head.

Khatib.

Xander reached down where he had laid the harpoon gun, took it in his hand, and looked over his shoulder at Kyle. Kyle held his fist high in the air. Xander in turn raised the harpoon and sped toward the boat. In his side mirror he noticed the light on Kyle's Jet Ski. Since they had turned on automatically when they started up the Jet Skis, he supposed he'd just forgotten the lights were even there. So much for sneaking up on Khatib. Kyle kept a safe distance, and just when Xander thought he might get to surprise Khatib, the boat in front of him swerved wildly to the right. Xander checked his watch. It was already twenty after five now, just fifteen minutes before Bob would be taking off in the G6. He couldn't be sure of exactly how far out they were; he just knew he would see it when the beach on his left turned into trees. At any rate, he had to make this quick. His grip tightened around the harpoon gun, and his hand pulled back the throttle. Instead of going straight for the back of the boat, Xander turned almost dead right and headed out toward the darkness. With no light switch in sight, he took the sharp end of the harpoon gun, leaned out over the handles, and smashed out the light. It was now apparent just how much of that light he had been using. It was dark. Much more so even than the rest of the night had been because a string of clouds now covered up his flashlight moon.

Even better.

Xander turned his Jet Ski back in Khatib's direction and pinned the throttle. The Jet Ski gurgled up some sea water, then screamed as it rocketed forward. In front of him, through the spray of ocean water, he could see the light on the front of Khatib's boat, then Kyle's Jet Ski trailing after it. He was closing fast. There was no way Khatib would see him. Xander brought the Jet Ski up to the exact speed same speed as Khatib's boat, alongside it but just far enough away so he would be able to inch his way in, undetected. He used the light from the front of the boat to match his pace. Khatib would most definitely have a gun ready. Xander inched his way along the water, slowly moving left, closer to the boat. The Jet Ski slapped against the rolling ocean and groaned with power as it kept pace with the boat. There was only about ten feet between them now, but it was so dark that Khatib's focus was pulled to the light of Kyle's Jet Ski in his rearview mirror. Xander continued to inch closer. The wake from Khatib's boat put extra stress on Xander's one arm that guided him in. His biceps burned as he held steady.

Just five feet away now.

If Khatib decided to swerve his way, Xander was finished. He was close enough now so that he could see Khatib's every movement. Fear had Khatib constantly jerking his head from side mirror to side mirror. Water from the boat's wake was spraying a heavy mist onto Xander as he raised the harpoon gun with his left arm and wrapped his index finger around the trigger. At that very moment Khatib turned his head toward Xander and looked him dead in the eye. The emotion of coming face-to-face with his parents' murderer made Xander pause, and when he did, Khatib had time to swerve the boat, hitting Xander's Jet Ski. Xander went flying onto his back, and the harpoon gun bounced out of his hand and fell to the floor of the Jet Ski, on the side closest to Khatib's boat. Khatib was close enough to touch for a moment, but then he pulled the boat away, and in the moonlight Xander could see him pick up a machine gun.

"Xander!" Kyle screamed over the roar of the engines. "He's got a gun!"

Xander reached down for the harpoon gun, but just before he could touch it, Khatib swerved again, almost completely toppling Xander's Jet Ski over.

Khatib screamed at Xander. "You think you can kill me? You die, motherfucker!"

Xander made another attempt for the harpoon, and as he did he could see Khatib raise the gun.

"Xander!" Kyle screamed.

It was too late. Xander knew he couldn't get to the harpoon gun. In a last-ditch effort he kicked the steering column, and just as his Jet Ski swerved away from Khatib's boat, he heard a gunshot. Xander winced and closed his eyes, bracing for the bullet, but the bullet never came. He squinted through his left eye to see if Khatib was readying to take another shot, but instead he heard a crash and Khatib went slamming down to the floor of the boat. Kyle had run his Jet Ski into the back of the boat, giving Xander a chance.

Khatib staggered to his feet at the same time Xander pulled himself back to a seated position on the Jet Ski. Kyle pulled his Jet Ski off to the left and around the other side of Khatib's boat. Xander pulled the steering to the left and back toward Khatib's boat as he raised the harpoon gun to shooting position. Khatib hadn't had time to get his gun, so he instead reached for the steering wheel. It was nearly impossible to get a clear shot with the harpoon over the Jet Ski shifting in the wake of the boat, but Xander had no choice. Khatib yanked the steering wheel in Xander's direction, and simultaneously Xander fired the harpoon. Just before the boat hit his Jet Ski, Xander felt the harpoon connect with something, but what it was he wouldn't know because Khatib had turned the boat on him with such force that Xander went flying off the Jet Ski into the ocean. The Jet Ski stalled when Xander's hand left the throttle and came to a stop as the other two water vehicles sped off into the darkness.

Sam and Kyle saw what had happened, and panic slammed both of them. Sam screamed into Kyle's ear.

"Get me close to the boat!"

"No, Sam, it's—"

"Just do it, Kyle! Xander needs me!"

Just as Xander had done, Kyle used the light on the front of Khatib's boat as a guide. He didn't have to be very precise. Sam had already pulled herself to a standing position on the seat of the Jet Ski, and as Khatib picked up his gun, she pounced like a panther across the three-foot gap between them and landed on top of him, sandwiching his machine gun between them. Immediately, Sam rose up and brought an elbow down, crushing Khatib's nose. As she rose up again in haste, Khatib shoved forward with the gun and sent Sam flying onto her back, her head slamming against the back rail of the boat. Everything went black.

Khatib used this moment to pull himself to his feet and point the barrel of his gun directly at Sam's head as the boat continued to race over the ocean. Sam opened her eyes to find herself trapped.

"Now, I finish what I started back on land!" Khatib screamed. He had one hand on the gun and the other steadying himself on the side rail. He was going to make sure he didn't lose his balance this time.

Sam didn't close her eyes; she didn't make a move to stop him. She knew Kyle was too far away.

Kyle turned the Jet Ski back toward the boat, but it was no use. When Sam jumped off the Jet Ski, the momentum forced him too far away. There was no way he could make it back to help her.

"Sam!" Kyle screamed to try to get Khatib's attention. But Khatib couldn't be distracted.

Sam was ready. She had known her entire career that death was not only a possibility but a probability. There is no man alive that she would rather give her life for. Just as Xander had been willing to do all those years ago for her, when he hadn't even known her. She just hoped that somehow Xander had survived the fall off the Jet Ski. She knew if he did, Khatib would die and she would get her shot at him on the other side. Khatib wrapped his finger around the trigger, but just as he went to squeeze, a hand wrapped around his arm that was steadying himself on the rail.

Xander's hand.

When Xander was thrown from the Jet Ski, he never let go of the harpoon gun. The harpoon had lodged in the side of the boat, and Xander had been pulling himself in against the violent rush of the water by the rope that attached the tip of the harpoon to the gun. He had used almost all of his remaining strength to pull himself through the impossible push of the ocean.

Almost all.

Xander held himself on the side of the boat by the rail he had vise-gripped with his right hand. The other hand he used to yank so hard on Khatib's arm that it actually spun Khatib around and gunshots clapped the air, momentarily drowning the sound of the hum of the boat's engine.

"No!" Kyle shouted from the opposite side of the boat. Seeing the flashes from the gun's barrel hollowed out a hole in his heart. "Sam!"

Sam looked down and noticed that the bullets danced all around her, but they didn't hit her. Water began to fill the holes that the bullets had left in the boat's floor. She looked up and saw Khatib had recovered and had his machine gun aimed over the rail.

Aimed at Xander.

There wasn't time to reach Khatib, so she rolled forward and slammed the throttle down, causing the boat to lurch forward, sending Khatib to his back at the front of the boat, and causing Xander to lose his grip on the boat's rail and fall into the water. The same fate as Khatib's gun. Sam motioned for Kyle to fall back and pick up Xander. He did. Sam had Sanharib Khatib alone on a boat, unarmed.

She couldn't help the smile that grew across her face.

Without a Trace

The boat sat still in the mostly calm ocean water. Sam did not. As Khatib rose to his feet, Sam rushed toward him. Her eyes were wild with anger, her fists clinched at her sides. Blood continued to run from Khatib's nose from Sam's earlier smashing elbow. It flooded from his beard and pooled below on his white robe-like attire. He moved forward to go on the offensive but not before Sam slammed him with a straight right hand, which blasted his already crushed nose. He grunted in pain and bent over at the knees, grasping at his busted face. Sam grabbed the black towel wrapped around his head and drove her knee into his forehead. With a loud smack, it sent Khatib flying onto his back to the boat's floor once again, but the towel stayed in Sam's hands.

As Khatib lay there groaning in pain, Sam wrapped his towel around her neck like a scarf and dropped on top of him in the mount position. His coal-black eyes stared up at her, masking the fear that trembled in his mind behind them. Sam smacked him in the face with an open hand.

"Did you kill Xander's mother and father?" she screamed and dropped another punishing elbow. She could feel his right cheekbone cave beneath it. Khatib was unconscious. "Did you? Answer me!" She forced her elbow down on him violently again, this time into his forehead. This one woke him back up, though he was battered and dazed.

She went to elbow him one last time, and somehow Khatib managed to move his arm, using it to catch her left wrist.

"Is that what this is about?" Khatib asked. His speech slurred through his broken face. "This is about Mommy and Daddy?"

Khatib began to laugh uncontrollably, maniacally. Sam couldn't stand that sound. She pounded him with another hammer of an elbow, but it didn't stop the laughing. He had yet to answer her question, but she couldn't stand the sound of him laughing. Each and every one of those laughs put her right back in the basement of the compound, as he had laughed the same way while letting one of his men rape her and while urinating on her, degrading her to as low as a woman can go. Sam wanted to know the answer for Xander, but she couldn't stand the laughing.

She had to stop the laughing!

Sam wrapped her hands around Khatib's throat. She began to squeeze so hard that she felt his Adam's apple pop. Somehow, even though the laughing had stopped, he maintained a smile on his face. She squeezed even harder and leaned hard down on him. The light from the moon left a glint in his charcoal eyes, and as life began to leave his body, so too did the smile leave his face. Sam squeezed so hard her hands began to cramp, but she clamped even harder in spite of it. She knew she would regret not getting the answer Xander was so desperately seeking, but she couldn't stop squeezing. She could still hear Khatib's haunting laugh, so she squeezed; she could still feel that terrorist inside of her, so she squeezed; she could still smell his nasty urine in her hair, so she squeezed. Khatib's eyes began to bulge beyond their lids. Behind her she heard the motor of a Jet Ski as Kyle and Xander approached. In front of her, she saw the moment life exited the body of Sanharib Khatib.

Water had begun to overcome the back of the boat, partially submerging it in the ocean. Kyle pulled up with Xander at his back and throttled down. Sam walked to the back of the boat, the light from Kyle's Jet Ski showing the wildness in her eyes. There was no need for words; they knew that she had finished him, and as she stood there she wore his turban as a trophy.

"Are you all right, Xander?" Sam asked, her chest heaving from exertion, the madness in her eyes finally subsiding.

"Are you?"

Sam didn't answer.

"What did you do? Did you get him?" Kyle broke the silence, excited to know the answer for certain.

Sam didn't answer at first; then the madness returned in the form of a smile. "Yes, yes I did. I taught that fucker to piss on me."

Xander smiled back at her as Kyle laughed hysterically and held up his arms in triumph. His laugh echoed over the water.

The celebration didn't last long.

Suddenly, through the middle of Kyle's sky-reaching arms, to Xander's horror, a massive explosion lit up the night and a cloud of orange-yellow fire billowed up into the darkness from the shore. The sound was like a crack of thunder, and all three of them jumped out of their skin and instinctively covered their heads.

"Please tell me that's not our way out!" Kyle shouted. Sam perked up from the sinking boat, eagerly awaiting Xander's answer.

"We have to hurry! Trade me spots, Kyle. We have to find the beach where we left on the speedboat earlier!" Xander answered.

Kyle didn't say anything; he just let Xander climb in front of him, and Sam hopped on the back. Xander sped off and just moments later banked the Jet Ski left and ran it up onto the beach.

"We've got to go, Xander. It's 5:31," Sam said before they could even dismount the Jet Ski.

Xander turned to her, then looked back to the blaze that just so happened to be in the exact direction of the hangar.

"I'm afraid it might not matter."

Kyle grabbed Xander's hand, pulling him up from the Jet Ski, and Sam led them back through the tree line that separated the beach from the landing strip. Their hearts were in their throats as the closer they got, the worse it looked. They made it through the trees and out into the grass, then onto the pavement. Sam took a direct line to the side of the hangar that was hot with flames. They peered around the corner, and inside a plane was engulfed in a raging fire.

"No! Shit! Now what the hell are we gonna do?" Kyle shouted. He looked back at Xander, panic burning in his eyes.

"That's not my jet."

The moment those words left his lips he heard the unmistakable sound of his G6 engine begin to wind up off to

314

their right. They all looked over and Bob was flashing the plane's lights on and off. A beacon for them to come aboard. Excitement bolted through Xander's body, and when he looked over at Sam and Kyle, they were already jumping up and down, hugging each other. They started toward the plane, and Xander looked back at the burning jet inside the hangar. This time, however, he noticed there were three bodies lying on the ground next to it. He looked back to his jet and Bob had lowered the stairs. Bob walked down to greet them, machine gun in hand and a smile on his face.

"Good to see you, sir," Bob said, grinning.

"Damn good to see you, Bob. Have some trouble, did you?" Xander asked, nodding back toward the hangar.

"Nothing I couldn't handle, sir."

"Good man!" Xander patted Bob on the shoulder.

"We must leave immediately. We'll have to stop for fuel somewhere on the way back to Kentucky. As you can see, the refueling tanks here are useless." Bob pointed to what was left of the burning fuel pumps. "It really needs to be Paris," he insisted.

"Paris?" Xander asked, his mind flashing to Natalie.

"An old war buddy mans the flight tower there. It's the only way we will be able to land without anyone truly knowing we left from here, our only real shot of leaving without a trace. He will cover for me," Bob explained.

"Hmm, Paris?" Kyle smiled at Xander.

Xander smiled back.

"Paris it is."

It Never Takes Me Long to Find Trouble

Bob chimed in over the jet's intercom system to let Sam, Kyle, and Xander know they were about twenty minutes from landing. His voice woke all three of the exhausted passengers. Xander took a deep breath and rubbed his face to clear the cobwebs. He felt a shooting pain in his shoulder as he stretched. Sam had become quite masterful at in-flight triage. He would undoubtedly have some pretty sick scars to commemorate this little outing. They had all taken turns showering and washing the smoke and death from their skin. Sam excused herself to the bathroom upon waking. Xander didn't like the look on her face. He didn't like anything about what they had just been through. Though Sanharib Khatib was dead, the mission was a failure. Xander looked over to the empty seat where Sean should have been.

"It's not your fault, Xander," Kyle said. "He wanted to—"

"Thanks. I know." Xander interrupted solemnly. And in his heart he did know, but that didn't make it any easier. Xander lifted the shade covering the window and stared out at the approaching city. He thought he could see the iconic Eiffel Tower far in the distance. His heart was heavy; however, he still allowed a sliver of it to let in the excitement of seeing Natalie. He unlocked his phone and scrolled to her name. He started to text her but thought a surprise might be more fun. He closed his phone and looked to Sam's empty seat. He wanted to talk to her about what happened. He wanted to apologize, but he knew she wouldn't have it. He knew she wouldn't want it. But he couldn't just act as if nothing had happened.

Xander excused himself and went to the bathroom door. He could see steam coming through the crack, and he pushed the door open slightly.

"Sam?"

The water shut off.

"Sam? Everything all right in there?"

"Yes, I'm fine, Xander. I just had to rinse off one last time."

It had been the fifth time she had showered since they left Lebanon. Xander knew she was trying to wash the disgusting filth off her, but even the hottest of water couldn't clean it away.

"Can I come in for a second?"

"Certainly."

Xander pushed the door open, and a waft of steam gave way to Sam standing at the opening of the shower, wrapped in a towel.

"Sam—"

Sam stopped him. "You know it isn't necessary. I knew the

risks. I've been a woman behind enemy lines before."

"Sam, you don't have to be the rock all the time. I know it hurts, I can't even imagine—"

Xander had to stop midsentence to step forward and catch her before she hit the ground. Everything had finally caught up with her. Xander took her in his arms and took a seat on top of the toilet. He laid her head on his shoulder and cradled her, brushing the still wet hair that clung to her face back behind her ear. She let her body fall against him. He squeezed her in his arms and gave her a kiss on her forehead, then looked into her big brown eyes.

"I love you, Sam. No one will ever do this to you again. I swear on my life, it won't happen."

Sam sat looking at him for a moment. Her bottom lip began to quiver, and tears pooled at the bottom of her eyelids.

"I love you, Xander. I would do it a thousand times over for you. You are the only family I have, and you have been better to me than anyone ever has in my life. Your enemies are mine, as mine have been yours in the past."

"I wouldn't even be here if it wasn't for you."

"Nor would I without you."

Not another word was spoken. Xander sat holding Sam as both of them let the many memories they had shared over the years—good and bad—play in their minds. Indescribable horrors and triumphs that had not only brought them together as partners but also united them in life. Wars that had formed a bond that would never ever be broken.

Natalie heard a knock at her hotel room door. She backed away from the window, returned her cup of coffee to its saucer, then headed for the door. She checked the peephole and sure enough it was Jean. He was even more handsome than she remembered. She looked down and noticed she was still in her robe. *Time flies*, she thought, *especially when you are a silly woman daydreaming about a man who's thousands of miles away.*

With an embarrassed smile on her face, Natalie cracked the door but didn't remove the chain.

"Jean! I am so sorry. Can you give me just one more minute?" She flashed a section of the robe to him. "You know us girls, never on time." She shut the door without his response, and then opened it again. "Hi, by the way. I'm so sorry. It's so good to see you!"

Jean just smiled.

"It is no problem, it is lovely to see you as well."

If it were possible, his French accent made him even sexier to her.

"Okay, I'll be out in just a second, I promise."

Jean managed to get a bouquet of flowers through the door before she could shut it. Natalie's eyes lit up at the sweet and thoughtful gesture. She looked into his deep brown eyes and felt a small, unexpected flutter in her stomach.

"Oh my, they're beautiful. Thank you so much."

"You are welcome, how about I wait for you in the café across the street? That way you can take your time?"

"Do you mind? I swear I'll only be a minute."

"Of course. They have a wonderful specialty cappuccino there. I will order us one." He smiled as he tucked his midneck-length, jet-black hair behind his ear. His white teeth sparkled against his olive skin.

Natalie smiled and shut the door. Once it was closed, she fell back against the door with a sigh. Then, with a playful smile, she ran to the closet for the perfect outfit.

"I don't feel much like sightseeing today," Sam told Xander and Kyle as they enjoyed a coffee at a small café across the street from their hotel. "Besides, I've been here more times than I care to count. Other than New York, this is the most overrated city in the world. The food is shit, the people are rude, and the wine is far better in California."

"Well, I agree about the wine, for sure, but where is your sense of romance, Sammy?" Xander asked.

"Not in the mood for romance today." Sam glanced at Kyle, and he quickly looked down at his coffee. He couldn't bear to see the pain from last night in her eyes.

"I totally understand. They said our suite will be ready in an hour."

"Well then, let's talk about a few things so that I can have something to work on this evening while the two of you are off sniffing after some cats in heat."

"Business? Already?" Kyle winced.

"Go ahead, Sam," Xander said. He knew she was looking for something to occupy her mind.

"All right, first, Darryl says he may have a lead on that anonymous text message you received before you were attacked at the house in Lexington. He says he knows where the burner phone was purchased."

"I may just have an idea of who sent that message as well." A vision of Sarah Gilbright flashed in Xander's mind. "But, yes, I don't care what time it is when you find out more on that, call me and let me know what it is. That is priority one."

"Of course. Also, one of my sources messaged me and said

he had something urgent about Khatib. Obviously it isn't all that urgent now, but he says he has details about what he was in trouble for in the States around the time of your parents' death. So I will obviously follow up, just so you have all the facts. Dirty as they may be. Lastly, and I know we have spoken about this before, but he keeps reaching out to me. Now he is insisting that he meet with you."

"Who?" Xander guffawed. "The big wig Director Manning?" The look on Xander's face was one of amusement.

"You know he wants us to work with the government and you know he'll use whatever info Gilbright has been gathering on us to do so."

"No, Sam, I have no interest in what he has to say."

"We cannot avoid him forever. He's the head of the CIA, for God's sake."

Xander paused. "Hell with him. I'll pay Sarah Gilbright a little visit when we get back."

Kyle couldn't help but smile. He had been going on and on about the gorgeous woman at the King's Ransom bourbon launch party in San Diego since they ran into her. He thought her all the more sexy when Sam told him she was a special agent for the CIA.

"Thank you," Sam replied, then turned to Kyle. "So, what are your plans today?"

"Well, that depends. Xander, are you going to try to see Natalie—"

Kyle's eyes shot over Xander's shoulder toward the entrance of the café.

"Well, speak of the devil and she shall appear."

Kyle nudged Xander and pointed to the other side of the café.

Natalie Rockwell.

"Go say hello!" Kyle nudged him again.

Xander slid back his chair, and just as soon as he got up, he sat right back down. Disappointed. It wasn't the fact that she'd met a man there. It wasn't the fact that she threw her arms around him. No . . . it was the look in her eyes when she did so. It reminded him of the way she had looked at him just one long week ago. At least it appeared that way from across the room.

"Ouch. You seemed to have frightened her away," Sam said, then immediately apologized because she realized how it sounded.

"Shit, X, I'm sorry," Kyle said.

"It's okay, no worries. Listen, I'm gonna run and check on the hotel room and then we can get a jump on the sights if you want."

"Sounds good. We'll just wait here."

"All right. I'll be back in a few."

Xander grabbed his duffel bag, and as he got up he accidentally pushed his chair too far back and it lightly hit a beautiful woman getting up from a table with her equally beautiful friend. The woman looked up at him, and her face turned from annoyed to one that clearly showed she found Xander attractive.

She smiled and spoke flirtatiously to Xander.

"Well, I don't mind being hit on, but I feel like there are better ways." She reached out her hand. "Shanda Bateman, this is my friend Elizabeth Hall. What's your name, handsome?" Her accent told Xander she was from the South.

Xander took her hand. "Xander King, and this is my friend Kyle Hamilton." Kyle bolted to his feet and said hello. Sam rolled her eyes. "Sounds like you ladies don't hail too far from where we come from; I'm guessing Georgia?"

"North Carolina actually. Kentucky?" she asked.

"You're good." Xander looked over at Kyle and knew exactly what the smile on his face meant. Especially after he noticed the tattoo on Elizabeth's ankle.

"We're here for our girlfriend's wedding. It's not till next Saturday, but we just thought we'd come out a little early and find some trouble."

"I promise, if it's trouble you seek, you needn't look any further." Xander smiled.

"Now that, I believe." Shanda laughed.

"Is it too early for a drink?" Xander asked.

Shanda looked over at Elizabeth and smiled. "You know it never takes me long to find trouble." Elizabeth nodded and Shanda turned back to Xander. "We'd love to."

"Perfect. I have to run across the street and check on our room and then I'll be right back," Xander told her as he winked at Kyle.

"Sounds good. Don't be too long, handsome." She smiled.

Sam interrupted. "If you're going to check on the room, remember, I had to put it in my name."

"Okay, thanks, Sam. Be right back, ladies."

Xander turned from them, walked along the back wall, and slinked out the side door of the café. Natalie never saw him. On his way across the street to the Hotel Le Bristol, he stopped and bought two dozen red roses from a street vendor. He didn't know Natalie's room number, but he figured that if she was on shoot here, the production company was picking up the tab. That meant a suite on the top floor. He passed through the lobby, hopped in the wrought iron–and–glass elevator, and rode it all the way to the top. When the elevator door opened, he stepped out into the hallway and found a maid's cart. A young lady in uniform walked out of a room with folded sheets in her hand.

Xander approached. "Excuse me, I'm sorry to bother you, do you speak English?" The woman shook her head no. He noticed on her hip sat the master key. "Um, let's see . . . Natalie Rockwell?"

She smiled, nodded her head excitedly, and as a reflex looked at Natalie's room. She practically pointed him to it.

Too easy.

"I-I love her," the woman managed to say in a thick accent, "b-but I—"

"It's okay," he interrupted. She had already given him all he needed. Xander smiled and took one of the roses from the bouquet and handed it to her. As he dropped his hand from hers, he swiped the master key from its clip. The young lady was so excited she didn't even notice.

"Merci! Merci beaucoup!" She smiled and turned down the hallway to the next room to show her fellow hotel maid. They looked back at him; Xander just waved. As the woman happily waved back, her coworker said something to her sternly and pulled her inside the next room. Xander took advantage, hurried across the hall, swiped the key to Natalie's locked door, and quickly shut the door behind him. Natalie had left the patio doors open to the view, and he could see an empty table out on the balcony. Traces of her perfume that she had sprayed before she left the room delighted his senses, and a flash of their night together in Lexington flickered inside his mind. He walked over to the balcony and set the roses down on the table. He reached inside his duffel bag, pulled out a bottle of his King's Ransom bourbon whiskey, and set it on the table beside the roses.

Xander took a step back to see what Natalie would see when she found it. In the distance, sitting directly over the top of the whiskey and the roses stood the Eiffel Tower.

He wanted to be with her, but it just wasn't meant to be.

Whiskey & Roses

"Gilbright, where the hell is he?"

Director Manning shouted at her from the other side of his desk. His face was as red as a crayon, and Sarah was sure he was going to pass out. She knew flying the Gulfstream all the way to Russia and not seeing a single sign of Xander King was going to cause him to blow a gasket, but she didn't think he *actually* would. Not until right now, his eyes bulging and veins popping. She knew her answer sure as hell wasn't going to help his gasket, either.

"I don't know."

"That's it? I don't know? That's all you're going to give me? Some special agent you're turning out to be. Did I make a mistake here? Are you helping him?"

"Helping him? Helping him what? I don't appreciate you—"

"I don't give a baker's *fuck* what you appreciate, Gilbright!"

Manning's decibel level had officially gone through the roof. It literally rattled her bones.

"There was a massive terrorist takedown in Syria last night. Somehow, no one knows a single goddamn thing about a scheduled operation, Black Ops or otherwise. Forty-five dead, including Sanharib Khatib and, imagine this, Sean Thompson. That mean anything to you?"

"Sean Thompson is dead?" Sarah asked.

"That's right, the same Sean Thompson that you said left on a plane with Xander King from the Bluegrass Airport in Lexington Kentucky."

Sarah's heart turned a flip and then sank to her gut.

"Xander?"

"Xander what, Gilbright?"

"Is he okay?"

"Are you listening to me at all? I just asked you where he is. You are the one who watched his plane leave."

"Yes, and then I went to Russia to find him. Not . . . Syria."

"Well, either you helped Xander, or you are just shit at your job."

"But why would Xander go after Khatib? It makes no sense."

"Obviously he is under the impression that Khatib killed his family. Is that true? Did you know this and run smoke for him in Russia?"

"What? No!" Sarah stood up and put her hands on her hips. "I went to Russia because our intel says it was Dragov who was involved with the killing of Xander's parents. Why would he think Khatib—"

"'Cause Khatib was in the oil business. Had dealings in the US around the same time King's parents were murdered. How the hell did you miss this?"

"I-I—"

"I-I-I . . . you had better get your shit together, Gilbright. And it had better be fast. Find out where the hell he is. Now that Khatib's operation is destroyed, Ahmed Abdallah—the nastiest son of a bitch in the Middle East—is going to become even stronger. The things he will be able to do with Khatib's money and operations will be devastating!"

Sarah was speechless. All of this information was too much to process at one time. She stood staring at the medals displayed on Manning's desk. She did so until Manning pounded his fist on the desk, violently shaking her from her trance.

"Are you listening to me, agent?"

She looked back up at him, lost.

"Y-yes. Yes sir. Just tell me what I need to do."

Manning took in a deep breath and calmed himself.

"Find King. He and Sam took out an entire terrorist cell, by themselves, as far as we know. Does that even compute to you? It doesn't to me. Everything I said in that meeting with the directors last week, all I did was undersell Xander King. He is far better than I even imagined. But if he's not working for us, he'll be working for no one. And, Agent Gilbright, that can't happen. He will save hundreds, maybe thousands of American lives if we use him in the fight against Abdallah. Use whatever it takes. I need to know if killing Khatib was killing Xander's parents' murderer. If so, we find something else. However, if it's Dragov who had them killed, Xander needs to know, and only when he promises—in writing—that he is again one of us. It goes without saying that if we don't get Xander, you don't have a job. Is that clear, Ms. Gilbright?"

"Crystal."

***

"Natalie, come sit! It is so good to see you," Jean said to her. She took a seat beside him, looking out across the street.

"It's good to see you, too, Jean. Sorry to keep you waiting. You are as handsome as ever." She smiled.

"And you are the most beautiful sight in Paris. How has your holiday been thus far?"

"It's been great. This is such a gorgeous city. I just love it." She took a sip of the specialty cappuccino he had waiting for her. "Wow, Jean, this is delicious! Thank you!" Her energy was infectious.

"You're very welcome. I knew you would love it. So, are you ready to start shooting tomorrow morning?"

"I think so. I've been over and over the script. I really think this movie is going to be a lot of fun to make."

"I agree. I am just happy to be a part of it with you," he said to her, but she did not reply. Natalie instead had a perplexed look on her face as she peered out the window to the street.

"Natalie? Are you all right?"

"W-what? Oh . . . yes, I'm sorry. You know what, I'm a little chilly. Would you mind if I run across the street and get my coat?" she asked him, still seemingly in another place.

"We can get it when we finish our cappuccino. No?"

"I'm sorry, I'm just gonna run across the street. I'll be right back," she insisted.

"Okay, okay sure . . . no problem."

Natalie hopped up from the table and almost ran out of that café. As Jean was asking her about starting the movie tomorrow, she was sure she had seen Xander at the flower stand. She knew it was silly, but as spontaneous as she knew him to be, she couldn't help but see for sure. If she didn't, it would ruin her entire day. She rushed across the street and glided through the hotel lobby. She looked all around the grand room, but there was no sign of Xander. She noticed the check-in desk and hurried over.

"Hello." She smiled at the gentleman behind the counter.

"Miss Rockwell! Yes! What can I do for you?" the attendant asked exuberantly.

"I need a big favor."

"Anything for you, Miss Rockwell, anything."

"Could you tell me if an Alexander King is staying here this evening?"

"Hmm, that doesn't sound familiar, but let me check." He began to tap away at his keyboard as he stared into the computer monitor. "I'm very sorry, Miss Rockwell. There is no one staying here by that name."

"Oh, okay. Well, thank you."

Disappointed, she walked to the center of the lobby. It was a bit chilly out, and besides, after interrupting Jean at the table, she couldn't possibly go back without getting her coat. She walked over to the elevator, rode it to the top, and walked down the hall to her room.

I swear that was Xander . . . Sheesh, pull it together, Natalie.

She laughed at herself as she opened the door. The first thing she saw stopped her dead in her tracks. Straight ahead of her, out on the balcony table, sat a bundle of red roses. The same roses she swore she saw Xander buying on the street just a few moments ago. Her heart raced as she whirled her head around, hoping her eyes would find him somewhere in the suite. But they didn't. As she moved closer to the balcony, she could see that something else was sitting beside the roses. The air escaped her lungs as she cupped her hand over her mouth.

"King's Ransom whiskey," she said aloud. "He was here . . . I knew it. I really did see him."

She bolted back for the door, flung it open, and looked frantically back and forth down both sides of the hallway. All she saw was the maid. The maid waved excitedly at her, a single red rose tucked inside her hair. Natalie forced a smile, waved to her, and then walked back inside her room. She paused just inside the door, and for a moment she thought she could smell his cologne. She let out a sigh and wandered her way back out onto the balcony. She ran her fingers across the soft, damp petals of the fresh red roses. She removed one from the bouquet and brought it to her nose. The sweet aroma filled her senses. Hundreds of thoughts raced through her mind, but the fact that Xander wasn't in the room meant he wasn't planning on seeing her. He must have seen her with Jean. She took a deep breath and took the bottle of whiskey in her hand. She missed him, and he clearly was thinking of her.

Below her, Xander and Kyle were walking out of the café, two beautiful women on their arms. She couldn't see this from where she stood; she could only see the beautiful city of Paris beyond the flower-covered rail. Natalie closed her eyes and took one more long inhale of the sweet rose. She knew her business with Alexander King wasn't finished just yet. What she didn't know was how long she could wait to be with him again. She had asked him for space, and though she was still so confused about who Xander really was, all she wanted to do was be with him. She clutched the whiskey bottle tightly against her chest. She could tell by the fact that he had been in Paris that he, too, struggled with the thought of life without her.

Xander remembered the sad but beautiful words she told him her father always used to say. It was in that moment she understood exactly what Xander meant by leaving whiskey and roses for her on that balcony. And how appropriate it was for the moment.

Roses to remember him.

Whiskey to numb the pain.

VANQUISH

The deeper the wound the sweeter the revenge

Book Two of the Xander King
Series is Available Now!

Order today exclusively at Amazon.

Letter From the Author

Dear Reader,

Thank you so much for taking time out of your inevitably busy schedule to read *Whiskey & Roses*. I realize there are a million other things you could have been doing, and I am so proud that you chose to spend a few of your precious hours with my imagination. I love hearing from readers, and you can reach out to me on social media or just use that old-fashioned thing called email: info@bradleywrightauthor.com. (That's right, email is now old-fashioned. Some twelve-year-old told me Facebook is too. You're welcome.)

funny guy

Xander says hello. He comes around and has a drink with me every once in a while. Son of a bitch always sticks me with the bill. Right now he is making his way back from Paris. He mentioned that he and Kyle are going to make a pit stop in Vegas. He invited me, but I reluctantly had to pass. I am just too busy writing.

Thanks again for reading. The second book in the series, *Vanquish,* is out now. Xander is thrown a major curveball, and you won't want to miss the twist the story takes.

All the best,
Bradley

Bradley Wright is the author of the Xander King series. He and his wife spend time in both sunny California and the great state of Kentucky, where he does his very best to be charming, witty, and clever. When those attempts inevitably fail, he locks himself in a room and makes up characters who seem to always find him far more interesting than real people do. Funny how that works.

Bradley has been writing since he was a child. He started with songs and poems, but finally gave in to writing stories when the voices in his head resorted to shouting. He is inspired by every author he reads, most notably, Stephen King, and Carsten Stroud.

For more information visit: www.bradleywrightauthor.com

Cheers!

Made in the USA
San Bernardino, CA
17 February 2019